Get the prequel to the Mars Frontier series FOR FREE

Sign up for the no-spam newsletter and get exclusive content, all for free.

Details can be found at the end of DISCOVERY.

COPYRIGHT

First published by P&J Books 2019

Copyright © 2019 Paul Rix

This novel is entirely a work of fiction. The names, characters and incidents portrayed in it are the work of the author's imagination. Any resemblance to actual persons, living or dead, events or localities is entirely coincidental.

Paul Rix asserts the moral right to be identified as the author of this work.

First edition

DISCOVERY

Book 1 of the Mars Frontier Series

DEDICATION

To Julia. The future is in the stars

Chapter 1

"Please don't throw up now. You've done this a hundred times," Georgia said to herself.

"What was that, Pyke?" She could hear the satisfaction in the captain's voice.

"Nothing, sir. Simply performing a comms check." She knew she was fooling no one.

The sound of laughter over her headset confirmed it. "Get to it then. I thought you'd appreciate something different to break the monotony of life on *Endeavour*. Isn't that how you described it to me last week?"

"Sir, you know I was only joking. I'll need to be more careful what I wish for next time."

One final visual inspection of her cumbersome spacesuit in the full-length mirror and she was as ready as she was going to be. But even a fake beaming smile at her reflection did nothing to lift her anxiety. A quick glance at the visor's heads-up display showed that her suit's systems were green.

"Okay, you've got this," she whispered as she pressed the release button on the wall.

The airlock door slid silently open, exposing the empty blackness beyond. Georgia sucked in her breath and held on tightly to the grab rail. Her heartbeat thumped loudly in her ears and she instinctively knew she was breathing too rapidly. Despite her years of training on simulators and on the lunar surface, this was her first experience from a spacecraft travelling at over eleven miles per second. It was a struggle to overcome her fears, but she knew she must remain calm. It didn't help that the little voice inside her head was listing all the catastrophic things that could go wrong and the countless painful ways she could die.

With a deep breath, Georgia released the grab rail and pushed herself gently forward until she was entirely outside the airlock before pausing and looking down the length of *Endeavour*. At the same time, her visor adjusted to filter the bright crisp light from the sun, allowing her to see the troublesome communications array at the rear.

The sunlight was intense, causing the brightness of the craft to be in stark contrast to the dark void of space. The sun made everything appear crisp and sharp and was a welcome relief after months of living under artificial light. She took her time to take in the view, relaxing with each passing second.

"Good of you to join me." The voice of Jim Grant, the flight engineer, affectionately called 'the chief', cut into her train of thought. "Take your time and you'll soon get your bearings. I remember my first proper spacewalk so I know it can be overwhelming at first." He had already reached the array and had secured his tether so as not to float away. "The LCS is a mess. Probably a micrometeorite strike. What are the odds of that?"

Georgia didn't want to think about it. Being struck by a grain of sand at this speed would be lethal. Instead, her gloved hands grabbed tight hold of the rope that the chief had already unfurled, allowing her to follow him slowly but steadily.

"We've done well to get this far with no significant issues," she replied. "I was expecting far more problems during this mission. This should be an easy swap out."

"Agreed. There's a spare LCS assembly in compartment C-One. Can you retrieve it on your way here?"

Georgia stopped to unlatch a large panel which swung open. Inside the unpressurized storage area, there were spare components as well as a selection of tools and a maintenance droid. She was able to reach in and extract the spare array at the same time as activating the droid.

The maintenance droid followed Georgia as she made her way to join the chief, a toolbox attached to its side and the replacement part held nimbly in its mechanical hand. It was basically a voice-controlled box with various appendages to carry tools or perform minor repairs. Twenty-four tiny jets made it highly maneuverable and the perfect assistant for astronauts conducting spacewalks. Georgia had programmed it to respond to MAUD, short for Maintenance and Utility Droid. "Come on MAUD, we don't want to keep our chief engineer waiting." While the droid used its gas jets to propel itself, Georgia was struggling with the exertion of pulling herself along the support cable. By the time she reached the array, she was breathing heavily.

The array comprised an eight foot antenna to transfer data to and from Earth, and a laser communications system, or LCS, which had a far quicker data transmission rate. It was the LCS that had failed the previous day and it was easy for Georgia to see why. A one-inch hole ran straight through the transducer unit. The clean edges of the entry and exit holes were a clear indicator that a meteorite travelling at high velocity had caused the damage. Looking at the hole, Georgia was reassured that steel plates were in place to protect the *Endeavour*'s hull to absorb such impacts.

With only ten days until they reached Mars it was essential that the communications equipment was fully functional. "Let's make this quick, Jim. I don't want to be out here any longer than I have to. I can't remember if I'm wearing my lucky pants."

"Roger that," came the reply.

Once she had safely tethered herself to the ship, Georgia instructed MAUD to hold station, allowing her to retrieve the necessary tools. It was slow, methodical work. Their thick Kevlar gloves made work very clumsy. For Georgia, this was taking too long even though she knew the task couldn't be rushed. Any repair activity outside the ship had to be performed carefully. They didn't want to lose any tools this far out in space, so every item had to be secured.

After two hours, the work was complete, and Georgia had to admit that she and Jim worked well together. Jim held up the broken array and asked, "Do you need this?"

"No, just toss it. We don't have any room for souvenirs on this trip. Make sure you put the effort in to your throw so that it doesn't return. Captain Winter won't be happy if we dent his ship."

The chief adjusted his stance as best he could, bracing his boots under a safety strap to give him more leverage. "I'm sure you'd sweet talk your way out of it and let me take the blame. You are his favorite after all."

Georgia knew that to be true. When she had first been assigned to Expedition Two, the captain had taken her under his wing. She wasn't sure why. Perhaps he saw something in her that she had missed. She'd learned so much from him and he was always willing to share his experience with her, and the rest of the crew.

She watched as Jim swung the defunct box in a wide arc before releasing it. The box slowly rotated in the sunlight as it headed away from and behind *Endeavour*, narrowly missing one of the ship's huge landing legs as it sailed by. "That was too close!" she gasped. "Next time, let me dispose of the rubbish."

"It looked perfect to me," replied Jim, with a smile. "We won't be seeing that again."

Georgia had long forgotten her fears and was almost reluctant to head back into the ship. "We should carry out a quick visual inspection," she suggested. "We finished ahead of time, so another thirty minutes won't impact our schedule. And it's been several months since you last ventured out."

"Okay, but we stay together as we trained. And MAUD comes too, to take video imagery."

Endeavour was fundamentally a large cylinder, two hundred and twenty feet long and thirty feet wide, which tapered to a point at the front where the flight deck and crew quarters were situated. The main body of the craft contained essential supplies, including oxygen and water, as well as some cargo. The bulk of the spaceship was taken up with the vast fuel tanks and the five powerful rockets used for take-off and landing.

Because of *Endeavour*'s size, the inspection took over an hour with Georgia and the chief carefully traversing along the side of the ship, inspecting for any obvious signs of damage. Although there were the odd scuff marks and scratches, the chief was content that there was nothing to worry about.

Before she re-entered the airlock, Georgia took the opportunity for one last look at the stars. As she turned slowly around, she was in awe at the millions of stars that made up the Milky Way. Although not an expert on constellations, she spotted Orion the hunter with the star Betelgeuse shining brightly above the three stars that made up Orion's Belt. But as she started to turn away, the three stars briefly disappeared as if something had passed in front of them. Georgia looked again and Orion's Belt was visible again. She quickly dismissed the incident as a trick of the light and made her way into the airlock, not mentioning what she'd seen to anyone.

***

Joe Mancuso, Endeavour's pilot, was waiting to help Georgia and the chief out of their bulky spacesuits. Although Mancuso's muscular build often made people think he was a boxer, his fingers were nimble enough to swiftly unclip the intricate latches, hoses and seals.

"Hey, Georgia," he said as he removed her helmet and placed it in its protective padded bag. "You did well not to puke. I wasn't so lucky on my first spacewalk. I can still smell it!"

Georgia had never met anyone as positive as Mancuso. The strapping former navy pilot from Brooklyn had a positive story for every scenario. She wasn't always convinced he was telling the truth but was grateful for his sympathetic support.

"You heard me too? I thought I'd gotten away with it," she replied, running the fingers through her short blonde hair. It stuck messily to her scalp after being trapped under her comms cap.

Mancuso's green eyes beamed from under his bushy eyebrows. "You know there are no secrets on this ship. By the way, the captain wants to see you both."

The chief nodded. "Thanks, Joe. But can you help me out of my suit too?"

***

Captain Winter was fifty-seven years old and would be sixty by the time he returned to Earth. His twenty years in the air force before joining the astronaut corps had taught him to exercise every day and eat a strict healthy diet, which was why he still had a lean frame and didn't look a day over fifty.

So far, the mission had gone much better than he could ever have hoped. The hardware was proving reliable and the crew of *Endeavour* had become a tightly knit unit. He was well aware, however, that the human element was the weakest link and he strove every day to ensure they stayed at the peak of their effectiveness.

He was in his cabin, taking a short break when Georgia and the chief arrived, pulling themselves through the hatchway and looping their feet into some Velcro restraints.

"Nice work out there today, both of you," Winter said as they steadied themselves. "We've just had confirmation from Ground Control that the LCS works again. We now have a steady data stream."

The chief, who had been sucking water through a straw to rehydrate, nodded nonchalantly. "All in a day's work for the finest chief engineer and his capable assistant." He didn't see Georgia roll her eyes, but correctly guessed the reaction, even though she kept silent. "Does that mean I get to upload the new *Die Hard* remake for movie night?" he added.

Winter sighed. "I guess so. But I'm leaving it to you to handle any fallout from Doctor Betts. You know action films aren't her thing. Before that happens though, tell me, how does the ship look from out there? Is she holding up okay?"

The chief replied, "Yes, nothing out of the ordinary. I don't expect any more EVAs at this stage, anyway. It's just general wear and tear but nothing to be concerned about ahead of next week's landing."

Satisfied with the response, Winter turned to Georgia, who had also been drinking to rehydrate. "How was the experience? Will you be volunteering for the next spacewalk?"

"I loved it, sir. I don't know why you need to ask. But I'd be willing to let someone else get the chance to experience deep space. Maybe you?"

Winter gave his widest, warmest grin. "I'll leave it to you youngsters to enjoy the fun. I've had more than my fair share. On that note, get something to eat and prepare for Jim's movie. I can't wait."

***

Ultimately, *Die Hard* was played without the presence of Doctor Betts. She spent the evening in her cabin counseling Grace Cooke, one of the science specialists. Grace was only thirty years old and finding it the hardest among the crew to adapt to the isolation of being so far away from home. Although she had passed all the psychological stress tests that were a mandatory part of the selection process, it had been less than a month after leaving Earth orbit that she had exhibited signs that worried the doctor.

Since then, the doctor had spent many hours with Grace, attempting to form a bond and establish in Grace's mind that she was not alone. Some days were more of a struggle for Grace than others and today had not been a good day because of the failed communications with Earth.

This was the first time Grace had been unable to contact her family in Toronto. Even though the communications were now repaired and had only been offline for nineteen hours, the situation had hit home to her how remote and alone they were. When not on duty she had avoided the crew, instead spending in her cabin her time looking at family photos and videos.

Doctor Betts had plenty of sympathy. Grace was a civilian who had never been in the armed forces and had to live away from home for extended periods of time. It was a huge change for her, and Betts had recommended improving the selection process so that future candidates were better screened.

Chapter 2

Two days later, the persistent sound of the master alarm had been ringing around the ship for nearly forty seconds with the crew working methodically to resolve the cause. Besides the alarm, several monitors were displaying error messages, assisting the crew to determine the problem. This was a new issue and had arisen at the worst possible time on re-entry. If not resolved in the next ten seconds, the results would be catastrophic.

Captain Winter looked across to his right at Joe Mancuso, strapped into the pilot's seat. "We're nearly out of time, Joe. Can you regain the correct attitude?"

Before Joe could answer, there was a shout from behind his seat. "Ventral thrusters back online, captain." Within a fraction of a second, the master alarm ceased and the error messages stopped flashing.

Mancuso pressed a series of controls on the touch sensitive console before replying. "Attitude recovered. Re-entry is now nominal, sir," He placed his hands on his lap and visibly relaxed.

"Well done, everyone, you can all stand down," said Captain Winter. "That's the final trial run completed with flying colors. Georgia, very well spotted with the jammed actuator. Ground Control went all out to lead us astray."

Georgia sat back smugly in her seat. "I have to admit, they very nearly caught me out this time. However, as they failed yet again, I'd like to remind you all that I'm entitled to the first shower once we set Alpha Base up."

The captain didn't reply but merely sighed to himself as he loosened the restraints that prevented him floating away from his command chair. Georgia would not let anyone forget about the shower. But after nearly four months of only being able to wash with a damp towel, the shower had been a suitable motivation to encourage the crew during the mock landing exercises.

Staring intently out of the main screen he noticed that Mars now looked much larger than it had a few days earlier when it had still just been a large bright orange speck. Today he could see that there were definite hints of orange, brown and ochre on what was now unmistakably a planet. It didn't take him long to detect the position of the small Martian moons, Deimos and Phobos.

After nearly three months' transit time from Earth orbit, *Endeavour* and the other vessels making up Expedition Two were quickly catching up with Mars. Winter was spending more time pondering what it was about to mean for him and his crew to become the first humans to land on the planet.

Over the past few days, he had noticed a buzz of excitement about the crew that had been missing since shortly after leaving Earth orbit. Mentally, each of the crew had put their lives on hold during that period, taking one day at a time. There had been plenty of mission planning and research to carry out during the transit to ensure that they were all prepared for the landing, as well as regular daily exercise. But it was fair to say that everyone on board had found the journey monotonous. He was sure they had all struggled with the confines of *Endeavour*, seeing the same five faces every day and dealing with loneliness and separation from loved ones. He knew that he had.

"Good work, Joe. Time for a coffee before the planned course correction?"

It was more an order than a request, but he knew that Mancuso wouldn't say no to a coffee.

***

Winter filled two pouches with hot black coffee from the machine and handed one to Mancuso. He was not surprised no one else had taken the opportunity to head to the galley during downtime. Over recent weeks he had noticed that the crew preferred the seclusion of their own cabins. When asked for her opinion, Doctor Betts said she wasn't concerned. It was a coping mechanism and the crew had probably run out of anything interesting to say to one another.

Mancuso was no different. When not on duty he spent most of his time in the gym, working out. And it showed. He had lost some muscle mass on the journey, but nowhere near as much as everyone else. At six feet two Mancuso will be the first bouncer on Mars, Winter thought to himself ruefully.

"Joe, I wanted to check in. Ensure you have no concerns with the ship or the maneuver in a few hours."

"Thanks, Cap. The ship's a beauty. You should also speak with the chief, but I couldn't ask for anything more. These practice drills are keeping us on our toes, I'll give you that." Mancuso's New York/Italian accent always reminded Winter of *The Godfather* movies. Yet behind all the brawn, there was a keen intelligence that could never be taken for granted.

"That's good to hear. I'm proud of *Endeavour* and her crew. I'm sure neither of you will let me down. How are you standing up so far?

"I'm missing my family. But everyone is. I speak to them most days and you know they'd grown used to my long endurance space missions anyway. Knowing this is my last time away from them helps. And the fact we're doing something spectacular." Mancuso downed his coffee and went for a refill.

Winter sipped his drink. Still not used to the pouches, he was counting down the days to be able to drink from a mug again.

"So, no doubts about the mission? No worries?" Winter pushed, wanting to ensure his pilot had the right mindset for when it mattered.

"None, sir. I know you'll not let us get in the same situation as Expedition One." The comment caught Winter off guard, but he had the answer he wanted.

Chapter 3

Mancuso, a veteran Dragon pilot, was looking at the two computer screens in front of him, reading the systems information he needed. He had already double-checked that the new trajectory and burn times received from Ground Control had been correctly entered into the nav computer. "All systems looking nominal sir. I've stirred the fuel tanks and they're all up to pressure."

"Good work. In that case it's time to get everyone buckled up." Captain Winter used the internal comms to summon the crew up to the flight deck to get strapped in. The maneuver was expected so the four remaining crew members were in their seats within two minutes of the call.

There was an air of anticipation with this particular correction. Although minor, it would put *Endeavour* on the final heading to Mars orbit. The end of their marathon trip was in sight. The crew members murmured among themselves while Joe and Captain Winter monitored the systems as the computers counted down to the final burn.

***

The one exception was Georgia who sat quietly in her seat with eyes closed, listening to the Foo Fighters through her headphones. She wasn't needed for the course correction and was content to relax while Mancuso and the chief oversaw the maneuver. Music was the coping mechanism she used to escape from her surroundings and crew mates. It blocked out everything else going on around her like nothing else could. Never the most social person anyway, she welcomed the solitude wherever she could find it.

Although she had built strong friendships with Captain Winter and Doctor Betts during the twelve months' training for this mission, she had struggled to form bonds with the rest of the Expedition Two crew. A quick sense of humor covered for the fact that she didn't like to get close to people and would rather spend time with her computers and robots. They never asked questions. She was happy taking care of herself and not having responsibility for others. Landing on Mars couldn't come quickly enough as the confines of *Endeavour* were weighing down on her.

Her music drowned out the sound of the chatter and the constant drone of the various computers and systems located throughout the ship. During those moments, she could be anywhere.

As her head rocked to the beat of the music, Georgia sensed the slightest of nudges as *Endeavour*'s thrusters commenced their seventy-five second burn, delicately adjusting the velocity and trajectory. This was the third and final course correction of the mission and she knew what to expect, even with her eyes closed. In her mind, she pictured the landing zone inside the northern rim of the Hellas Planitia crater. With this course correction, it was becoming a reality.

The song finished as the engine burn ended, allowing her to hear and feel the rockets being shut down. Reluctantly she opened her blue eyes as the next song began, blinking a few times at the brightness of the LED lighting in the cabin. Unfastening her restraints, she noticed that Doctor Betts was trying to speak with her. Georgia turned off her device, removed her headphones, and smiled.

"Sorry, Megan, you were trying to tell me something?"

"I'm guessing that was Dave Grohl again." More of a statement than a question. "I was trying to let you know that you can have your medical check now rather than later. The captain has agreed to answer some questions from NBC reporters, so he's moved his time."

"Thanks, give me fifteen minutes to pack these seats away."

***

As the crew unbuckled themselves and returned to their duties, Mancuso looked at the data on his computer screens. "Course correction complete, captain. New trajectory is nominal for *Endeavour*."

Chief Grant floated over from his position. "All engines shut down as planned. Power was marginally down with engine three but well within safety limits."

"Good work, gentlemen," said Captain Winter. "Can you complete your detailed reports and send to Ground Control to confirm? Chief, how's the latest telemetry from the supply ships?"

"They continue to track well and are on course to arrive a day ahead of us. It couldn't be going smoother."

"Don't count your chickens just yet. We're still in the easy part." Winter pushed himself out of his chair. "I'm heading to my quarters to answer the latest batch of reporters' questions if you need me. I'll check in with Commander Anders on *Eden* to ensure he's prepared for his maneuver tomorrow."

Captain Winter floated deftly from his command seat, through the crew galley and into his cabin. Questions from journalists had dried up within a week of leaving Earth. With no dramas, Expedition Two's news had been overtaken by the latest political scandals to rock Washington, as well as rising tensions with Russia. Winter was more than happy with that scenario as it allowed him to focus on his job.

However, now that they were fast approaching Mars, he was well aware that the public relations people were in overdrive to make the mission front and center again.

Answering the public's questions wasn't something Captain Winter enjoyed, but he had a natural skill. His laid-back approach created an instant rapport with whoever he spoke to and his thirty years with NASA gave him instant authority on the subject of spaceflight. Winter was no fool. He knew that any questions he received would have already been filtered and approved by the public relations experts to ensure there was nothing contentious and that the right questions were being responded to. Those same experts would also review and probably amend his written responses so that he didn't inadvertently reveal any mission critical secrets. It had been exactly the same during his two command missions on the International Space Station.

He opened the message from Ground Control and inwardly sighed when he saw that he had eighteen questions to answer. None of them were difficult but they would take the next hour to deal with. He noticed he'd also received a message from his wife, which he quickly decided to delay opening until he'd addressed the questions. He wanted something to look forward to.

Chapter 4

In the medical center, Georgia had just completed her examination. Without thinking, she hooked her feet into the restraints to prevent her floating around and tapped the nearest console repetitively with her fingernails as she waited for Doctor Betts to provide her results. Like the rest of the crew, she was subjected to weekly physical examinations since leaving Earth orbit to monitor the effects of deep space travel. While Georgia knew they were necessary, the examinations had revealed nothing she didn't already know.

Due to size constraints, the medical facility was no bigger than an elevator and could only comfortably fit four people at any one time. They had conducted the physical tests in the gym with Megan looking on as Georgia completed cardio and resistance weight exercises.

Looking around the medical center, Georgia still didn't know what most of the equipment did. Luckily, there had been no medical emergencies so far. One wall was lined with a multitude of drawers, each neatly labeled with the medication it contained. Another wall had a bank of computers and monitors as well as a medical scanner. She knew this was all highly advanced technology. It had to be this far from home. There was still a faint metallic antiseptic smell, which always reminded her of her doctor's surgery back on Earth.

Doctor Betts, who had been reading data from her equipment and typing in copious notes to her computer, finally looked up and in her normal relaxed manner said, "Those two-hour daily runs we've been doing have done the trick. Nice to see that you do listen to me sometimes. You won't be able to complete a marathon, but at least you've not lost too much muscle and bone mass. Enough to cope with the Martian gravity anyway."

Although she didn't show it, the news relieved Georgia. It had worried her that her fatigue on the recent spacewalk was a sign her fitness was not where it needed to be for Mars' excursions. "No problem, Megan. It's easier to stay accountable with you as my running partner. And I appreciate the new expletives you've taught me."

Doctor Betts smiled. "You can thank my years at medical school for the language," she joked. "Eyesight and bloods have come back all clear too. Other than Mancuso, who is an absolute beast for his age, you're my healthiest patient."

Both laughed out loud. Georgia couldn't remember the last time she'd done that. The strain of the mission had been getting to her over recent weeks. The hardest part was dealing with the same people day after day. They invaded her personal space and she found even the smallest habit annoying. She'd bitten her tongue so many times but occasionally had vented her frustration. Captain Winter had gently spoken to her several times about controlling her anger and she often wished that she could be more like him. He never got flustered.

When she'd signed up to the Expedition Two mission she had not truly considered having to live with people in cramped and basic conditions. What had attracted her to the mission was actually the solitude and being away from the rest of humanity for a period of time. So, while most of the crew were experiencing isolation from their loved ones, Georgia was overwhelmed by the handful of people she came into daily contact with. Megan was the exception, but Georgia still found it difficult to speak openly with the doctor.

"Can I go now? I want to send Jackson a birthday message before I go back on duty."

Georgia didn't wait for an answer, pushing herself toward the door. Megan nodded. "We're done here for today. I'll book you in for my first Mars clinic next week."

***

As she entered her cabin and closed the door behind her, Georgia noticed a green flashing light on her computer terminal, indicating she had a new message. Switching on the screen, it thrilled her to see that it was a video message from her brother, Jackson.

She hit 'play' and a smiling image of her brother Jackson appeared. Behind him was Cocoa Beach Pier and the bright blue ocean. There was no mistaking that they were siblings. They both had the same blue eyes and short wavy blonde hair. Many times, people had thought they were twins, even though he was four years younger than her.

"Hey, sis, I just wanted to wish you well before you land on Mars next week. You know how incredibly proud of you I am. And how envious I am that you're getting there before me. Training is going well with my group lifting-off to Armstrong Base tomorrow for two weeks of fieldwork on the lunar surface. I'm excited about getting back into space again and preparing for Expedition Three. So, I really need your mission to go well for me and for you to save me the best cabin in Alpha Base." Georgia smiled at how ridiculous that sounded but knew she'd have to find him a special bunk.

"Mum and Dad would be proud of both of us. I know they're looking over us all the time. I'll be watching closely next week and will be in touch again once you've landed.

Love you loads, sis."

Georgia wiped a tear from her eye and touched the image of her brother on the monitor. Jackson was the only person back on Earth that she missed. He was the only family she had and the one person who had nearly held her back from joining this expedition. It had been difficult to say goodbye. But he had insisted that she take this opportunity and that he would follow in her footsteps.

She hit the record button to prepare her own message.

"Hey, Jacko. Just calling to wish my little brother a happy thirtieth birthday. I'm sure you didn't think I'd forget, even though you sent me that message. You look good for your age. Thanks also for en-suring you were standing in front of the beach and pier. That place is full of so many happy memories. Nearly every day I wish I was there rather than here. I hope Mars is worth it.

"No doubt you know the mission is still on track and that you'll be watching us land. I cannot wait to get there. I'm like a coiled spring some days. A little tip for your trip, take something that lets you escape because the people will drive you insane. I promise to try and get you a room upgrade at Alpha Base. It will cost you though and my preferred currency is chocolate. You know which brand. Make sure you work hard on your lunar field trip. You have to ensure you're part of Expedition Three otherwise I'm coming home on the first available rocket to kick your ass.

"Love you loads, bro."

Chapter 5

On board *Endeavour's* sister ship, *Eden*, the crew were experiencing issues with an aquaponics unit in the agriculture lab. There were three aquaponics units in total. Each was basically a large centrifuge which fooled the plants that there was gravity and ensuring the roots grew strong and in the right direction. The fluid provided the correct minerals and nutrients. A system had detected a leak in one tube feeding the plants but not before five liters of mineralized water had escaped which was now floating in multiple large bubbles around the bay. The lab was contained and, although there was no imminent danger to the ship itself, there was a risk of damage to important equipment monitoring the health of the plants.

Commander Anders had just arrived in the agriculture lab to get an update from the two botanists on board, Harry and Nicola King, and the flight engineer, Rashid Qadir. His eyes were quickly adjusting to the intense LED lights that mimicked natural sunlight and which were far brighter than in the rest of the ship. "Good work on scooping most of the water out. No impact on the plants I hope. They look healthy to me, but I'm not the expert."

"It's thanks to Rashid for quickly identifying the faulty valve," Harry King replied, at the same time patting Rashid on the shoulder. Rashid blushed at the compliment and smiled shyly. "We've turned off the circulation pumps, but the plants can handle it for several days with no lasting impact."

Anders turned to the still-blushing Rashid and asked, "How soon can you change the valve? I assume we carry spares."

"Let me check, commander." Rashid checked the personal device strapped to his wrist. "The computer confirms we have two in stores. If I can isolate the water, I can get it fixed within an hour."

"In that case, I'll leave the matter in your capable hands." Rashid nodded and left the lab, carefully ensuring he closed the hatch behind him. Anders liked Rashid's enthusiasm. Even after three months, he could still be relied on to quietly and efficiently get on with any tasks given to him. He wished he could say that for the rest of the crew who seemed to want to make his life as hard and miserable as possible.

Turning to the Kings he said, "I'll leave you to it unless you have any questions. I assume you'll scoop up the remaining droplets."

Nicola King grabbed his forearm to prevent him from leaving. "Actually, before you go, I would like to remind you we asked for additional spares. This equipment is vital for our studies on the effects of space travel on plants. It's unacceptable we have to nursemaid these delicate machines."

Anders had heard this several times. "Yes, I understand. But you know as well as I that we were limited on the cargo space. Ground Control decided on what we carried so blame them."

"I have spoken to them frequently and they are always unhelpful." Anders ensured he kept a straight face although he could imagine Nicola giving some poor unsuspecting soul a hard time.

"All we need to do is make it to Mars. Then you can have all the spares you need from the supply ships or the 3D printer."

This didn't placate Nicola's mood in any way. Anders could tell she wanted to launch into a debate on the matter. He was therefore relieved when his personal device chimed to advise him that Captain Winter was trying to contact him. He excused himself, ignoring Nicola's irritated stare, and returned to his cabin where he turned on his monitor to speak with the captain.

"Good afternoon, captain. I assume the course correction went without a hitch."

After a ten second delay, Winter replied, "Yes, Lars, we're now on final trajectory. *Endeavour* continues to operate flawlessly. The upgrades introduced after Expedition One continue to work perfectly. They give me complete confidence for this mission's success. I know it's early, but I thought I'd check in to see how you're shaping up for your burn tomorrow."

"*Eden* is doing great too. We have an issue with aquaponics where we have a leak, but I've got Harry and Nicola mopping that up at the moment. It shouldn't have an impact though."

"That's good to hear. And the crew?"

"Not as excited as I'd like them to be. Lots of gripes about lack of personal space and inadequate resources. It's like traveling with a ship full of infants."

Winter's laugh didn't help the commander's mood on the subject. "It looks like I have the star pupils on *Endeavour*. They're quiet but not mean. The good news is we have Mars in our sights and she's looking beautiful. Satellite imagery of the landing zone is not detecting any adverse atmospheric conditions that could cause dust clouds. At this stage, it's likely we'll be going for a direct landing. I'll check on before your maneuver but keep me informed if any issues arise."

"Will do, sir. *Eden* out." Lars switched off his monitor and reluctantly headed back to see how Harry and Nicola were progressing.

Harry and Nicola King were the only married couple on the mission. Now in their mid-forties, they'd originally met while studying for a Plant Science BSc at Canterbury Christ Church University. Their shared passion in plant genetics and microbiology had soon made them inseparable and it was no surprise to anyone that they'd qualified top of their year. They had both gone on to study for master's degrees and worked together at a bio pharmaceuticals company with the aim of improving crop yield to support the ever-growing population on Earth. It was there, when Nicola turned thirty, that Harry had asked her to marry him.

Their work had been noticed by NASA. They'd had a number of successes in being able to dramatically increase the yield per acre and produced a number of papers, even performed a TED talk on the subject. Initially they had been extremely reluctant to even speak with NASA representatives. The failure of Expedition One had put a huge question mark over the viability of safely landing on Mars. Let alone colonizing it. But the upgrades to the systems architecture, combined with a wealth of testing on the Moon reduced some of their fears. Once the space agency had promised further funding for their research and allowed the Kings to design sixty percent of the proposed experiments, they were finally convinced to set up the infrastructure on Mars. After all, they could always return to Earth after two years. Harry had been the keener of them to agree to the mission and after some gentle persuading, Nicola also came around to the idea. After all, their work would be benefiting the chances of mankind successfully colonizing another planet. And that legacy was too hard to resist.

By the time Commander Anders returned, the Kings had collected the remaining fluid and returned it to the irrigation system. Rashid had also returned and was half hidden under the aquaponics bay as he carried out his repairs.

"Excellent work, both of you. Does that mean we'll still have something to eat in a few weeks?"

Harry smiled, and gave a mock salute. "Have no worries, Mon Capitan. You will soon be eating green beans and lettuce. We know that everyone is looking forward to fresh vegetables after the months of processed meals."

***

While the excitement was happening in the agriculture lab, Thomas Redmayne Ph.D. was locked away in his science lab, preparing a new round of experiments on four mice. As Expedition Two's chief scientist, he was beginning to resent some of the menial research he was being asked to do. In his opinion, much of it was more suited to Grace Cooke's skills over on *Endeavour*. Although she also had a full roster of experiments to conduct, it would allow him more time to focus on more important research. It was bad enough that she'd been assigned to *Endeavour* and would be setting foot on Mars before him.

As he brooded over the situation, he roughly grabbed one of the white mice which was helplessly flailing its legs. Without any hesitation, Redmayne injected the mouse with a radioactive compound before placing it back in its tank and sealing the lid. After taking a few notes, he repeated the exercise with two of the other mice with different concentrations of the compound. He knew that the mice would be dead within a week. The fourth should survive, at least until the next experiment.

His dark thoughts were interrupted by Emily Pope hesitantly knocking on the door to his lab, her face peering through the glass window. She was by far his favorite crew member. He found her blue eyes, wavy brown hair and tight lips exciting and erotic. Add to that her understated intelligence and she could have been the perfect woman for him. He considered it such a waste that she was married.

Redmayne knew that his own rugged looks and intense blue eyes were attractive to women. He'd had no lack of attention from females over the years but had never found one who came close to his intellect. Emily was probably the closest to being his ideal partner but had made it blatantly clear early on that she was not interested in him.

He floated over to the door and unlocked it. "What do you want?" he asked brusquely. "I'm in the middle of my experiments."

Emily was used to Redmayne's manner and had long ago learned to ignore it. "Commander Anders wanted to know when you'll be providing your revised itinerary as part of the preparation for landing. Do we need to make special provision for any of your ongoing experiments?"

"He could have asked me that directly."

"The commander is dealing with an issue the Kings have with their aquaponics system. He sent me instead."

"Thanks, Emily, I'll inform the commander when I'm ready to give an answer." Redmayne closed the door and turned back to his computer, entirely missing the tirade of expletives coming from Emily's mouth.

**

"Commander Anders. I just sent you the information you're after." Redmayne pulled himself into Anders' cabin without waiting for an invitation and hovered in the middle of the room

Anders was annoyed by the sudden intrusion but knew it was pointless raising any objections. Instead, he replied, "Thanks Tom. I assume there aren't any nasty surprises in there for me."

"Of course not, Lars. You know how I like to make life easy for you."

Anders couldn't tell if Redmayne was being serious. From day one, he'd been unable to read the man but always had a gut feeling that there was more to him than met the eye. To be fair, Redmayne was very supportive to him and always first to offer clear thoughts on any problems that arose. He wasn't sure he would have been so confident in some of his decisions without his chief scientist's assurances.

"Is there anything else, Tom? I assume you're here for a reason."

Redmayne gave a knowing smile. "Perceptive as always, sir. Yes, I wanted to know if you'd made any further requests to Ground Control to delay *Endeavour*'s landing in favor of ours? The more I think about it, the more sense it makes to be able to get on the ground and set up my experiments in a pristine environment, before those idiots contaminate everything within one hundred miles."

Anders was expecting the question. It was one Redmayne had asked on numerous occasions. "General Stockton denied the request. Again. It's no use asking any more. Ground Control have been explicit that Captain Winter and his crew will be landing as scheduled."

Redmayne looked deflated. If he thought Anders hadn't been forceful enough, he kept it to himself. "That's highly disappointing. The general is being extremely short-sighted. Not only because of the risks to my work but also overlooking you to be the first man to set foot on Mars. Winter is only there because of public relations. You should have been chosen through merit."

"It's kind of you to say so, Tom. But we both know that's not true. Captain Winter has had a long and distinguished career. He deserves every honor he is going to receive."

"Okay, Lars. I won't ask again. But I do believe it's a missed opportunity." With nothing more to say on the subject, Redmayne immediately headed back to his lab, leaving Commander Anders to contemplate if maybe he should be the first man on Mars.

Chapter 6

The following day, Georgia and Captain Winter were strapped to the running machines, halfway through their daily run. Even though Winter had never learned to enjoy running, whether on Earth or in space, he had learned from his missions on the International Space Station that the time allowed him to work through problems in more detail without being interrupted.

This morning, he was concerned with the latest telemetry from one of the supply ships, *Aquarius*. The guidance systems were not performing entirely as planned but were still waiting operational limits. Ground Control had suggested rebooting the systems but Georgia, as mission specialist for those systems, wasn't entirely sure a full reboot was necessary.

"There's not much we can do when we're only four days out from Mars," Winter commented, his breathing sounding slightly strained. "But I don't want to leave it to chance and risk losing *Aquarius* and its supplies. Tell me why we don't need to reboot."

Georgia couldn't remember the last time she'd run with the captain, but she was pleased he was asking for her opinion. "It's exactly the same guidance system as the other two supply ships and, for that matter, *Endeavour* and *Eden*. *Aquarius* is the only ship experiencing anomalous energy spikes. I think those spikes are causing the guidance issues, not the system itself."

"Do you know what's causing the energy spikes?"

"That's the confusing part. The energy spikes are a reaction to another energy source emanating from outside *Aquarius*. I've double-checked the numbers with Ground Control, and they stack up. So, a system reboot will make no difference at all."

Winter pressed stop on his machine. Picking up a towel to wipe sweat from his face, he asked, "Any theories?"

"Mars is still too far away to have any effect. Maybe there's an energy leak from one of the other supply ships, but the data doesn't back that up. I could suggest there's another craft nearby, but we know the Russians are over one week behind us. Unfortunately, we don't have the sensors to pinpoint the cause."

"Honest assessment. Are you concerned?"

Georgia stopped her machine. "I'm frustrated I don't have an answer. But I have no concerns about the reliability of the guidance system."

"Okay, I trust your judgment on this. But monitor the telemetry closely. If there is a bug in the system, we'll need it fixed before touchdown."

Georgia was about to reply when Joe Mancuso's voice boomed over the internal communications. "An ultra-fast coronal mass ejection has occurred. We've just been advised an X8-class solar flare has been detected and heading in our direction. It's going to hit in just under twelve minutes. Everyone head to the refuge until further notice."

Recognizing the seriousness of the situation, Georgia and Caption Winter immediately unstrapped themselves and headed to the corridor leading back to the refuge, situated between the living quarters and the hold.

The crew quickly gathered their immediate belongings and calmly headed for the refuge, which was protected by a thick layer of tungsten as well as the primary water tanks. At the same time, and to further protect the crew from the bombardment of solar radiation, Mancuso oriented *Endeavour* so that the engines and fuel tanks directly faced the fast-approaching solar flare.

There had been fortnightly training drills for this scenario and in less than three minutes everyone was in the refuge, waiting for the solar flare to strike. All critical inboard systems, except for life support, were switched off. *Eden*'s crew were advised to move to their refuge despite it looking as though they were safely out of the path of the solar particles.

"Two minutes until impact." There was a nervousness in Winter's voice. An X8 flare was at the top end of what the refuge had been designed to withstand. A potentially lethal dose of radiation was about to envelope the ship, and possibly affect onboard systems. While his main concern was the crew's safety, he was worried that some of *Endeavour's* critical systems could be disabled this close to Mars. "Joe, I should have checked but are all systems turned off and the communications array retracted?"

Winter could see that Mancuso was mentally running through all the activities he'd completed. As soon as Mancuso's jaw dropped, he knew something was wrong. "Fuck! I can't remember what I did with comms! I need to check."

Winter raised his hand in protest. "No, it's okay. You stay here. I'll deal with it." Without waiting for a response, he opened the heavy tungsten door, quickly making his way back along the ship's corridor, which was now bathed in red emergency lighting.

"Damn," he thought, "if communications fail then we'll have to abort the mission." He returned to the flight deck to key in the commands that would rotate the array out of danger. Nothing happened. He tried again, but with the same result.

"Georgia!" he shouted through to the refuge. "The computer is not responding to commands. I need your help. Get up here fast."

As soon as Georgia reached the flight deck, she could see that the captain was in trouble. Winter moved out of her way to allow her to assess the problem. She keyed in a string of commands, but still there was no reaction.

"Get back to safety, Georgia. We're too late. The computer's not responding, and we've run out of time. We can repair comms when it's safe."

"Right behind you, captain. Let me try one more sub-routine."

As Winter drifted back to the safety of the crew quarters, Georgia tried one last trick up her sleeve. She was desperate to succeed and knew that it would take days to repair the damage caused by the flare, if repairs were possible at all. It would fry many electronics systems. This time, a green light signified she'd been successful, and the comms array was retracting. Relieved, she pushed off in the direction of the refuge. At that same moment, the alarm signaled that she was out of time as the solar flare hit and enveloped *Endeavour*.

There was a strange buzzing sound in the cabin and her whole body started tingling. She could see hundreds of black dots appear in her eyes as the charged particles coursed through her brain, destroying brain cells in their path.

"Oh shit," were her last thoughts as she passed out.

Chapter 7

Approximately nine hundred and fifty thousand miles away, *Eden* avoided the main brunt of the solar flare. As soon as it was safe to leave the refuge, Commander Anders had the crew perform a complete systems check. Within an hour, all critical systems were deemed operational and the commander was able to send a report to Ground Control.

The main concern for the botanists was any long-term radiation impact on the plants. The Kings had spent all of their time in the refuge, helpless and frustrated that their work may be destroyed. The walls of the agriculture lab weren't as well shielded as the refuge and there was not sufficient research to tell what damage cosmic rays could have to the delicate nature of the plants. It wouldn't necessarily be a disaster if the crops were inedible. However, if the plants were decimated there was a very limited supply of seeds until Expedition Three arrived in two years' time.

After a tense thirty minutes frantically analyzing a record of the radiation levels, Nicola confirmed, "Radiation exposure doesn't appear to have spiked into the red. We dodged a bullet this time and the crop should be safe."

Harry breathed a sigh of relief. "The equipment remained fully functioning too. And no more leaks."

"Thank goodness for small miracles," agreed Nicola. "I dread to think how *Endeavour* got on. They were in the eye of the storm and had very little time to react."

***

On the flight deck, Anders was trying to regain contact with *Endeavour*, but was receiving only static.

"No need to worry yet," he said to his co-pilot, Emily Pope. "Captain Winter may still be experiencing the effects of the solar flare. Keep listening out for them while I report to Ground Control from my quarters. Let me know as soon as you receive a response."

"Yes, sir. Is there any other action we can take?" Emily was almost pleading with Anders to do more, betraying her young age and lack of experience.

"I'm sorry, Emily. There's not much we can do out here. We have to trust that *Endeavour* survived. I'm sure they'll make contact as soon as they are able."

Anders slid from his chair and floated effortlessly to his cabin, sliding the door closed behind him. But before he could send an update to Ground Control, there was a knock on his door. "Captain? It's Tom. Do you have a few minutes?"

"Come in, Tom."

Tom floated in and grabbed a handrail to steady himself. If he has any worries, he's certainly not showing them, thought Anders who knew that the chief scientist was more interested in proving his research than empathy for people. "I wanted to let you know that I was able to monitor the strength of the solar flare that *Endeavour* encountered. It was an X-twenty-class flare, far more powerful than any spacecraft has previously experienced. The dose of radiation the crew just experienced is far higher than they were expecting. Or what any of our ships were designed to withstand. The refuge may have provided sufficient protection, but it's not guaranteed. The shielding on many of the electronics systems will not have prevented damage. Have you been able to establish contact yet?"

Anders' concerns for the safety of *Endeavour* and her crew suddenly increased. He absently rubbed the stubble on his chin and replied, "Not yet. We've tried several times to make contact on different channels but with no success. I've left Emily with the task while I make a report to Earth. Forward me your readings and I'll add them to my report."

Thirty minutes later he returned to the flight deck. "Any news?" he asked, knowing the answer already.

"Nothing yet," Emily Pope replied, slowly shaking her head. "I have telemetry from both supply ships to confirm that they are still on course with all systems nominal, although *Aquarius* is continuing to drift marginally."

Anders knew that there could be a dozen reasons *Endeavour* hadn't been in contact because of the solar storm, not all of them catastrophic. He had to retain hope until he knew for sure otherwise. Redmayne's readings on the flare confirmed it was highly likely that systems would have been affected. Perhaps communications was one of those systems. He hoped that the crew would be able to correct the system failures at the earliest opportunity. It was just a waiting game.

He smiled encouragingly at the Kings as they entered the flight deck. "All good below I understand."

Nicola nodded and said, "Yes, no problems as far as we can see. What's the news from *Endeavour*?"

"Still silence. It's likely the storm fried their comms, but we really don't know for sure. I'll give a crew update after Ground Control have responded." Anders was clinging to a thin hope that Ground Control could contact *Endeavour* directly. The prolonged silence was ominous though.

Chapter 8

Georgia came around and opened her eyes to see a worried expression on the face of Doctor Betts. Looking around she saw she was back in the refuge with the rest of the crew. She found it hard to focus and there was a constant buzzing in her ears. Her head wanted to explode.

Captain Winter was trying to speak to her, although his voice sounded very distant. "Georgia, thank goodness you're okay. What were you thinking?"

She blinked twice, trying hard to concentrate and gather her thoughts. "I'm not sure I thought it through, sir. I just reacted to save the mission."

"We'll see if you did that. Thank you for retracting the array before the flare hit, but it wasn't worth the huge personal risk. Doctor Betts says you were hit by a massive dose of radiation from cosmic particles. I've told her to watch you closely for the next seventy-two hours."

Megan looked extremely worried and was more sympathetic. "You were exposed for only a few seconds before the captain pulled you to safety. How are you feeling?"

"Light-headed and nauseous, but I'll live."

"You had us worried there. You were out cold for a couple of minutes. I'll prescribe you painkillers and anti-radiation tablets. I'll also need to take some blood and you must rest. No excuses."

"Sorry, doctor," interrupted Captain Winter, "but I'll need Georgia back on the flight deck with Mancuso and the chief to effect repairs. This flare is likely to have knocked out many of our systems. I will need all the expertise I can to get everything back online."

Megan protested. "You can see she's in no fit state. Can't you give her an hour at least?"

Georgia pulled herself upright, concentrating hard on not throwing up. "I'll be fine, Meg. Let me help the captain for as long as I can. Then I promise to take some rest and you can carry out all the tests you want to."

The doctor wasn't happy but knew when she was outnumbered. "I'll be watching you closely, Georgia. I know what you're like."

"And I know what I'm capable of doing," Georgia replied defiantly. "No one else knows the computer systems like I do."

An hour later, the radiation levels had dropped to a safe enough level for the crew to exit the refuge. Captain Winter directed Georgia to work with Mancuso to prioritize the communications equipment. The communications array itself had been saved by Georgia's actions. The problem was with the fried circuitry on the flight deck, but that was easier to diagnose and replace.

Once the captain had left to help the chief in engineering, Mancuso said, "I'm sorry, Georgia. I should have retracted the array. I don't know how I forgot."

"You didn't. The controls were offline. As a safety precaution, I turned them off when I carried out the EVA to replace the LCS the other day. You weren't to know. It's my mistake."

"That was still a ballsy thing you did. Bat shit crazy but you did a great job."

"Thanks, Joe. Now you must excuse me." Georgia made a dash for the crew toilet as a wave of nausea came over her, just closing the door behind her before she was violently sick.

***

Winter left Mancuso and Georgia on the flight deck and floated down to engineering to assist the chief to determine the level of damage and what repairs were essential prior to even considering a landing. The flare could not have happened at a worse time, he thought.

There would be a lot of worried people on *Eden* and on Earth waiting desperately to hear that they were safe.

He hoped that Georgia wouldn't suffer any side effects from the radiation exposure. He had pulled her into the refuge within seconds of the solar flare striking. And although the chief had just informed him of the strength of the flare, he had done all that he could to protect her. If Georgia was affected, then he knew he would feel guilty for a very long time.

***

Georgia returned from the toilet looking pale and weak but determined to help Mancuso. After two hours of testing and replacing components, they repaired the communications equipment. But the effort had taken it out of Georgia, and she put up no resistance when Captain Winter suggested she should return to her cabin to rest. Once in bed, she took the pills given to her by Megan, slipped on her headphones to listen to her favorite rock compilation, dimmed the lights, and fell into a deep sleep.

Back on the flight deck, Winter was more relaxed. Repairs of the main systems were nearly complete, and the chief had advised him that all systems would be functional within twenty-four hours. He had a mixed sense of pride and relief that *Endeavour* and its crew were standing up to all the challenges. Mancuso was looking at him expectantly, awaiting his next instructions.

"Okay, Joe. Before I contact Ground Control, let's see how *Eden* faired."

Mancuso pressed a button on his console. "*Endeavour* to *Eden*. This is Mancuso. Comm check."

Following the standard delay, they heard the excited voice of Commander Anders. "Great to hear you, Joe. You've been off air for a while and had us worried. What's your status?"

"Commander, it's Winter. We took a hit, but systems are coming back online. Nothing that the chief can't fix. How's *Eden*?"

"Everything is green here. We caught the edge of the solar flare so had it easier than you. There's some people waiting to hear from you back at Control."

Winter nodded, sure that General Stockton and Kristen would be concerned about their fate. Although he always tried to reassure his wife before any mission, she'd always remind him he wasn't indestructible. "That's my next call, Lars. I knew you'd be worried about me too. As far as I'm concerned, we're still a go for landing."

"Nice to have you back, sir. I'll inform the *Eden* crew there's no need for a search party."

"Okay, Lars. Time for me to speak to the general. *Endeavour* out."

Winter would have much rather spoken with Kristen first. She was strong but would still be frantic until he spoke with her. But protocol dictated that he up-date the general as a priority. The best he could do was keep his report as concise as possible.

Chapter 9

The following day, and unable to keep any food down, Georgia was strapped to the bed in the medical bay attached to an infusion drip with Doctor Betts for company. Each of the crew dropped in at different points to check on her progress but didn't stay for long. Georgia was not in the mood for visitors and it hadn't taken long for any of the crew to get the hint.

The doctor and the captain were the only ones she had time for. To pass the time, she had watched three romantic movies from Megan's personal collection. They weren't really her type of film, but they had kept Megan from talking for several hours, which was enough for Georgia.

She had been asleep for maybe half an hour when she woke to see that Captain Winter had replaced Megan. "Back with us?" he said as he saw her eyes flicker open. "Doctor Betts has gone for her evening meal so you have me to talk to."

He gave her his warmest fatherly smile, and it was impossible for Georgia to argue. "Anything interesting to talk about?" she asked.

"I thought you'd like to know about *Aquarius*."

Georgia sat forward, looking eager to find out. "Was I right?"

"Yes, you were. The anomalous energy spikes stopped shortly after the solar flare. The guidance systems have self-corrected the course and now *Aquarius* is back on its optimal trajectory. There has to be a connection, but I don't know what it can be."

"I can't help with that either but at least it proved me right. What do Ground Control want to do?"

Captain Winter absently scratched his head. "They're as perplexed as me. Even more so because they detected a similar energy spike on *Endeavour* about three hours after *Aquarius* recovered. It lasted for only a couple of minutes and it didn't affect any of our systems."

"Perhaps some kind of natural phenomena that we've not previously encountered?" Georgia suggested.

"Possible, but the pattern of the spikes is too regular. Something to watch out for, I guess. Maybe a mystery for Doctor Redmayne to look into."

"Agreed. As long as you don't expect me to work with him. He's not the easiest person to get on with."

"That's rich coming from you," snorted the captain.

"True, but I'm the best at what I do," laughed Georgia, feeling better already.

Chapter 10

Captain Winter sat in his command chair on the flight deck, pondering what the next few hours might hold for all of them. Mars was now a little over a day away. Within two hours, the supply ships, *Challenger*, *Intrepid* and *Aquarius*, would land on the surface. It would be the first true test of the new systems introduced since the failure of Expedition One, six years earlier. Despite the rigorous testing, re-testing and training, there was still a huge element of danger with what was being attempted. And there was no option for failure this time. Further loss of life was not an acceptable outcome after the six astronauts already lost.

Assuming the supply ships all landed safely and without incident, there would be a go/no go decision to make. Winter was grateful that the final decision was not his alone. He trusted that Ground Control would make the right decision based on the available data, rather than pressure from the investors who had pumped trillions of dollars into the program. Those companies expected a return on the investments, but they wouldn't want bad publicity.

He knew there was a huge worldwide interest in their mission. The stakes were enormous; not merely financial but also reputational. Now that the lunar colony was firmly established, Mars was the next big frontier for humanity. It was an honor to be leading the advance party that would establish a permanent Martian base. And, if successful, Mars would be the perfect stepping-stone for mankind to explore the solar system and ultimately the galaxy.

The tragic failure of Expedition One had been a shock at the time. He had known all the astronauts on that flight and flown with three of them on missions to the ISS. They had been good men and women. The best. He didn't want the world to mourn his mission as well.

It was only because of the public enquiry to understand what had gone so catastrophically wrong, that the extent of the industry's greed and arrogance had been revealed. Quality had been compromised because of budget, time constraints and national pride. It was reminiscent of the Cold War of the 1960s between the former USSR and the USA. Only this time, it was the egos of billionaire businessmen as well as politicians that had caused Enterprise to crash, resulting in the deaths of its crew.

NASA's Aerospace Safety Advisory Panel had been particularly scathing in their findings and made many thousands of recommendations to be applied to any future missions.

Although it was widely accepted that travel to Mars would never be entirely risk-free, measures were implemented to mitigate the dangers as much as was reasonably possible.

And so, wholesale changes were made to the management of the program. The spacecraft were redesigned and upgraded to allow for more system redundancy and safety features. Increased emphasis was placed on crew wellbeing, both mental and physical, to help them cope with the stresses of a long-duration mission. The mission profile had been completely re-written and Expedition Two's crew rigorously selected and trained. Although these changes had led to years of delay, they reassured Captain Winter that *Endeavour* and its sister ships were far more capable for this challenge.

And yet, because they were the first, there was still a huge element of trust in the engineers and scientists back on Earth. If further lives were lost it would be a massive setback for America's Mars ambitions. The joint Mars mission between China and Russia was breathing down their necks, only a week behind them. There was no doubt in Winter's mind that the Chinese and Russians wanted to be the first to step on Mars and were hoping for another American failure. He would do his damnedest to make sure that didn't happen.

For the hundredth time, he studied the map of the landing zone pinned to his wall. He already knew the area like the back of his hand but was constantly drawn back to it. The site within the crater known as Hellas Planitia had been carefully selected many years before as a result of detailed analysis by robotic landers. It was the lowest point on the Mars surface, with a depth of almost four miles below the standard ground level, the result of an enormous asteroid crashing into the planet some four billion years in the past.

Being such a low elevation had a range of benefits for the mission. Firstly, the increased amount of atmosphere to travel through would allow the ships to slow down prior to a controlled landing. Secondly, the Mars atmospheric pressure was at its greatest, although it was still far too thin to sustain life. But it was sufficient to allow for water to flow without boiling away. Thirdly—and most importantly—a vast reservoir of subsurface water had been detected. They would use this to create rocket propellant for the return journey, as well as water to sustain the colonists.

***

The Expedition Two crews on both *Endeavour* and *Eden*, along with most of the population on Earth, watched and held their collective breaths as the three supply ships entered Mars' upper atmosphere for their final approach and landing. The *Endeavour* crew were gathered in silence watching a video transmission from *Challenger* on the large monitor in the galley. They could see the Martian surface hurtling past, close enough for Winter to identify certain geographical features. He watched in awe as the image changed from day to night, the Martian surface fading from brown to black in less than a minute.

A smaller screen showed the direct feed from an orbiting satellite that was tracking the rockets from ten thousand miles' altitude. Despite the distance, the feed clearly showed the supply ships glowing bright against the Martian night as super-heated gases enveloped them. As expected, telemetry from *Challenger* was interrupted because of the ionized gas. It was an anxious wait for confirmation that the landing had been successful. Winter couldn't take his eyes away from the seconds ticking by on the digital clock. Time almost stopped. He whispered a silent prayer for a positive outcome.

Exactly on cue, the signal from *Challenger* was received that it had touched down, quickly followed by *Intrepid* and then *Aquarius*. Winter released the breath he'd been holding, and a cheer rang through the ship from the crew. Several seconds later, video images arrived from *Challenger* showing that the supply ships had made pinpoint landings at their designated landing zones.

Despite his elation, Winter felt sick in the pit of his stomach. They had come too far to turn back, but the safe landing of the supply ships made it almost inevitable that by this time tomorrow he would be standing on Mars—or smeared across its surface. I guess I should be more careful about what I wish for, he thought ruefully to himself. For now, though, it was a time for celebration with his brave crew.

***

Following the successful landings of the supply ships, it was clear in Captain Winter's mind that the decision to continue the mission would be a mere formality. The telemetry and flight profiles of the ships needed to be analyzed in detail to ensure that they had followed flight parameters but from the information he had seen, nothing jumped out as being unusual. However, it took nine hours for Ground Control to make their decision, with General Stockton detailing the instructions via a video message.

After he'd viewed it in his quarters, Winter sighed wearily, switched off the monitor and gathered the crew in the galley to update them. "Ground Control has been analyzing the telemetry and confirmed that all systems operated well within safe flight parameters. I've just received orders from General Stockton." He paused for dramatic effect, looking at the five eager faces waiting to hear the news. Once he had everyone's attention he loudly exclaimed, "It's a go for landing!"

A loud cheer echoed around the small galley as the crew's relief at the news was expressed. "This is finally it, ladies and gentlemen," Winter continued, once everyone had hugged each other and the room was quiet again. "You have all sacrificed a great deal, trained hard and traveled an awful long way but we're going to Mars." He could see the excitement and intensity in everyone's face. He knew that, once the euphoria of the moment wore off, they would get their game faces on and prepare for the greatest moment in their lives.

"I also have a personal video message from the US President to share." Winter turned on the large monitor to show an image of the presidential seal, before switching to a view of the President sitting at his desk in the Oval Office. The President, knowing his message would be shared publicly, had put on his best reassuring smile, used so many times in his addresses to the nation.

"Captain Winter and the crews of *Endeavour* and *Eden*, it's an honor to speak with you from the Oval Office. Within a matter of hours, you will have achieved the greatest triumph for mankind. I do not need to tell you that the entire world is watching with anticipation. Not since the Moon landings of the 1960s and '70s has man dared to reach further out into space.

"As a child growing up in Texas, I watched the moon landings with my folks. I remember a huge sense of pride at what America had achieved. For too long, talk of human settlements on the Moon and Mars never became a reality. I, along with many Americans, have been left frustrated at the lack of imagination and foresight shown by successive administrations. Ultimately, it took fifty-five years from Neil Armstrong landing on the moon to the first permanent lunar settlement. And finally, ten years later, mankind stands on the brink of colonizing a new planet and extending our reach into the universe. I sense we're starting to make small but consistent steps.

"We are all explorers and we seek new challenges thanks to heroes such as yourselves who are willing to sacrifice so much for the advancement of mankind. I speak for all Americans and everyone in the free world when I say a sincere thank you. Good luck to you all. And God speed."

The message ended and Captain Winter spun round to face the crew. "Rousing stuff from the President. You all know what you need to do. I have absolute faith in every one of you. We'll commence entry procedures in six hours. I suggest you all get some rest and gather your thoughts. Are there any questions?" Winter paused for a few seconds and, when no one spoke up, said, "You know the world is watching and praying for our success. Let's get this thing done, guys."

The crew dispersed into smaller groups. Doctor Betts floated over to Winter and said, "Nice presidential speech. He's bound to get re-elected if we land and survive, and I never even voted for him. Typical politician, now he's trying to take credit for decisions made by his predecessors."

"It's been a long journey, Megan, and we're still not there. But we have every chance of pulling this off and establishing another level in our understanding of the universe."

"Sounds like you're channeling the President himself," Megan replied with a wry smile. "I hope you've planned what to say when you step onto Mars tomorrow. You know they will repeat your words for generations to come."

Winter looked exasperated. "Because my moment will be broadcast live, the PR guys have given me some suggestions. They're nervous I may screw it up. To be honest, I'm nervous I'll screw it up! They want me to be inclusive and to not offend anyone. But I have a few ideas of my own which I'll go with instead. I hope I don't upset anyone. Kristen would never forgive me if I did." Kristen had helped write his words before he left Earth. She had always been far better with language. And she knew to keep it simple enough for him to memorize.

Winter noticed that the galley had quickly emptied. He supposed that the crew was eager to send final messages to their loved ones back home before settling down to rest. But he had one other matter on his mind for the doctor. "On another subject, how's the patient?"

"Too early to tell, although I am worried about her. Georgia was subjected to a huge dose of radiation, so the nausea and vomiting doesn't come as a surprise. But thanks to your quick reactions, her exposure time was extremely brief. She tells me she's fit and able to work and I have no doubt that she'll do her duties tomorrow."

"Thanks, doctor. We need her computer skills. I'd hate to be a man down."

"You mean a person down," Megan corrected.

"You know what I mean. Each member of this crew is invaluable and has earned their own place on the mission. Georgia is no different, but I need you to assure me that she will be ready for re-entry. It's going to be a highly stressful time until touchdown."

"From what I've observed, I have no reason to believe she will perform anything other than to her optimum. She's not going to let you down, Liam."

"Thanks, Megan. That's all I need to know."

With that, Winter made his way to the flight deck, climbed into his command chair and sat alone, staring at the red planet that now dominated the view. He didn't know how long he stayed there but, as he looked at the familiar features, he was at peace with the decision to land. He knew they would succeed.

Chapter 11

Georgia slipped on her bright orange flight suit in her cabin. Shortly before leaving Earth orbit, she had mischievously started a debate among the crew why the flight suits were required. After all, if anything went wrong during the landing phase, who would rescue any survivors? *Eden* was the only ship equipped to mount a rescue attempt but would certainly not be allowed to do so for fear of losing both crews. It had surprised her when most of the Expedition Two crew threatened to boycott wearing the flight suits. In the end, however, Ground Control convinced them there was a public expectation that all safety measures be in place, even if some of them were a token gesture.

Her flight suit was looser than the last time she'd worn it almost three months earlier. Although it had been hard work, she was now grateful for the daily hours of exercise and running Megan had insisted upon to keep her in shape and prevent total muscle atrophy.

The doctor's medication had proved very effective. She'd slept for four hours and was feeling better than she had done in days. Although she still had no appetite, the nausea had gone, and she was fairly confident that she wouldn't throw up before touchdown. Instead, she could actually enjoy the experience and the excitement inside her was building.

Collecting her gloves and helmet she floated out of her cabin, through the hatch leading to the mid-deck containing the common room and galley before heading up to the flight deck to take her position sitting next to the chief and behind Mancuso. She viewed Mars out of the front windows, clearly being able to make out craters, mountains and valleys. There were also wisps of cloud. It looked so close she was convinced she could almost reach out and touch it.

After pulling the straps tightly to secure herself into her seat, Georgia secured her helmet with the visor still up. The captain and

Mancuso were busy up front going through the long checklist required to make the ship ready for landing. The captain briefly glanced over his shoulder and gave Georgia an encouraging smile that she couldn't help but return. "Good to have you back, Pyke. How are you feeling?"

"Exhilarated! This will be the ride of a lifetime. I wouldn't be anywhere else." As Georgia said it, she knew it to be true. At that moment she was exactly where she wanted to be. It didn't matter what happened next, although failure was the furthest thing from her mind.

Chief Grant looked up briefly from his panel of instruments and simply nodded at her. Not one for many words, she thought. But then what was there to say when you were responsible for the rockets working correctly to take *Endeavour* in for a smooth landing?

***

The four of them worked in unison for the next forty-five minutes to complete all the tasks on the checklist. Having done this a hundred times in training, it was as if someone had choreographed their every move. With thirty minutes until they entered the Martian atmosphere, they were a few minutes ahead of where they needed to be.

Winter looked at Mancuso and asked, "Can you patch me into *Eden*, please?" Once the channel was open, the captain pressed the switch on his microphone. "Commander Anders, we're showing green lights across the board and all good to go. We'll try to put on a good display for you."

"Good luck, Liam," came the reply a few seconds later. "I expect a warm welcome when we join you."

"Thanks, Anders. You'll get one if you nail the landing. *Endeavour* out."

Winter took a moment to look around and noted that Megan and Grace had also quietly taken their places at the rear of the flight deck. Grace looked pale and sweaty, and she was staring down at her lap as if she didn't want to be there. Although Winter had some sympathy for her, there was no going back now even if they wanted. There wasn't enough fuel to escape Mars' gravity. He tried to lighten the tone and in his most formal voice said, "This is your captain speaking. Can everyone please return their seats to the upright position, fold their trays and stow any loose luggage in the overhead compartments."

Grace raised her eyes and gave him a nervous grin to confirm that she was okay.

Mancuso joined in by commenting, "I was waiting for the drinks trolley. Have I missed it?"

He'd broken the tension that was running though everyone. But, all too soon, the computer warned them that *Endeavour* was about to enter the upper atmosphere and the crew were focused once more on tracking the various readouts in front of them.

***

Strong vibrations ran through the deck plates as soon as *Endeavour* began to encounter Mars' upper atmosphere. It wasn't long before the intensity increased, causing the fixtures to shake and rattle.

"Oxygen to primary and visors locked," commanded Winter and, the staccato sound of latches locking in place, was enough to tell him everyone had complied.

The computer was now controlling entry, with Mancuso paying close attention in case the captain ordered him to switch to manual. Small thrusters fore and aft fired to turn *Endeavour* around, so it was now flying tail first. With Mars now behind and below them, they could see only the blackness of space through the main windows.

"Distance three fifty," Mancuso called out as the main engines fired for a ninety second de-orbit burn, reducing the speed by three thousand miles per hour. The sudden deceleration slammed the crew hard into their seats at the same time as the deafening roar from the rocket motors reached the flight deck. Breathing became a struggle and Georgia found it easier to take short rapid breaths until she began to feel light-headed. It was a relief when the engines cut out.

"Engine status, chief?" Winter queried, concerned for the next phase.

"Nominal. All pressures where they need to be," came the immediate reply from behind him.

Thrusters fired again to orient *Endeavour* so that the vast belly of the ship, covered in an adaptive heatshield coating, was facing the oncoming planet.

Georgia could see plasma dancing across the nose of *Endeavour* as the ship's speed caused gases at this altitude to ionize. While mesmerizing, the plasma meant they were now entering the most dangerous part of the mission, and the point where Enterprise had failed. Pushing that thought swiftly from her mind she paid close attention to her console for any heat spikes that would be the first warning the heat shield was not up to the job. As *Endeavour* swooped ever closer to the planet's surface, she spotted that two sensors were showing the aft port fin was getting hotter. Within fifteen seconds, the temperature was creeping toward the red line.

Calmly, she called out, "Captain, we have thermal issues on the port fin. Another ten seconds to structural integrity being compromised. All other temps are normal."

Winter switched the view on his monitor to confirm Georgia's readings. "Shit!" he muttered. "Joe, can you adjust the flight profile to reduce stress on the port side?"

Mancuso reacted before the captain had completed his order. He deftly moved the small joystick in front of him and *Endeavour* slowly twisted. It was now crabbing into the upper atmosphere, but the effect on the affected fin was almost instant. Georgia saw the temperatures return to normal as *Endeavour* continued to bleed off speed.

"Thanks, Joe," she said.

Velocity had reduced by eighty percent by the time the rim of the Hellas crater came into view on the horizon. Altitude was still twenty-eight miles when, once again *Endeavour* returned to its tail first orientation for its final series of burns. The engines re-fired, sounding much louder this time and with a greater jolt. By now, the vibrations were too much for Georgia to read the data on her screens. The force from the rapid deceleration meant that she couldn't move her head or arms anyway. All she could now was look past Mancuso's helmet at the ever-brightening Martian sky and wait for the pain to stop.

Endeavour touched down with a slight jolt three seconds early and within ten feet of its target. The roar of the engines disappeared to be replaced by creaking sounds as *Endeavour* swayed and then settled into its new location. As the crew lay in their seats, absorbing the fact they had landed, there was an eager wait for engine shutdown confirmation. The chief, looking up from his instruments for the first time, gave a thumbs-up to let everyone know the ship was okay.

The crew were now effectively laid on their backs in their seats. There was complete silence as each of them absorbed what they had just achieved. Against all odds they had landed safely on Mars. Georgia smiled to herself and lifted her arms to experience the odd sensation of Martian gravity on her body.

Winter broke the silence. "Congratulations, everyone. I can confirm that we have safely arrived. You can now remove your flight suits and resume your duties to make the ship safe. But first, let's all meet in the galley in five minutes for a small celebration."

By the time Georgia had struggled out of her seat and climbed down the central ladder to the crew quarters, she was breathless. Her body was heavy and sluggish. Despite Mars' gravity being roughly forty percent that of Earth's it was a struggle to walk after three months of weightlessness. Maybe I'm not as fit as I thought, she mused.

Chapter 12

Captain Winter was back in his cabin, viewing the latest message from Earth. The Vice President of the United States was standing next to General Stockton, each holding a glass of champagne. From the expression on their faces, these weren't their first drinks and Winter could hear the raucous sounds of celebrations in the background.

"An absolutely astounding job, Captain Winter," exclaimed the vice president, slightly slurring his words. "The nation is so proud of you and your crew. This is another glorious day in the history of American spaceflight. And yet again we've shown those Russians how to get things done. The general tells me that you don't have any alcohol to toast this momentous occasion. That's very sad but you can rest assured that we're more than making up for it here." The vice president held his glass up to toast the moment before continuing. "You've already demonstrated the best of mankind and will be an inspiration for generations to come. We're now all eager to watch as you plant your American boot on Martian soil for the first time. I have a surprise guest who wants to say something." The vice president looked to his left and motioned someone to enter the screenshot. It was Kristen, and it looked like she'd been crying. Even after thirty years of marriage Liam couldn't tell if they were tears of joy.

"Hello, my darling," she said softly. Her blue eyes looked watery, but her make-up remained immaculate. As always, she looked gorgeous and Winter had a sudden urge to hold her in his arms. "I'm sorry for the tears. You know that I always worry for you. I can't tell you how relieved I am that you landed safely. The VP and his wife invited me and Maisie to watch the landing with them here at the Cape. Everyone is being very kind. You won't believe the press coverage you're getting. Maisie sends her love and wants me to tell you you're going to become a grandpa. I've only just found out myself.

She and Roger are expecting a boy in the spring. I'm so proud of both of you. Keep safe. I love you."

The camera panned back to the vice president who was holding a freshly filled glass of champagne. Winter paused the message before the vice president could say anything else. He was too overcome with emotion to pay any attention and tears started to roll down his cheeks. Surprised at himself, he wiped the tears away. The news that his only daughter was pregnant put landing on Mars into perspective. Now he could look forward to meeting his first grandchild when he returned home.

He pressed play to finish watching the message but by now he wasn't listening to the platitudes that the vice president continued to shower on him and the rest of Expedition Two. He was already thinking about what it would mean to arrive back on Earth to his loving family.

Chapter 13

It was a fitful sleep for everyone as they re-adjusted to the effects of gravity on their bodies. Georgia, in particular, was struggling to sleep even though completing the post-landing checks had exhausted her far more than she had expected. Her legs were heavy and fatigued as every step she took was like wading through treacle. Lying down in her bunk was not helping. The thin mattress was hard and unforgiving. She told herself that it was reassuring to have gravity again and to know which way was up. But it was a painful experience. After thirty minutes she swallowed a sleeping tablet, but that still took time to have the desired effect.

Lying in the darkness of her cabin, she listened to the familiar sounds of the life support system circulating and processing the air, as well as the steady hum of the three computers in her room. But she was aware of a new eerie sound. The creaking of *Endeavour* as the metal hull continued to cool and contract from the fiery re-entry. It was disconcerting and she could imagine the ship cracking and causing her to be sucked out into the thin Martian atmosphere. She finally drifted to sleep, dreaming of a large hand peeling the skin off the ship as if it was a banana.

***

The following morning, their first full day on Mars, the *Endeavour* crew were awoken just before dawn. Georgia was sluggish from the poor night's sleep and the constant drag of the Martian gravity. She considered how she would cope when she went home to Earth. At least her own bed in Miami had a thick, comfortable mattress.

She sat up and swung her feet out of her bunk to stand but was immediately overpowered by a wave of nausea and dizziness. Waiting a couple of minutes for it to pass, she tried again with more success. Still nauseous, she put on a clean tee shirt and shorts, opened her cabin door and climbed the steps to the galley area.

The smell of fresh coffee would normally have been welcoming, but it did nothing to ease her nausea. She poured herself a mug of black coffee from the machine, anyway, taking some pleasure out of the ability to drink from a mug rather than sucking through a straw. Feeling invigorated from the first few sips, she was more prepared to face the world. But only just.

The rest of the crew were already standing on the observation deck, taking their first real opportunity to look outside at the strange and barren landscape that was now their home until they returned to Earth. They were lost in their own thoughts as Georgia joined them. She doubted any of them noticed she was there. Looking out of the ten-foot-wide circular window, she could understand why.

The sun was rising over the eastern horizon in the far distance, casting long shadows across Hellas Planitia. While the base of the crater looked flat from space, the sun's low angle betrayed the many humps and valleys and the many rocks and boulders that littered the ground in all directions. It was a mesmerizing view, far exceeding what she could have ever imagined. Georgia forgot all her aches and pains as she tried to take in the vista. It was surreal to be standing here and not in a simulation inside a warehouse in the Californian desert.

Her eyes followed the rim of the crater around to her right. Their landing site was only four miles from the twenty-six-thousand-foot cliff on the northwestern side of the crater. The near vertical cliff loomed ominously over *Endeavour*, and Georgia had to lean in close to the window and crook her neck to look up at the cliff face. That will be an interesting challenge to climb, she thought.

Looking back across the plain, Georgia spotted *Challenger*, *Intrepid* and *Aquarius* two miles away, gleaming in the morning sunlight, their sharp shiny edges a stark contrast to the rough, dusty Martian surface.

Past those three ships, she could also make out the distinctive shapes of the two supply ships, *Excalibur* and *Merlin*, that had been part of Expedition One and which had successfully managed a soft landing. They had been standing there patiently for the past six years waiting for the next crew to arrive. Georgia hoped she would be able to access their computer systems as the supplies on board would make their lives easier.

"Incredible isn't it?" Georgia had been so absorbed by the view that she hadn't seen Captain Winter walk up to her. He was also drinking coffee and was looking more alert than she was feeling.

"I'm not sure I have words to describe my thoughts as I look out there. You probably need Joe for that," she replied without turning around. "It's absolutely awe-inspiring. I never imagined it to be this beautiful."

Mancuso smiled at the sound of his name. "Thank you, Pyke. My mother is a poet and taught me well. Though even she might be at a loss for words to describe this view and capture the beauty and desolation." He turned his face back to the window, but not before Georgia noticed a tear in his eye.

After another five minutes lost in her own thoughts, Georgia broke away from the view. She was now more eager than ever to get down to the surface as soon as possible.

***

Following a short briefing, it was time for the landing party to be lowered to the surface. The group, comprising Captain Winter, Chief Grant and Georgia, lined up in the hold, with Mancuso operating the crane from the flight deck. Wearing their specially designed Mars mobility suits, or MMS for short, the three of them waited as the hold depressurized.

Georgia held her breath as the large external hatch silently slid open, exposing the landing party to the Martian atmosphere. As a motorized boom arm extended out from the roof of the hold, the astronauts stepped onto an open cradle attached to the crane by four metal ropes.

As the cradle swung out to the end of the boom, Georgia gripped her seat tightly. The eighty-foot drop to the surface looked a long way as she leaned forward to peer over the edge of the cradle. She could see scorch marks caused by the landing engines and a pattern of rock and debris that had been blasted away from the immediate vicinity. The scorching stopped about fifteen feet from the base of the ship with the ground returning to the monotonous dark orange color that permeated the landscape all around. The cradle swayed slightly as it stopped at the end of the boom before Winter instructed Mancuso to lower them gently to the surface.

The three of them sat in silence during the descent, taking in as much detail of the scenery as they could. To their left, the imposing precipice of the crater wall dominated the view. The sun cast shadows across the cliff face, exposing details that had not been visible in the darkness. Numerous outcrops and gullies revealed weathering that had occurred over millions of years. It reminded Georgia of a trip she'd taken to the Grand Canyon with her parents, although she couldn't see any sedimentary layers and the cliff face seemed to go up forever.

Straight ahead and to their right, all they could see was the unforgiving, relentless view of the Hellas plain, which continued as far as the eye could see. Although the plain had initially looked flat, the shadows created by the low sun now revealed numerous hills, depressions, and boulders.

Sitting beside Georgia, the chief was equally inspired by the spectacular Martian scenery. However, his main purpose for being part of the first landing party was to assess the exterior of *Endeavour* during their descent. As the cradle slowly continued its journey downwards, his keen eyes studied the ship, inspecting for any damage resulting from the journey or the fiery entry through the atmosphere. He was not surprised that the hull of the ship had suffered no ill effects other than a few holes caused by meteorite strikes and scorch marks from super-heated plasma during entry. His main concern was the aft fin that had overheated, but that was on the far side and would require a far more detailed inspection. By the time they reached the surface, the chief was quietly confident that *Endeavour* was in good shape to return to Earth once it was refueled and orbital alignment was optimal.

Winter was trying hard not to be overawed by the whole experience as he looked across Hellas plain. He was acutely aware that six billion people were currently watching what he did and said over the next few minutes. Inside his MMS, he was clammy and so adjusted the temperature on the environmental system.

To calm himself, he recited the words he'd been rehearsing for the last week. His mind went blank though as his carefully worded speech deserted him. His mouth was dry with the anticipation of what he was going to say to all those people eagerly hanging on his first words. Closing his eyes, Winter silently cursed Neil Armstrong for setting such a high benchmark over sixty years before.

There was a gentle bump as the cradle reached the surface and Winter noticed a puff of fine red dust float into the air. He nervously undid the safety bar, concentrating hard so that his trembling hands didn't fumble the simple mechanism. Standing up, he stepped to the edge of the cradle, pausing for a moment before he carefully placed one foot on the scorched Martian soil. Taking a deep breath, he uttered, "The first step in mankind's colonization of the solar system. Mars is now the new frontier." It wasn't what he'd rehearsed, but he was happy with the sentiment. Turning, he saw that Georgia and Grant were applauding him with admiration on their faces. Winter shrugged unapologetically and took two deliberate steps away from the cradle, allowing the others to follow.

Georgia tentatively placed her right boot on the Martian surface, watching it sink a half inch into the dust. She carefully took another step forward, fully conscious that her legs were still unsteady and the last thing she wanted was to fall flat on her face.

Once all the landing party had adapted to walking on the surface, it was time to have a more detailed look around the landing zone. They lumbered to the severely scorched area directly below *Endeavour* where the giant rocket engines had blasted away the top layer of rocks and dust to leave a solid black patch that looked like polished glass. Looking up at the monstrous engines, the chief was satisfied with his preliminary visual inspection. "I can't see any obvious problems, captain. There aren't any cracks in the engine casings and, other than a build-up of carbon deposits, the heat shield is intact and performed as designed."

"Thanks, chief. I'd like similar inspections of the supply ships to see what state they're in and to ensure we have remote access to the supplies when we need them. I'll get Joe to lower two of the speeders for you and Georgia to take. Straight there and back, as I'm not taking any risks. We'll leave the legacy ships for the time being as they're too far away."

"Yes, sir," came the reply from both.

Chapter 14

Georgia and the chief returned excitedly to *Endeavour*'s mid-deck for a debrief with Captain Winter soon after midday. The captain was in the middle of completing his report to Ground Control and answering further questions from the press. It was taking longer than he wanted, but he understood that Ground Control were keen to keep this event newsworthy for as long as possible to keep public interest. They had learned harsh lessons from the Apollo missions to the moon in the 1970s. When the public stopped being interested, they would want money spent on the next important issue and the Mars' budget would dry up. It was as simple as that.

Winter listened intently and made a few notes on his computer as the chief summarized what they'd discovered at each of the supply ships. Georgia then explained the access issues she had encountered at *Challenger*. She was confident that it was only a problem with the power relays and had already worked out a solution in her head.

Once she had finished outlining her solution, Winter sat back in his chair and read the notes he had typed. Looking first at Georgia, he said, "The priority has to be to access *Challenger*. We need to offload the rovers so that they can start surveying the cave complex while we settle in here. The speeders don't have any sensors and offer no protection against falling rocks. We need to know that at least one cave is viable to convert into Alpha Base. Take Grace with you if you need some help and let me know if you can't have a rover ready by tomorrow."

"That won't be a problem, sir, but I will of course keep you informed."

"Thanks, Georgia. Chief, I'd like you to carry out a detailed inspection of *Endeavour*, especially the aft fin. There looked to be some severe scorching along the edge where we registered the super heating. I want to understand how bad the damage is and if you can complete necessary repairs. I need to know the status and whether she'll fly again. And the same applies for *Eden* when Anders arrives later today."

The chief nodded. "Can I borrow Mancuso for a few hours? The external inspection will be far easier with two of us. Plus, I can rely on him to carry out some of the systems checks."

"Whatever you need. If you need to use Emily or Rashid for *Eden*, check-in with Commander Anders."

Georgia and the chief stood to leave the room before Winter added, "Oh, and Georgia? Doctor Betts would like to see you now."

Georgia grimaced. She didn't need this now but knew there was no point in delaying a visit to Megan. She would only become more persistent. And in any case, medication would help her cope with the headaches that were becoming more regular. The additional painkillers won't go amiss to help me through the next few days so I can keep on top of all my tasks, she thought. So, with a sense of reluctant acceptance she slowly made her way to the medical bay.

***

"Liam says you want to see me," Georgia said, poking her head through the curtain.

"Hi, Georgia, come in." Megan glanced up from her computer screen. "Now that we've landed, I need to check you over. Especially as you removed the monitor you're supposed to be wearing so I can track your vitals."

Georgia could feel herself blush yet tried to brazen it out. "It was uncomfortable and getting in the way. What was I supposed to do?"

"I gave it to you for a reason."

"All you have to do is ask." Georgia stared, challenging Megan for a reaction.

Megan knew the game being played and shrugged her shoulders in resignation. "Okay, talk to me. And be honest."

Georgia sat to rest her legs. "I've not been sleeping well despite the sleeping pills. I'm still getting headaches, but the painkillers are helping. On the plus side, I've not vomited for over a day."

"Is that it?"

"Yes, I believe so. Like everyone else, I'm still becoming accustomed again to gravity, so I have plenty of aches and pains. But none of that is preventing me from doing my job. I do find it difficult to concentrate unless I take the painkillers. My appetite has not yet returned. But I figured that's a side effect of the painkillers."

Megan was taking written notes on a writing pad as Georgia spoke. Despite all the technology around her, she still preferred some tried and trusted methods. "It could be the painkillers. Or it could be something entirely different. I'm not going to jump to conclusions. The captain needs to know you're fit and well. And able to do your job. It's down to me to assess that you are."

"Oh, I am able. But with all the work that now needs to be done I would like some stronger painkillers if possible. And something to help me sleep."

Megan slowly shook her head. "You're already on the strongest painkillers I can prescribe. They should be dealing with your headaches and nausea. Why haven't you come to me sooner?" Georgia looked back at her blankly, so Megan continued. "Something else is going on with you. I don't know what it is. Possibly the effects of the solar flare. Georgia, please come back here tomorrow morning so that I can conduct further tests. I'll take a blood sample now, but we really need to get to the bottom of what's affecting you. No one else on board is suffering with similar symptoms."

"Okay, I promise to be back here first thing tomorrow. But please don't take me off duty. I have too much to do for the captain."

"I'll reserve judgment on that. I have a duty to you and the rest of the crew to ensure that you don't endanger anyone, including yourself. But that means you need to be honest with me Georgia. I know you think you know best, but you have to trust me to do what is right for you. You can continue with your assignments for the time being, as long as you promise to let me know immediately if you have any other problems."

Georgia attempted her most genuine face. "Megan. I'd be a fool not to."

Megan sighed. "You're fooling no one other than yourself if you don't. Please be careful. You could put more than just yourself at risk."

Part of Georgia knew that Megan was right. Any mistakes she may make could easily impact any member of the crew. And she didn't want that on her conscience. However, there was also a stubborn streak within her she recognized she would have to keep in check. She smiled and nodded at Megan before heading off to find Grace.

Chapter 15

Captain Winter sat quietly in his cabin, finally with a chance to contemplate what he and the crew had achieved. The chief and Mancuso were outside inspecting the *Endeavour's* hull and heat shield. Georgia had taken Grace with her to unlock *Challenger*. And Megan was most likely in the medical center preparing for the next round of crew medicals.

It really had been a monumental effort, not only by *Endeavour's* crew and Ground Control but also from the thousands of unseen workers around the world who had contributed to the design, build and ultimate success of the millions of components required for the mission. And he couldn't be more thrilled to have commanded Expedition Two. He knew his family would be proud and were probably planning his welcome home party as he sat in his room. He tried to ignore the fact that there would be a multitude of other functions to celebrate him and his achievements when he returned to Earth. In his heart, all he wanted to do was return to Kristen, retire to a smallholding and grow old with his grandchildren.

The thought of his wife persuaded him to send her a personal message to thank her. As his hand moved over the keyboard to hit the record button, he noticed his computer screen showed he was receiving an encrypted message from Ground Control that was marked for his eyes only. This was most unusual and Winter was immediately intrigued. It took about thirty seconds for the message to finish downloading and allow Winter to view it.

General Stockton's lined face appeared in the middle of the screen, looking stern and worried. He had recorded the message from his office and with him was Doctor Alison Jackson, the chief scientist supporting Expedition Two. Any hope that Winter may have had that the two of them would heap more praise on him immediately evaporated.

The general, as always, was gruff and to the point. "Captain Winter, on behalf of everyone here at Ground Control I'd like to thank you and *Endeavour*'s crew for your faultless landing. I know the vice president gave you his personal thanks yesterday, in his own style. This news has gripped the entire world and we've been inundated with reporters and well-wishers. You're all heroes and celebrities now to the seven billion inhabitants of Earth.

But you know as well as I that the mission has only really just begun. Landing was the easy part. Without overstating the obvious, you now have to survive on the surface for just over six hundred days and establish a viable outpost before returning safely. Although you landed yesterday, the next seven days is really going to be vital because we're going to be moving up some tasks originally assigned to later in the mission. Without sounding too dramatic, it's a matter of life or death. I'll let Alison explain why."

The camera panned around slightly to allow Doctor Jackson, affectionately called AJ, to be front and center. She looked self-conscious, and Liam could see that she was carefully concentrating on what she had to say. He had worked with her for fifteen years and had the utmost respect for her knowledge and honesty. "Thanks, general. Liam, I'd also like to say really well done. I'm very envious that I'm not part of your crew. Anyway, down to more important matters."

The image on Winter's screen changed to that of what looked like a long-range photo of an asteroid. "Three days ago, we detected this asteroid heading toward Mars. Initial estimates suggest it's about one hundred and fifty yards across which is why we only recently spotted it. Since then, we've been urgently calculating its trajectory and have determined that there is currently an eighty percent probability of it impacting Mars in nine days. The modeling we've carried out shows that although the Martian gravity would cause the asteroid to break up, the atmosphere is too thin for those pieces to burn up. A good proportion will reach the ground, resulting in numerous impact craters and a large dust cloud, possibly in your current vicinity. We're still carrying out further assessments to narrow down the probability of impact, but there is a high risk to you and the expedition.

"While the ships will give you protection except against a direct hit by debris, the dust clouds will severely hamper your operations for weeks, maybe months. Solar power generation will be limited which means that you'll have to carefully conserve the remaining battery power you have."

Winter could see where this was heading. He didn't need to be told he had limited options.

The image returned to that of General Stockton. "The safety of the Expedition Two crew is paramount. That means you must establish Alpha Base and commission the nuclear reactor before the asteroid reaches you. I know that is a lot to ask of you. The mission profilers are developing a new set of tasks for you as we speak. I intend to send them through to you within the next six hours. It will mean delaying most of the scientific experiments and the setting up of the Sabatier Reactor, but I figure you'll have plenty of time to do those things once the danger has passed. Sorry if this news spoils your celebrations. Let me know your thoughts, captain. Stockton out."

Winter sat looking at the frozen image of General Stockton with AJ sitting behind him. He cursed, unhappy that the carefully laid out plans were already heading south. But he knew that he and his crew were both resourceful and adaptable. He typed a quick reply to signify he'd received and watched the message. He then tried to put the news to the back of his mind as he recorded a message to send to his wife without mentioning the possible asteroid threat.

Chapter 16

Two hours later and the outside temperature had plummeted to minus one hundred degrees Fahrenheit. It was pitch black outside, with only the stars visible. All the crew was back on-board *Endeavour* and in good spirits. During the day, each of them had taken some time from their busy routines to take photos and videos from the Martian surface. Before dinner, the captain had allowed them to send messages to friends and loved ones back home.

They were now gathered in front of the large screen, watching the approach of *Eden*. Except for Georgia, they had eaten their rations for the evening. The crew had worked hard all day and, as they relaxed, the effects of gravity were draining their bodies of what little energy remained. Doctor Betts had advised the crew to drink plenty of fluids and rest as much as possible.

Captain Winter looked around the room at each of his fellow pioneers, extremely proud of each one but fully aware from the silence that they were all ready for a well-earned rest. The anticipation of seeing *Eden* land, however, was too much for any of them to consider sleeping just yet.

Winter had spoken with Commander Anders two hours earlier to send his best wishes to the crew of the *Eden* for a safe landing. Anders had sounded understandably anxious. Winter wondered if that was how he had sounded yesterday. Probably, he thought with a wry grin.

As *Eden* performed its aero braking maneuvers at the extremes of Mars' atmosphere, communication and telemetry was lost and the screen went blank. Georgia moved to one of the windows, eager to be the first to glimpse *Eden*'s approach over the horizon.

It was ultimately Mancuso who shouted and pointed to a glowing point of light streaking across the ink black sky. Within ten minutes *Eden* made a perfect vertical landing a short distance from

Endeavour, its thundering rocket engines lighting up the night and blasting dust in all directions, before settling onto the ground.

The crew of *Endeavour* gave a loud cheer as the bright flare of *Eden*'s rocket motors and the rumble through the deck plates died away to leave a serene darkness outside, although they could see the thick dust cloud slowly dispersing.

"Great landing, *Eden*," radioed Captain Winter. "Good of you to join us."

With all the Expedition Two craft safely on Mars, it was finally time to rest for the crews of both *Endeavour* and *Eden*. There would be plenty of work ahead of them over the coming days.

***

Georgia laid in her cabin later that night and again couldn't sleep. The intense headaches had returned with a vengeance and she'd vomited twice since eating what little food she'd had for dinner. She had never felt this sick in her life and was finally anxious that she was more ill than she'd wanted to accept. She would have to be more honest with Megan.

At just after three in the morning she weakly rose from her bed and slowly made her way to the doctor's cabin. The ship was silent except for the constant whirring of pumps and fans, and the odd snoring sound from the heavy sleepers. The corridor was dim except for the faint red overhead lights as Georgia reached the doctor's cabin and quietly whispered, "Megan, are you awake? It's Georgia."

Georgia heard Megan turning over as she said, "Is anything wrong?"

Before Georgia could reply, Megan switched on her lamp. Georgia squinted, her eyes getting used to the light. "I really need something stronger for the headaches. I can't sleep and the painkillers you gave me are not making any difference. I need some sleep to function properly tomorrow."

By now, Megan was sitting up in her bed. "You should have come to me sooner. I knew you weren't telling me the full story earlier but didn't want to push it. I can't give you any more painkillers, but I will give you a stronger sedative to help you sleep. That's all though. And make sure you come and see me again first thing in the morning."

Georgia had no fight in her to argue. She gratefully took the sedative and returned to her cabin. Within minutes she was in a deep sleep, filled with nightmares.

Chapter 17

The next morning, the crew was awake early for breakfast. Georgia was one of the last to climb up into the galley area to the smell of fresh coffee. Her head was pounding and what sleep she'd managed had not dented the overwhelming fatigue she was fighting.

Someone, probably Mancuso, had microwaved bacon for breakfast and the smell made her want to throw up. However, she controlled her stomach, poured herself a black coffee and huddled down in a corner, cupping the hot mug in her hands.

"I'm no doctor but you look like shit," said Chief Grant, a look of genuine concern on his face despite his jovial tone. "Are you okay?"

"Thanks, chief, you know how to make a girl feel better. I'm sure it's just my body adjusting to gravity. I'm checking in with Doctor Betts in a few minutes. Then I'll be fit and ready to unload *Challenger*."

The chief looked at Georgia doubtfully. Everyone aboard was having to deal with Martian gravity, but no one looked anywhere near as bad as she did. "Take care of yourself and pay attention to what the doctor says to you. We all know what you're like at taking advice! I'll check on you later. For now, I've got an inspection report to complete for Captain Winter before heading over to the *Eden*." The chief whistled an old tune as he headed back to his quarters with a steaming coffee in his hand.

Georgia looked around the galley and made brief eye contact with Megan, who was eating breakfast at another table with Mancuso. Georgia vainly tried a smile, nodded and made her way down to the medical facility, with the doctor following not far behind.

***

Forty-five minutes later and the medical scan was complete. Megan looked at the results and Georgia could tell from her expression that the initial prognosis wasn't good. Then, before she could say anything, Megan suddenly and unexpectedly began to cry, quickly wiping away her tears with her sleeve. "I'm sorry, Georgia, that was unprofessional of me. As your doctor, I shouldn't have reacted like that. It's hard when I'm also your friend."

Georgia looked at her in stunned silence. Megan was normally a tough nut. A million questions were going through her head, but she didn't know which one to ask.

Once she had composed herself, Megan continued to analyze the results in front of her. "The ultrasound scan results aren't good. I'll send them to Earth for confirmation. It looks like you have several tumors in your head, with one behind your right eye. They could be what's causing the symptoms you're experiencing. They weren't there during your last medical, so probably they result from that solar flare. That's only my best guess, but if that is the case then the tumors are likely to be malignant. I am so sorry, Georgia, but at the rate they've grown, there is not sufficient time to get you back to Earth in time to have them operated on. And I don't have the equipment or the skills to operate on you here."

The blood drained from Georgia's face. The news confirmed her worst fears. "So, how long do I have?"

"I can't be sure just on these tests, and I'm no expert. I would say a matter of months, three at the outside. It's not an exact science and, of course, there are no similar cases like yours that I can compare with."

"That's no time at all! You must be mistaken. Perhaps the scanner needs recalibrating after the landing."

"I'm sorry, Georgia. The scan simply confirms what the drop in your white blood cell count is telling me. The only thing I'm not sure of is how much time you have."

Georgia stared numbly down at her hands for several minutes, desperately struggling to hold back the tears that were threatening to engulf her. She felt broken. She was so used to being in control and now she was suddenly in a position where she would never have control again. She almost laughed at the twisted irony. Eventually, her emotions back in check, she looked back at Megan and, almost in a whisper, asked. "Is there any way you could you have misinterpreted the results? How soon will you get a reply from Earth?"

Megan had been waiting patiently, knowing that Georgia would need time to absorb the tragic news. "I'm not an oncologist but I'm fairly positive about my diagnosis. I wouldn't have given you this news without a high degree of confidence. I'd expect to have the results confirmed later today."

"So, it's not definite! Am I able to continue working? I have so much to do here and I don't want to be a burden to the captain and the rest of the crew."

"You'd never be a burden. And we wouldn't be here if it wasn't for you. I'll talk to the captain. Physically, there is a high chance of seizures and vision blurring and the symptoms you're already showing. But to be honest, my immediate concern is the psychological impact to you. If you want it, I would seriously suggest some counseling to help you come to terms with the diagnosis and what options you have available. You know that you can talk to me at any time but talk to family and friends as well. Is there anyone other than your brother who you're close to?"

"No, there's only Jackson. Hell, I have no idea what I'll tell him. Or anyone else for that matter." The thought of speaking to Jackson was the last straw for Georgia. There was no holding back the tears this time as her body convulsed in grief.

All that Megan could do to comfort her friend was hold her tightly until the brutal sobbing subsided.

***

An hour later, Georgia was sitting in Captain Winter's cabin, staring at the photos of his wife and daughter pinned to his wall. Judging from the various hairstyles and fashions, they'd been taken over many years. One more thing to regret she thought to herself. She'd never found time to have a meaningful relationship, let alone start a family. Although her career had always come first, she had always expected to have a family at some point in her life. Now, it was too late.

She stood up to attention as Winter entered the room, although he quickly waved her to sit back down. "No need for formalities, Georgia." He sat down wearily and took a few seconds to consider what he would say next. "Doctor Betts has obviously just spoken to me about your news. As captain, I take full responsibility for the health and welfare of all my crew. I'm therefore absolutely devastated by your diagnosis."

Georgia could see that he was genuinely upset and trying hard to find the right words. Despite her situation, part of her sympathized with him. He was a good man, and she knew he would be blaming himself.

"You're one of the finest members of *Endeavour* and you know you hold a very special place with me. I had such high hopes for you. You have lived up to the trust placed in you when I selected you for this mission. I understand from Doctor Betts that you want to carry on working."

"That's correct, sir. There's still a chance that the specialists will come up with a more positive diagnosis. I'm not giving up yet. I joined the mission because I'm the best in my field and I want to continue as long as I'm able to. I don't want to sit around on the sidelines when I still have plenty to offer. There is so much to do here to make Mars a viable future for humanity. And even if I'm not around to enjoy it, I'd like to leave a legacy."

"That sounds like a speech I would have made." Winter considered his options. "Okay. I suggest you wait for confirmation of the scan results. If Doctor Betts is correct, then just take as much time as you need to let the news sink in. It has to be a huge shock. For the moment I'll leave the choice to carry on with your assignment up to you."

"Thank you, sir."

"I have several conditions that you must comply with. Firstly, I don't want you outside the ship on your own. Although you will be monitored, Doctor Betts advises that one symptom will be blackouts and I can't have you alone if that happens."

Georgia nodded. She had expected it.

"Secondly, I'd like you to train Joe up to be your replacement should the worst happen. He already has some robotics and computing skills and you two work well together. You don't need to tell Joe about your condition unless you want to. Until Earth confirms the scan results, we'll carry on as if nothing is wrong. I don't intend letting the crew know anything until we have to."

"Thank you again, sir. I'm still hoping that Megan is wrong. I'm more than happy to work with Joe. We spent some time on Earth working on the rovers, so I agree that he is more than capable of picking up most of my tasks. Other than that, I want no special favors."

Winter could see from Georgia's determined expression that she wanted to put this devastating news to one side. He couldn't blame her. He did not know how he would deal with a similar situation.

"As far as I'm concerned there won't be any special favors. But please come and speak to me if you ever need to. You don't have to face this alone and you know you have plenty of friends here. I'd like to help in any way I can."

"I appreciate that, sir. I still need to process the information myself but will wait until Ground Control comes back with good or bad news. For now, I'm happy to get back to work. First stop will be *Challenger* if that's okay with you."

Winter smiled. "You're a braver person than I could ever imagine being, Georgia. And an inspiration. Before you go to *Challenger*, I need to debrief you and the other senior crew members on an urgent change of orders."

Chapter 18

The senior crew of both ships were waiting patiently in the *Endeavour*'s galley area when Captain Winter climbed the stairs from his quarters. Georgia had just arrived and was sitting with Chief Grant and Doctor Betts at one table with Commander Anders, Harry King and Tom Redmayne at another. All five of them had spent the last ten minutes catching up and comparing information on the fiery entry and landing on Mars. It had been over three months since they'd last sat down face to face and there was a lot to talk about, not least of which was how amazing it was that the mission was going so well.

Commander Anders was sharing his initial impression of Mars. "It's strange to deal with the effects of gravity again. It made sleeping last night very uncomfortable. But it's not as bad as the times I returned to Earth after trips to the Moon or either of the space stations."

Winter waited until there was silence in the room. "Lars, Harry, Tom. It is so good to see you all again." He walked up to each of them to shake their hands and to pat Commander Anders on the back. "We'll get the whole of both crews in here later for a proper celebration. It's only right for what is a collective historic achievement. But first, I need to update you on some urgent orders I've received from Ground Control."

***

After he'd given them details about the asteroid, Redmayne asked, "Captain, how sure is Ground Control that the asteroid will actually strike? Is there anything I can do to provide additional readings to assist with their calculations?"

"Good questions, Tom. I don't think Ground Control will know for sure until the asteroid is only several days away. But the margins are small enough to take seriously. If you can help in any way, then please do. Contact AJ directly and offer your services."

Captain Winter continued. "Late yesterday I received new assignments and task lists from Ground Control. They replace what we currently have, effective as of the end of this meeting, and will enable us to erect the basic infrastructure for Alpha Base in the lava tube. That means the inflatable habitats, nuclear reactor for power, water and oxygen recyclers and possibly the hydroponics facility. I have put all other research and science on hold, as well as construction of the propellant factory."

Harry was not happy. "Captain, I wanted to establish the greenhouse over the next few weeks. We've been nurturing our crops to be able to re-plant them over that timescale. There is a danger that many plants will die or at least be stunted."

"I understand, Harry. But the priority has to be the safety of the crew first and foremost. I know it's not ideal for you, but I will do my utmost to maintain the power and light you need for your plants, even if they have to remain on Eden for a while longer. I'm giving Lars overall responsibility for getting Alpha Base operational in the next seven days. Give him whatever help he needs. General Stockton recognizes that this will put a lot of strain on the crews and will involve long hours. But we were each chosen because we can work under pressure and are highly resourceful. And this could be critical to the success of our mission."

Anders asked, "This is reliant on the lava tubes being suitable. When will we be able to survey them?"

"I'll have the rovers unloaded from *Challenger* by nightfall," said Georgia. "They should have sufficient power to start work immediately."

"Good work," said Winter. "Chief, I want you to start the *Eden* inspection immediately. If the inspection of *Endeavour* is anything to go by, you shouldn't discover any serious issues. After that, the nuclear reactor should probably be the focus for you and Rashid."

"Yes, that makes sense," replied Grant.

After all tasks were assigned, Winter dismissed everyone except Commander Anders. "Lars, I'd appreciate your thoughts on the detailed task list. It's challenging but necessary. However, you need to be totally on board with it if you're taking charge. I know you'll give me your honest opinion. And I also need to inform you about Georgia Pyke."

Chapter 19

It didn't take long for Georgia to suit up, pass through the airlock to the hold, and take the cradle down to the surface. It was now early afternoon, and the sun was high in the sky, its faint hue casting slight shadows on the red dust. Georgia looked at the vast Hellas plains in front of her and couldn't help but think how beautiful they were. They reminded her of the time in the Nevada desert when she had spent many weekends seeking solitude in the wilderness with her horse. She doubted she'd ever get those opportunities again but quickly put that thought to the back of her mind as her tears threatened to return.

The commander assigned Mancuso instead of Grace to help Georgia offload the rovers. He had prepared two speeders and was waiting for her with a satisfied look. The speeders were modified Segways, allowing individual astronauts to stand on a platform and freely move around the planet's surface. Although the speeder's top speed was only twenty miles per hour, the designer had, ironically, called them speeders. Although not as pleasant as driving in the comfort and safety of the pressurized MEV, they were a better and more convenient alternative to walking.

"I have been ordered to work with you by Commander Anders. What's the emergency?" Mancuso asked.

"We're heading to *Challenger* to offload the rovers and MEV. Surveys of the lava tubes start tomorrow so the captain is relying on us."

"That's quicker than was scheduled," said Joe. "Although I suppose there's no time like the present. And it's a good excuse to be out here. Is there any reason for the urgency?"

"I'll tell you more about it on the way."

It wasn't long before both Georgia and Mancuso arrived at their destination. Having pulled up a few yards away, Georgia walked to the main landing fin, opened an access panel, and activated the controls to get them up to the hold.

***

The remote rovers were the size of golf buggies and packed with cameras and scientific instruments. They had been folded for the journey to minimize their size in what were cramped conditions. Ground Control had left no spare inch of room on any of the supply ships and it took some careful maneuvering to release the first rover from its transit clamps for it to be then lowered down to the ground by crane.

"It will get easier," Mancuso said to encourage Georgia as she struggled to manhandle the bulky rover. "I had similar issues with unloading the first few items from *Endeavour*."

Georgia hoped that was the case. It frustrated her how long it was taking. But the rovers had to be unloaded in sequence so they could access the MEV components. Each of the ships could only be unloaded in a specific logical sequence.

Once the two robotic rovers were safely on the ground, they automatically unfurled their six-wheeled legs, opened their solar panels and slowly set off toward the imposing cliff wall, four miles away. Georgia watched them for a few minutes as she stood at the cargo bay entrance and was pleased to see that they were operating as planned. She contacted Commander Anders to inform him of progress and to advise that the rovers could now be tracked.

"You were right about timing, Joe. It's going to be tight to complete before the end of the day."

Joe was loading a pallet onto the winch. "Maybe if you stop daydreaming out of the hatch and help me instead, we'll get this done quicker," he joked.

"Point taken." She winced. She had to admit she had been distracted by the view again. It was far too alluring, and she hoped that the novelty would eventually wear off. She reluctantly turned away from the scenery to help Joe align the pallet before lowering it to the surface.

***

It was strenuous work to unpack the seven pallets and chassis unit. The original task sheet allowed the astronauts five days to recover from their flight before any physical activity. Because of the impending asteroid, this was only their second full day on the planet and by the time the chassis was lowered, they were both severely fatigued.

Georgia was sitting in the cradle with Joe as it descended from the cargo bay, stretching her arm when Commander Anders radioed to her. "Pyke? What's the latest update at *Challenger*?"

"Commander, we are fifteen minutes behind schedule. We've lowered the chassis and are about to head down to begin assembly," she replied.

"Excellent work. I'm sure you're both struggling with the effects of the work. Chief Grant is on his way to assist you."

"Thank you, sir, that is much appreciated." Georgia did not try to hide her gratitude. For the past thirty minutes, she had doubted how they would assemble the MEV before nightfall. Her limbs were leaden, and she could see that Mancuso was moving slower than he had earlier that day.

Five minutes later, a wave of relief swept through her, giving her a new burst of energy, as she saw the chief approaching. She walked over to him as he stepped off his speeder and clapped him on the shoulder. "You're a sight for sore eyes. And legs! I thought you were working on the reactor though."

The chief smiled at Georgia and started walking toward Mancuso, who was attaching the main cabin to the chassis of the MEV with a series of bolts. "I was. It took us less time than planned to unpack it and put it in location. I've left the cabling in Rashid's capable hands.

I suggested to Commander Anders that you two needed some assistance and I'm always glad to help. Remember, I saw how you were looking early this morning."

Mancuso looked up from his work. "We're doing fine. But as you're here, I suppose you can make yourself useful. I assume you know what a wrench looks like."

"Yes, Mancuso, and I know where to shove it when navy jocks get too lippy."

***

Even with the three of them it was nearly dark by the time they test drove the MEV back to *Endeavour*. Georgia was dead on her feet and was looking absently out of the front window as the MEV bounced its way across the terrain. She barely registered that they'd arrived back at *Endeavour*. The chief tapped her on the arm to bring her back to the present. "Come on, sleeping beauty," he said. "That's definitely enough for one day."

Georgia could hardly move. Every nerve and muscle screamed from the day's physical exertion and all she wanted to do was sleep. Somehow, she managed to find the energy to put her helmet back on and step through the airlock before slumping in the cradle to be taken up to *Endeavour*.

She hardly noticed being helped on board. Captain Winter was waiting for them as they stepped out of the airlock into the crew quarters. Georgia immediately stood straight, brushing the chief's supporting hand from her elbow. If Captain Winter noticed, he chose not to say anything.

"Great job, all of you. Now I suggest you get some refreshment and rest. Are there any issues with the MEV I need to know about?"

Before Georgia could answer, Mancuso said, "No sir, it worked like a dream. It's on charge now and will be ready for action tomorrow."

Georgia was lightheaded and finding it difficult to concentrate. She was pleased that the captain didn't continue the conversation. After staggering to her room, she swiftly drank a pint of water and collapsed onto her bed. She was asleep within seconds and missed the message light flashing on her terminal.

Chapter 20

It was shortly after eight o'clock when Redmayne received an encrypted message. He was writing the outline for a research paper in his quarters when the symbol flashed on his tablet device to inform him of the new message. This one was typed rather than video and the first one he'd received since Expedition Two had departed Earth orbit. He had wondered if there was a problem with communications.

He quickly saved and closed the document he was working on, eager to read the message. However, he was disappointed to discover that the note was short and vague. He had been hoping for more action after what was a mundane mission to date.

'We are aware of the imminent threat to the expedition and the revised plans for Alpha. We have delayed landing of the Kiev pending asteroid impact and will remain in orbit. Continue with your primary mission and await further instructions. Alex'

Whoever Alex was, and Redmayne had never met him or her, they knew how to use words sparingly. He had been giving the asteroid a lot of thought since the morning's meeting and had already determined that the Russians would not consider landing until the threat level had reduced. The cosmonauts and taikonauts on board could orbit Mars for many months and wait out the dust storm. It was even possible for them to return to Earth without ever landing on Mars, although Redmayne considered that to be unlikely.

For now, however, it would be a waiting game to see what transpired. He was a patient man and knew he'd be prepared when his moment finally came. After all, he had been waiting six years to reach this moment so what difference would several days or weeks make? And, he'd given up too much to fail now.

Chapter 21

Georgia was awake before six the next morning. Her body still ached from the previous day but was refreshed from the best night's sleep since landing on Mars. As she swung her legs out of bed and sat up, the dull throbbing in her head returned and she let out a soft groan. She reached for the painkillers on the table next to her bed and swallowed two, helping them down with several large gulps of water, hoping their effect would kick in quickly.

It was still dark outside her cabin window and there was only a pale glow silhouetting the rugged horizon to show that dawn was approaching. *Endeavour* was quiet and Georgia figured that she was the only one awake. Time to get a few tasks out of the way to keep me occupied, she thought.

After stopping briefly in the galley for a black coffee and nutrition bar, she quietly made her way to the airlock. She was keen to see if the MEV was fully charged. Although confident that it would be, there was no point in taking any chances with the timescales they had to work to. And, although the captain had ordered her not to undertake any more solo EVAs, she hoped to be back on-board *Endeavour* before anyone discovered her.

As the cradle slowly descended, she realized that the winch mechanism was noisier than she remembered. She was sure that the sound would disturb someone, but it was too late to turn back. Instead, she looked down at the MEV bathed in spotlights, and urged the cradle to move quicker.

Once inside the MEV it took her less than five minutes to complete the start-up sequence and confirm that the two banks of batteries were fully charged. The systems check was all clear too. It satisfied Georgia that the MEV was ready to start its mission. She patted the computer console, taking a small amount of parental pride in her baby not letting her down.

Stepping out of the MEV's airlock, she stopped moving when she noticed the chief walking in her direction. Even though it was still too dark to see Jim's face, his bouncy step as he strode in her direction was unmistakable. Georgia had a sinking feeling but caught the humor in his voice as he asked, "Couldn't you sleep?"

Georgia laughed and held her hands up. "Yes, you caught me, Detective Grant. I've been very naughty but I'm not sorry."

Jim laughed. "I may have to take you in for questioning, miss." He continued, keeping up the pretence. "This place isn't safe to be out at this time of the morning."

"I promise never to do it again. What are you doing out here, anyway?" Georgia asked, happy to have some friendly banter with Jim. "If you were planning on checking out the MEV you're too late. I've already done it."

"The sound of the cradle woke me up. I came to see who had the nerve to disturb my sleep. I should have known it would be you!"

"Maybe you should try wearing earplugs."

"To be honest, I came down to check out the MEV as well. I had no idea anyone was out here until I saw someone had lowered the cradle."

Now that she had company, Georgia wasn't ready to go back inside. The surrounding landscape was brightening and there was a faint mist hovering over patches of ground that were in sunlight. She had the sudden urge to go exploring. The scene took her back to her childhood when she'd wake up on cold winter mornings. She would often get dressed and sneak outside to be the first person to leave footprints in the crisp fresh snow.

"Do you fancy going for a ride on the speeders before breakfast? We can check the legacy ships and be back within the hour."

The chief looked doubtful. "The captain won't be happy."

"Only if he finds out. And I'm not going to tell him," she replied mischievously. "Come on! Live a little."

"Okay, but only because I know you'll go without me, anyway."

Georgia beamed as she stepped onto the nearest speeder and drove quickly toward the rising orange sun. She knew that she had caught Jim off guard, as she heard him curse under his breath. She looked over her shoulder to see him following a short distance behind, dodging the stones and dust that her speeder was kicking up.

Georgia's visor adjusted to compensate for the sun now shining directly in her face as she reveled in the scenery, enjoying the rhythmic bouncing of the speeder over the rocky terrain. It was a wonderful sense of freedom she'd not felt for a very long time.

Georgia hardly noticed as she passed *Challenger*, *Intrepid* and finally *Aquarius*. She was focusing her attention on the immense solar farm next to the Legacy ships. Flimsy solar panel sheets had been delivered on *Excalibur* with construction robots building the farm. They covered an area roughly the size of three football pitches and were designed to provide enough energy to satisfy the power requirements for Expedition One.

Six years on and the requirements for Alpha Base far exceeded the output the solar farm could generate. The nuclear reactor Expedition Two had brought with them would now provide the energy demands with capacity to spare. But instead of being obsolete, the solar farm would be re-purposed to support the propellant depot, once that began operating. The solar panels gleamed dully in the sun, having accumulated a layer of dust while waiting for humans to arrive.

The Expedition One ships stood like a pair of monoliths marking the location of the solar farm. "Are they still operational?" Georgia asked. "In theory, the batteries should still have enough juice to at least give us access. Let's take a quick look and find out."

The chief raised no objections as their speeders kicked up a trail of orange dust behind them as they bounced effortlessly over the small rocks and stones that littered the floor of Hellas Plain. Georgia paid close attention to her heads-up display to ensure she had a sufficient supply of air. She still had nearly five hours' worth, which she figured should be plenty with *Endeavour* less than thirty minutes away at top speed.

The radio suddenly crackled with the voice of Captain Winter, and Georgia immediately knew that he was not happy. "Pyke! Grant! What the hell are you doing?"

The chief, being the senior of the two, replied. "Good morning, sir. I thought we should get ahead with a few tasks and check out the two old birds. We'll only take thirty minutes and it will be useful to know how much work it still requires getting the solar farm online."

"We'll be back for breakfast, captain," Georgia chipped in, ignoring Winter's irritation. "By the way, the MEV is fully charged and ready to be loaded."

They heard Winter sigh in defeat. "Okay, you've convinced me this time but don't make this a habit. I'm supposed to be the captain so, next time, clear it with me first. Make sure you're both back inside *Endeavour* at the earliest for a full debrief. Winter out."

Two minutes later, they arrived at the first of the Expedition One ships, *Merlin*. From a distance, it looked the same as the Expedition Two supply ships. It was only as Georgia drew closer that she could see it had become weathered during its six years on Mars. The landing feet were covered in several feet of red dust and the bodywork looked like it had rusted. But it was only the effect of the dust where it had lodged in welds and joins.

Jim rubbed the tail fin with his gloved left hand to brush the accumulation of dust from around the access panel. He slowly unfastened the screws that held it in place and lowered the panel to the ground. "Here goes nothing," he muttered as he keyed in the access code. He couldn't hide a surprised grin as he was rewarded with a green light and the display lit up.

Unfortunately, it was not the same story with the second ship, *Merlin*. This was the ship that had provided the solar sheets and the construction robots. The three construction robots now stood motionless, directly beneath the crane boom arm, their power supplies long depleted. Looking up, Georgia could see that the cargo hatch was still open, waiting for the next delivery to be requested. After opening the access panel, it was soon obvious that there was no power left in the batteries.

"It looks as if I'm going to have to jump start this one," the chief said, making a mental note to add it to his ever-growing list of tasks. "Luckily, I don't think there's any equipment on board that's urgently required. Most of the solar panels were deployed by the robot crew before the power ran out."

He re-attached the plate before they started the long return journey back to *Endeavour*.

They had already passed *Challenger* when, as they crested a low mound, the chief laughed out loud and released a huge shout of joy. Alarmed by the sudden outburst, Georgia slowed down. "What's wrong, chief?"

"Absolutely nothing, Georgia. I'm sorry if I startled you. I guess it's just the exhilaration of being here. It's intoxicating! How lucky are we to be here on Mars? We actually made it. Billions of dollars and millions of miles and we're now two of the first humans to land on a new planet. And look at us. You'd think we were out for a Sunday drive. Thank you for being a rule breaker."

"I am so glad you feel the same as I do," replied Georgia. She had never seen the chief so effusive. "I don't remember the virtual reality training being this much fun or giving the sense of space and freedom, or how the crater wall would loom above us. Impressive doesn't even come close to describing it." She tried to tilt her head back to see the top of the precipice. "It must have been spectacular when the meteor impacted. And look at how uniform the rim is. There's some sign of weathering but I bet this cliff face has hardly changed in millions of years. The benefit of no atmos—"

Georgia suddenly stopped her speeder and pointed at a spot on the crater's rim almost directly above the *Endeavour*'s landing site. "Chief, up there on top of the ridge. I just saw something glinting in the sunlight. It looked metallic." She looked again but whatever it was had gone. She pointed to help Grant see where she had been looking, but he saw nothing unusual.

"It may just have been a rock outcrop catching the early morning sun," Grant said. "If that's the case, it will give the geologists an easier time if minerals are accessible on the surface."

Georgia wasn't convinced, but she had no alternative explanation. However, it wasn't long before the scenery made her forget the experience as they completed the journey back to *Endeavour*.

As they pulled up, the chief said, "Thanks, Georgia, that was fun. Let's do it again sometime."

Georgia surprised herself by hoping that she could repeat the experience with him sooner rather than later.

Chapter 22

Georgia hurried to see Captain Winter, allowing Jim to get his breakfast in the galley. Ignoring the pain in her forehead, she hummed her favorite song as she eagerly made her way along the corridor, remembering how fabulous the early morning outing had been. Her heart quickly sank as she saw that Doctor Betts was also in the captain's cabin. It could only mean bad news and a glance at Megan's solemn face confirmed her worst fears. She'd never seen her look so pale and distressed.

Winter stood as Georgia entered the room and sat down, looking at her with pity in his eyes. Speaking softly, he said, "Doctor Betts has your results back from Ground Control. I am sorry to say that they confirm what we thought. I'll let Megan go through the details."

The room began to spin, and nausea engulfed her as Georgia's world fell apart.

Megan, trying hard to remain professional, spoke quietly and slowly as she explained the diagnosis. "Georgia, you have what we call stage four glioblastoma tumors. Three in your head and a fourth on your lungs. They are inoperable while we are here on Mars. Even if you were on Earth, the success rate would be less than twenty percent because the cancers are so aggressive. I hope you understand that means all we can offer you is palliative care to ease the pain. I know that's no comfort but there is not much more we can do."

The tears that Georgia had desperately been fighting off finally erupted. Her emotions threatened to overwhelm her completely. They were a mixture of anger and fear. How could this happen to her now when she had finally achieved her dream of reaching Mars? It was devastating. For the past day she had tried to believe that there must be some kind of mistake but now there was no more denying to herself that she was dying. It was only a matter of time.

"How long do I have," she managed to ask, once she'd pulled herself together.

Megan was also crying now, desperately sad that she couldn't save her friend. "I still can't say exactly. We're looking at possibly two to three months maximum. I am so sorry we could not give you better news."

Georgia was stunned by how short her remaining time was. The news was too distressing to absorb properly. Megan had to be talking about someone else in the room. It couldn't be happening to her. There was a vague sense of someone putting their arms around her to comfort her, but the sobbing would not subside. She heard voices, but no longer heard the words. This was so unfair. She couldn't die on Mars so far away from her brother.

She didn't know how long she was crying before she finally had her emotions back under control. "I'm okay," she lied, wiping away tears with a paper tissue.

"Of course, your condition remains absolutely confidential for as long as you want," said Captain Winter. "There will come a point when we have to advise the crew, but we will try to leave that for you to determine. Ground Control will have to issue a press release to explain what has happened. For the time being, I suggest you take today to rest and absorb the news. Megan will stay with you."

Georgia no longer knew what to think. Her mind couldn't focus for more than a few seconds. "Thank you, sir. I just want time to myself. I'll need to let my brother know. He's supposed to be arriving on the next mission and is training in Texas. I don't know what to say to him or anyone else at the moment. It's so hard to take in."

"I understand. We'll arrange some counseling for you. As I mentioned yesterday, you're not alone. We'll support you as much as we can and in any way you want."

Georgia slowly rose from her seat and wandered back to her cabin with Megan, both of them in tears. Megan hugged her tightly and whispered, "You can talk to me at any time, day or night. I'm there for you to help you through this." Georgia nodded but didn't reply. She swallowed the sedative Megan had given her and lay on her bed, slipping on her headphones but neither hearing the music nor realizing that tears had streamed down her face again as she fell asleep.

Chapter 23

Georgia awoke shortly after midday. Her eyes were sore and her headache had returned with a vengeance. She wasn't sure she had ever cried so much in her life. And then she remembered how she had been, aged only seventeen, when her mum had died.

"Come on, Georgia," she chastised herself as she sat up on her bed. "Why are you feeling sorry for yourself? You will not let this thing beat you." She knew that she was still lying to herself, but denial had seen her through many situations in the past. She wasn't one to wallow in self-pity; she'd rather take action to overcome any negative thoughts. And she had determined that now wasn't the time for weakness. If she wanted to stay in the game, she had to move forward and face the world.

Georgia stood up, holding onto her desk for support. Leaning forward to look at her reflection in the mirror, she groaned at what she saw. She needed to do something with her hair and maybe apply some make-up to hide the bags under her swollen red eyes. But she was too weary to do either. Her crew mates would have to take her as she was.

She slowly climbed the stairs to the midships area, not sure who would be there. As it happened, the whole of the Expedition Two crew were present, listening to Commander Anders instructions for the afternoon. Georgia was acutely aware that the room went silent as she walked in and could sense some of them looking in her direction. Not necessarily staring, but definitely taking an interest as she walked by.

Before anyone had the chance to speak to her, she steeled herself to deal with the matter face on. Hiding the panic running through her, she boldly strode to the middle of the room and took a deep breath. Looking across at Captain Winter, she said, "Good afternoon, everyone. No doubt you've noticed I've not been myself for the past few days and you're wondering what's wrong with me. You wouldn't be the first." There were a few intrigued laughs, but Georgia was disappointed that her attempt at humor had fallen flat. Tough crowd! She continued regardless. "The captain and the doctor already know, and I want you to know what is really wrong with me." Georgia stopped, not sure of the words to say or if she could actually say them.

She could still see the sadness in Captain Winter's eyes, but he nodded his encouragement. "I've not been well for almost a week and have been getting steadily worse despite trying to fight it. I blamed it on a number of reasons. In the end, I finally went to see Doctor Betts three days ago. In her usual style, she insisted on testing me. And... she discovered I have a number of tumors." Georgia rushed the last few words and suppressed a sob. The room was totally silent, everyone in shock at the revelation. "I only had it confirmed yesterday morning. Doctor Betts advises that the tumors are malignant, and the prognosis is... well I have maybe three months. If I'm lucky. But you all know how stubborn I am. I intend hanging around far longer."

Georgia had nothing else to say and looked down at her feet, wishing a hole would appear to swallow her up. She was aware of a shuffling in the room, but no one else spoke until Megan took over. "What Georgia's just told you is true. Our best guess is it's the effect of the solar flare she was caught in, but we can't be sure. So, if anyone is suffering with nausea or headaches, come and see me immediately. We can give Georgia some medication to ease the pain, but there are tumors in her brain and we can't operate. I know this comes as a huge shock to you..." Megan also burst into tears and couldn't say any more. She went up to Georgia and the two of them hugged each other tightly. It was becoming a habit.

"This isn't the time for a eulogy," added Captain Winter after a few more moments of silence. "Georgia's not gone, and she still has plenty to offer as a valued member of this crew. I know that she doesn't want our pity or for any of us to treat her any differently. So, we go on as if nothing has changed and continue to treat Georgia with respect and dignity. All she wants is our support, and we'll deal with this one day at a time. As we do with every other curveball that comes our way. I would, however, ask you to watch out for Georgia and each other even more than you do already. Thank you."

With the announcement made, to Georgia's relief, the chatter resumed to the previous level as everyone returned to what they had been doing. Joe Mancuso was the first to walk over to her as she poured herself a coffee. "So now I understand why I've been asked to work more closely with you. I promise to be a good learner." He tried one of his winning smiles but couldn't quite carry it off.

"I know you will, Joe. You've one of the best AI minds that I know. You'll do great." Georgia felt a huge weight had been lifted as a result of sharing her news. It didn't solve her situation, but she hoped she would be treated normally for as long as possible. After some small talk with Mancuso, Georgia spotted Captain Winter and Commander Anders talking together by the far wall.

They stopped their conversation as she walked over to them. "I know what you're going to ask, Georgia," said Captain Winter before she spoke. "You want to get back to your duties."

"Yes, sir," she replied, nodding. "I would rather you allow me to work than force me to sit around with nothing but my condition to worry about. Physically I'm still capable."

"I know. But I'd like you to take some time to consider it properly. You only found out several hours ago. You need more time to process that news."

"I'm good for it, sir. At least until we move into Alpha Base. Then there will be plenty of time to sit back and take stock."

Captain Winter looked doubtful as he rocked on his feet, stroked his chin and looked across at Anders. "Commander? You're looking after the move. Are you happy for Pyke here to resume her duties?"

Georgia could see Anders blush as the captain put him on the spot. He looked at the captain, then at Georgia before saying, "Well sir, I er... think that may be okay. We are stretched to move to the base in time. Do we need Doctor Betts' opinion?"

"That's not necessary," replied the captain. "I'm happy for you to make a command decision."

"In that case, consider yourself back on duty, Pyke. You're back with Redmayne and Chief Grant in the MEV." Anders patted her on the shoulder and smiled.

"Thanks, both of you." Georgia was thrilled. "You won't regret this."

***

That evening, the chief helped Georgia and Redmayne prepare the MEV for the trip to the nearby cave system. The MEV, or Manned Excursion Vehicle, could comfortably carry up to six astronauts in a pressurized cabin so there would be plenty of room for equipment. The MEV was about twenty feet long and had six large wheels, each with its own independent electric motor, to help it maneuver across the rugged terrain. There was an older, smaller version of the MEV on *Excalibur* they would also need to construct once Alpha Base was built.

Georgia was pleased to have Jim with her. She had never really bonded with Tom Redmayne during their training. There was something about him she didn't trust. He had kept to himself and on more than one occasion had to be reminded that he was part of a team. She'd also noticed more than once that he would furtively look at her. The man had an issue with her, but she did not understand what that could be. It had been a relief to be assigned to *Endeavour* for the mission.

Redmayne identified the two equipment pallets he wanted, each about the size of a small refrigerator. "We'll attach those to the side of the MEV. They contain seismic detectors that can be left in the lava tube. We need to ensure that the cave system is stable and will withstand any Martian quakes. If that asteroid hits, I don't know how severe the tremors may be."

The chief and Georgia gently carried the pallets one at a time for Redmayne to lash onto the side of the MEV with an elastic cord. "These are going nowhere," Jim said, once they secured both pallets. He rocked them with his right hand to prove his point.

The physical exertion had taken its toll on Georgia. "Time out, guys. I need a few minutes to recover. Gravity's a bitch!"

"No worries, Pyke. Take a seat in the cabin while we load the rest of the supplies."

Although guilty at taking a break, she knew it was the right thing to do. Her weakened body was taking longer to acclimate to Mars than her colleagues' but at least she now knew why. She climbed the five steps that led into the airlock, using the handrail to pull herself up and once inside, she stepped straight through into the cabin area and slumped into the driver's seat.

Through the front canopy of the MEV, Georgia could see that the sun was setting. It would soon be too cold to remain outside. She pressed the blank control screen on the console in front of her and it sprang into life, its blue screen detailing a myriad of information that would be useful when they were in transit. The lack of any red warning lights indicated that all systems and functions were operating. Swiveling her chair, she turned to see the chief had followed her with a box of rations and a water container.

"Thanks, chief. I only need a few minutes then I'll be good to go again."

"There's no hurry. I've got this covered with Redmayne. You need to learn to pace yourself. And to rely on others," he said as he placed the rations in one of the storage compartments.

"Easy for you to say. I've never had to rely on anyone in my life. I don't want to start now."

"I can understand that. But your situation has changed whether or not you like it. I'm here for you though. And please call me Jim." He blushed at possibly overstepping the mark and quickly tried to recover the situation. "I mean, we all are. You'd do the same if the roles were reversed," he blustered.

Georgia enjoyed his discomfort. "Thanks, Jim. I don't want to sound ungrateful, but can we not talk about this? I'm not in denial. I just don't need to be reminded about it all the time."

He nodded and headed back out without saying another word.

Georgia sat for another minute, berating herself for being so hard on Jim. She knew that she was only trying to help. As was the captain and the rest of the crew. But she didn't want their pity. She wanted to keep busy and feel that she was still useful. Recovering her resolve, she stood and stepped back outside to carry on loading supplies. She was surprised to see that only Redmayne was there.

"Where's the chief?" she asked.

Redmayne was carrying another ration box. He stopped to look at her. "He went back up in the cradle." Georgia detected a sneer as he added, "It may have been something you said."

Chapter 24

As the sun rose above the distant horizon early the next morning, the chief and Redmayne set off in the MEV, waved off by Captain Winter and half of *Endeavour*'s crew. Georgia missed the departure, suffering from another severe headache.

The ride in the MEV was surprisingly smooth, with pneumatics cushioning any bumps they experienced. There wasn't a great deal for the two men to do. The autonomous driving program guided them to their destination while avoiding any large obstacles. It wasn't long before the rear viewing cameras showed *Endeavour* and *Eden* as small white dots, while out of the front canopy, the sheer cliff face of the crater wall grew ever larger and more imposing.

Although geology wasn't Redmayne's primary discipline, he was the most knowledgeable on the subject among the landing party and his name had always been in the frame for this part of the mission. The chief had not really spent much time getting to know Redmayne, although from what he'd heard, the chief scientist was not the easiest person. This proved to be true during the trip as Redmayne kept his attention on the instruments and preparation of his equipment, with no interest in striking up a conversation. Jim tried several times but was met with short abrupt responses that cut short any extended dialogue. After a while he gave up, sat back and tried to enjoy the view.

His mind wandered to Georgia. He enjoyed working with her and spending time with her and although he'd seen how difficult she could be, he found her easy to speak to. He hadn't always been comfortable around women, but she was different. Her tragic news had come as a blow to any hopes he'd had of forming a relationship with her. He didn't understand how she could be so calm and matter of fact about her fate but told himself he would be there for her as a friend.

The MEV slowed as it approached the entrance to the first cave. The chief switched the controls to manual and slowed the MEV down to a walking pace. The entrance to the cave was roughly semi circular, about sixteen feet high and twenty-five feet across. The edges appeared relatively smooth, but there were a number of large boulders in front of and close to the entrance. The chief managed to navigate the boulders and drive the MEV to the mouth of the cave, where he turned on the powerful spotlights.

The floor of the cave was flat. No boulders, but a significant number of rocks that would need to be cleared away. The first seventy-five feet of the cave was a tunnel and the MEV moved slowly forward until the tunnel opened up into a massive cave.

"Stop here while I take some readings," requested Redmayne.

The chief stopped and sent a message to *Endeavour* to confirm their status. Meanwhile, Redmayne checked the readings on three screens in front of him. Satisfied with what he saw, he asked Jim Grant to move forward a further fifteen yards. Once the MEV was stationary, Tom said he had to go outside and take samples. They both suited up and, once the chief had set the external cameras running and turned on all the MEV lights, they exited through the airlock.

Redmayne carefully stepped down onto the ground. "Don't disturb too much of the dust until I've taken some air samples. You can take some soil samples from the tunnel entrance back there. I'm going to move further in toward the back of the cave. Could you also collect a few rock samples? I don't need anything too large." And with that, Redmayne disappeared down the side of the MEV, leaving the chief lost for words.

The two men spent almost an hour walking round the cave, collecting samples and taking photos. The walls were smooth but with vertical grooves. Unlike caverns the chief had seen on earth, there were no stalactites hanging from the roof. It was as if something had flowed through and left a huge space behind it. To his eyes, the cave was more than sufficient for the plans they had, but then he wasn't the expert. He did find the space a bit eerie and, even though he knew better, expected to see bats flying around.

Returning to the comfort of the MEV, the two men remained in their spacesuits and carried the sample cases into the main cabin area. Redmayne kept the cases closed but put the samples containing the air into one of his machines. "Until we know there is nothing lethal inside this cave, I don't want to contaminate us," he said. "Once we've placed the seismic detectors, it will be okay for us to return to *Endeavour* so I can complete my analysis."

"Okay, whatever you say, Tom. But I also want to have a quick drive along the base of the cliff to ensure there are no obvious loose rocks."

After the pallets had been unloaded, the chief expertly turned the MEV around inside the cave and soon they were back in natural daylight. After a quick inspection of the rock face, he was happy that there was no obvious danger and signaled *Endeavour* that they were returning before switching on the nav computer for the drive back.

***

If anything, Redmayne was quieter on the journey back to *Endeavour* as he studied the results from the experiments he'd already started to perform. The chief was grateful for the silence and managed to doze for a short while. He awoke when he felt the MEV slow and he knew they were approaching *Endeavour*.

Once safely back inside *Endeavour*, Redmayne took all the samples to his small laboratory next to the mid-deck, where Grace joined him. Jim grabbed himself a coffee before heading to the captain's cabin to speak with Winter.

"First impressions?" Winter asked before the chief sat down.

"He's rude and an arrogant bastard, but I'm sure he's good at his job. Otherwise he wouldn't be here."

Winter hid his amusement. "I didn't mean Redmayne. I know what he's like! Will the cave be suitable for our needs? Do we have a home for Alpha Base?"

"Ah..." Jim blushed, not for the first time that week. "It's certainly large enough to house all of our habitats. There'll be some minor work required to level out areas of the floor and clear some rocks but that shouldn't take more than a day or two. You'll have to wait for Redmayne to come up with his results on the structure and composition of the cave. But I would say it's a good prospect for our base."

"Excellent news. Thanks, Jim. Start preparing your equipment to make the cave ready to move into."

"Will do. I'll get Georgia involved too. I know that she's looking to keep herself busy. She can help with programming the robots to level the floor before we erect the modules."

***

After lunch, Captain Winter read Redmayne's survey report with some satisfaction. The cave checked out. He ordered Jim Grant to start the clearance exercise as soon as possible that afternoon, then forwarded the report to Ground Control. The response from General Stockton two hours later was not what he'd expected.

"Congratulations on finding a safe haven for your crew, Captain Winter. While I approve your request to commence clearance activities, you must not populate the cave without further directions from me. I want you and your team to proceed with caution until further notice.

"As regards Georgia Pyke, we do not believe the timing is right to share her tragic news with the public. We are trying to build several positive news stories to exploit the ongoing public support and the high ratings your success is attracting. The last thing we need right now is any negative press, especially as we are hoping to seek an extension of funding from the government. While I respect her decision, it is unfortunate that she has shared her news with the crew. I trust that you understand I'm taking a holistic view of the Mars Project. There is far more at stake than one individual, whoever they may be. So, I'm sure you will not allow this mishap, self-inflicted by Pyke I must add, to have a negative impact in any way. To that extent, please ensure that the status of her health remains confined to those of you on Mars until further notice. Thank you and continued good fortune. Stockton out."

Winter looked at the frozen image of the general. "You gutless bastard," he said, clenching his fists in anger. He stayed in his chair for several minutes before the anger inside him subsided. There were aspects of his job he didn't enjoy, and this was one of them.

It was easy for the general, Winter thought bitterly. He was remote and had not forged attachments to any of the crew. Stockton's priority was solely the success of the mission and the crew were a means to an end. Winter was sure his role as captain would be far easier if he didn't care so much.

Chapter 25

It was the start of the mission's fourth day on Mars and Captain Winter was sitting at his desk, contemplating the latest orders received overnight from Earth, when there was a knock on the door. "Come in, commander. I'm ready for you."

Commander Anders entered and sat down opposite. Winter thought he looked weary. He wasn't surprised. He had noticed over the past few days that nearly all the crew were looking tired. Doctor Betts knew of his concerns and understood he needed all of them to be working at peak efficiency. It was vital for the mission.

"Good morning, commander. I've just been reviewing the latest update from Ground Control. At present, they're still estimating high probability that the asteroid will strike Mars in four days, although they are still refining their calculations. The percentage odds continue to drop so we may get away with it, but that doesn't mean we can slacken our efforts on completing Alpha Base."

"Agreed, sir. That's good to hear. Do we know where the asteroid could strike?"

"Yes. If it comes down, it will be just north of the equator, just under two thousand miles from here. So, we're not in immediate danger. It's the effects of the fallout that will hamper this mission. I'm told that the Russians and Chinese are in orbit keeping a watching brief. They have the luxury of being able to wait in safety while this plays out. A smart move. How are we progressing with the base so far?"

"Generally, we're on track, I would say. Most of the urgent components are now in situ at the mouth of the lava tube. I've had the rovers acting as tractor units ferrying urgent supplies from the supply ships. Joe and Emily are monitoring those elements. The one concern I have is wear and tear. Dust is a constant issue, getting into the tractors and causing them to malfunction. An increasing amount of time is being wasted having to clean and repair motor assemblies."

"Understood. When do you anticipate being able to place the habitat units inside the lava tube?"

"I'm confident we can start tomorrow. I've given Redmayne two construction robots to prepare the inside of the tube. They're sealing any cracks and preparing the surface. Tom's not found too many deep crevices and he advises that the tube is close to being totally sealed. The ground has been rougher and more abrasive than expected though."

"Excellent. And how about power? When will the reactor be commissioned?"

"That's a good news story, sir. The reactor is complete. The chief and Rashid have done an amazing job to finish it ahead of schedule and carry out all the testing. There's still some cabling to be laid, but the reactor is basically ready to be switched on when you give the word. It means Jim and Rashid are free to carry out other tasks, such as repair the rovers."

Winter was impressed with how Anders was efficiently overseeing the work. There had been no real doubt that the commander was up to the job, but it gave Winter additional confidence in his second in command.

"Fantastic work, Lars. Is there anything else you'd like to raise?"

Anders was about to reply when he was interrupted by Doctor Betts knocking and poking her head around the door. "Perfect timing, doctor," he said. "Please come and sit down." She looked at Captain Winter, who nodded that she could enter.

As she sat down next to him, Anders continued. "Two concerns, which the doctor may be able to help with. First, the health of the crew. I know that I've been struggling with fatigue since we landed. There's been no time to get used to Mars as we had hoped, and the crew are undertaking physical activity. What are your thoughts, captain?"

"Yes, commander. It's not gone unnoticed by me. I am concerned by the workload and I've shared those concerns with Ground Control. They are more focused on getting us to safety before the asteroid strikes. Doctor Betts, what are your observations?"

"If you want my honest opinion, and that's the only one I give, I'd say you're pushing the crew too hard. There have already been several strains, and that trend is likely to continue. Our bodies are in a weakened state because of three months in zero gravity. You cannot seriously expect people to act as if they were born to be builders. I've been prescribing plenty of painkillers and sleeping tablets. More than I would like to give. If I was a betting woman, I'd say an accident was highly likely."

Winter thought carefully for a moment. "Thanks, Megan. That's basically where I thought we were too. Although the medication worries me. Any recommendations, bearing in mind the imminent asteroid?"

Doctor Betts shook her head. "If it wasn't for the threat, I'd say the crew needed several rest days. I'll continue to monitor all of them and patch up any injuries as best I can, but once we're inside the base, you need to allow the crew some recovery time."

"That won't be a problem, doctor," said the captain.

"The second item from me," said Anders. "Georgia is trying hard. Everyone can see that. But she is really struggling. I'm worried about her. Not just her state of mind. She's getting easily fatigued. I've suggested lighter duties for her, but she simply refuses."

Winter knew how stubborn Georgia was. He had already spoken to her to see how she was and could see that she was putting on a brave front. He knew that he had a duty of care to look out for her, as well as ensure she didn't inadvertently harm the crew. "Let me have a word with her again, as her captain. Megan, you may also want to have a chat."

"As her doctor or as her friend?"

"Whichever is best. I'll let you decide. At the moment, she's her own worst enemy and we need to look out for her."

***

It was later that afternoon when the first serious accident happened. Two of the rovers, towing component pallets and accompanied by Mancuso and Emily who were on their speeder bikes, pulled up at the entrance to the lava tube. On the journey from *Intrepid*, Mancuso had noticed that his rover was drawing more power than expected, which was normally the first sign of a problem with the motor.

"It looks like we need another motor replacement," he said to Emily. "Let me carry out a quick visual inspection to see if it will last one more trip while you unload. I'd rather change the motor overnight than miss out on one more trip."

"Okay, Joe." By now, they both had plenty of practice unloading the pallets from the sleds with the help of a small robotic crane. This time, however, Emily was not paying full attention as she untied the sled and two pallets tumbled on top of her, trapping her left leg before she had time to react.

Mancuso was kneeling down next to the rover, brushing away the red dust that had accumulated around the motor housing unit when he heard Emily's scream of pain over his comms channel. "Emily, are you okay?" he said, standing up to get a better view. Fifty feet away he could see Emily lying on the ground with the pallets on top of her.

"My leg's stuck. I think it's broken. Can you give me a hand here?"

Mancuso could hear the pain in Emily's voice. Her breathing sounded ragged. Running as quickly as he could he reached her and tried to lift the pallets. Realizing they were too heavy for him, and with Emily grimacing at his efforts he commanded the crane to lift them. "Hold on, Emily. We'll soon have you out of here." He held her hand to reassure her but, looking at her face, he knew she was in excruciating pain. She screamed out in agony as the first pallet moved and Mancuso saw her body tense before relaxing as she passed out.

As soon as the pallets were out of the way, he could tell that the leg was indeed fractured. Worse still, there was a small tear in Emily's suit. He frowned in dismay, knowing that her suit must be venting air. Reaching into the utility pouch on his belt, he found a patch and applied it to the rip, preventing any further leakage.

By this time, the chief had heard what had happened and rushed over to see if he could help. Seeing that Mancuso had everything under control he called *Endeavour* to send the MEV for Emily and to inform Doctor Betts that she would be receiving a patient.

***

That evening, Captain Winter visited Emily in the medical center where Doctor Betts had operated on her broken leg to insert two titanium pins. He had been told about the accident shortly after it happened and before they had returned Emily to the ship. The incident only confirmed his fears, but he was relieved that it had not been fatal this time. He'd have to file a report to Ground Control, which would probably be the most annoying aspect for him.

Winter sat on the edge of Emily's bed and smiled encouragingly. "I hear from the doctor that you suffered a proximal tibia fracture and soft tissue damage. You'll be on light duties for some time but thank God it wasn't a whole lot worse."

It was clear that the embarrassment was far worse than any pain she was suffering. "I'm sorry, sir, I don't know what I was doing. We've been unloading as a pair all day. It was a lapse of judgment."

"We're all working under pressure. Accidents happen," Winter replied. "It could have been any of us and I understand it could have been much worse if Joe hadn't been there to patch your suit."

"I was lucky. Another few minutes and I'd have been out of air. I don't even want to think about it."

"The main thing is you'll be okay. Make sure you listen to Megan's instructions."

Emily winced. "I'll do that, captain."

***

At the same time Winter was talking with Emily, Georgia was in the canteen, forcing herself to eat a bowl of chicken soup which was all that she could manage without throwing up. Fortunately, she'd ordered it as part of her personal meal inventory. The aromas reminded her of being a young girl when her mum would often make soup and bake fresh bread for herself and Jackson and the soup now gave her some comfort just as she needed it most. Thoughts of her mother came with mixed blessings though. They acted as a stark reminder of how much Georgia missed being able to speak with her mum. She'd still not found the courage to contact her brother and inform him of her condition.

Just as she was once again becoming overwhelmed by emotions, Megan sat next to her at the table with what looked like a bowl of pasta and asked, "Are you okay, Georgia?"

Quickly composing herself and wiping her eyes, Georgia forced a smile, knowing full well that she was fooling no one, least of all Megan. "Not really. To be honest, I was just thinking about my mum. I miss her so much. I should stop feeling sorry for myself."

"That's understandable. I'm close to my mum too and try to talk to her at least once a week. I don't know what I'd do if she wasn't around any longer. But you still have Jackson. And you can always talk with me. I know it's not the same, but I am a very good listener."

"Thanks, Megan. I'm not sure I know where to start. I'm constantly tired and unable to stay focused for more than a few minutes at a time. Maybe I was wrong to insist on working."

"Do you want me to sign you off for few days? It will give you a chance to recover some strength until you are ready for light duties."

Georgia gave it some thought. It was tempting as she'd found the day a real struggle. Her arms and legs were throbbing, her neck ached, and it felt like someone was stabbing needles into her head. But she couldn't really see herself sitting around when everyone else was working so hard to build the base before the asteroid strike. "Thanks, but I'll get through it. I can't bear doing nothing. And I hear we're a person down already. How is Emily by the way?"

"A stress fracture in her left tibia. I've pinned it but she won't be able to walk on it for a few weeks. I'm not entirely sure how long it will take to heal properly. I'm breaking new ground here." Megan knew that Georgia had subtly changed the subject but decided not to push it for the time being.

"At least she's in good hands. I know you're worried about me. That's your job but I promise I'll be okay. I'm resilient. I just need some rest to recover from today. I don't suppose there are any spare mattresses you're aware of?"

Megan laughed. "I'm sure everyone has now asked me that question. I could have made my fortune selling spare bedding if I'd thought about it."

At that moment, Captain Winter joined them. He had a bowl of steaming fish and vegetables, which looked colorful and appetizing. "Ah, my two favorite ladies," he said, sitting down before waiting for an invitation.

Georgia considered whether this was a coordinated effort by the pair of them. They weren't the most subtle, but they were good friends and a large part of her was secretly grateful that she had people who cared for her.

As Winter ate his dinner, he explained that he'd spent some time with Emily and reassured her she was not to blame. There would always be accidents, and Emily had agreed to light duties for several weeks at least, although she didn't really have a choice.

"Actually," Megan interrupted, "she'll be laid up in the medical center for the next two days under observation."

"If only all your patients were so amenable," commented Winter, winking at Georgia. "You don't have to push yourself so hard. It's no good raising your eyebrows. I don't want you to have an accident like Emily because you're not ready."

"Thanks for your concern, captain. I've just been speaking with Megan about this. I know my limits and for the moment I'm okay to carry on. You can't really afford me not to."

"And I can't afford for you to injure yourself or anyone else. I can get one of the Kings to take over what Emily was doing."

"They're horticulturists. They won't be able to replace Emily. And they have enough to do transplanting all the crops. I can do this. Really."

"Okay," Winter conceded reluctantly. "But watch out for yourself."

Chapter 26

Tom also had some doubts about Georgia's ability to carry on her work. He was sitting in Commander Anders' quarters on the *Eden*, discussing the matter.

"Have you heard how Emily is recovering?" he asked.

"Yes, Doctor Betts has informed me that Emily suffered a broken leg and will be out of action for a while. Luckily it was nothing more serious than that."

"I hope you're not being blamed."

"Why should I be? It was an accident. Emily admitted that she made a mistake but there's no apportioning of blame."

"Maybe not yet. Winter put you in charge of the operation to build Alpha Base. Which makes you responsible for the crew safety. What will happen if there's another accident?"

"I've already reported my concerns that the crew are tired. We're under pressure to complete tasks that were planned to take twice the time we have, and when we had all recovered our strength. Ground Control will see that." Tom noticed a hint of doubt in Anders' response. It was the chink he was looking for.

"If you're sure, Lars. I just believe that the captain is setting you up to fail. You're now a person down and faced with a much harder job. And one of your crew is in the Medical Center. Winter is strengthening his own position."

"He does not need to do that. He's already captain. And there is only one Expedition Two crew. It doesn't matter which ship Emily arrived on."

"Winter's an old man on his final mission. He was the first human to set foot on Mars and will be a global hero when he returns home. He wants to cement his place in history and probably looks at you and feels threatened. Haven't you noticed that he surrounds himself with the *Endeavour* crew and ignores you, treats you like an outsider?"

Anders paused, almost afraid to air his thoughts aloud. "That's how command leadership works. The captain is making the most efficient use of the resources available to him."

"And what about Georgia Pyke? He has a weak spot for her. She shouldn't be on duty and could be a liability."

"It's no secret that he sees her as a daughter figure. It may cloud his judgment sometimes, but I don't believe it's affecting the overall mission."

"Spoken like a true second in command. You need to stand up for yourself more if you want to be considered for leadership. And that means there's no room for sentiment. Separate the captain from his trusted followers and do what needs to be done. And that means benching Pyke. It's only a matter of time before she gets herself killed. Or, worse still, one of us."

"I'm not sure, Tom. Pyke still has much to offer. And we need her skills to complete the base. We can't afford to drop anyone in the limited time we have available. Perhaps once the base is complete, we can look at easing her workload."

"That's your decision. But you may be making a mistake and putting the crew in unnecessary danger. I'm only thinking about you, Lars. It's unfair they have not given you the opportunities you deserve and are being sidelined by Winter. Being given responsibility for the base may have seemed important but it's a poisoned chalice."

"I appreciate your concern. And I'll definitely consider what you've had to say. To be honest though, I'm not sure what I can do at the moment."

"I understand. But rest assured that I have your back."

"Thanks, Tom."

Redmayne left and went back to his own cabin, pleased with the seeds of doubt he'd just sown. He knew that the commander was weak, and he would continue to play on that weakness.

Chapter 27

The sun had been above the horizon for an hour as Georgia descended in the cradle, back down to the surface. To her, the scene was beautiful yet desolate. She took in as much detail as she could, desperately attempting to remember everything. She could see a few wispy clouds high on the edge of Mars' atmosphere, lit up by rays from the sun. A red tinge made them look like autumn leaves. To her mind, Mars was eternally autumnal with the reds and browns dominating everywhere she looked. And for a second they transported her back to her home, kicking through leaves with her mum on a damp October morning.

The drive to the base had become so routine that it was almost like a daily commute. Georgia and the chief had hitched up a trailer with another load of supplies. No time for wasted trips at the moment. Joining them on this trip were Captain Winter and Rashid Qadir. Inflating the modules was a huge step in the mission's progress and would require the four of them to play their part.

Once inside the cave, Georgia could see how much work they had already completed. A series of arc lamps were set up around the cave to provide plenty of light. A plethora of cables ran along the floor from a huge junction box. And in the middle of the cave were the four expandable habitation modules which, when inflated, would be the first components of their permanent base. It would be their shelter, protecting them not only from the imminent asteroid with the thick rock of the cave providing a shield from the solar radiation raining down on the planet.

"Okay, let's get this thing moving," said Captain Winter to the chief. "I'm happy with the location. I suggest starting with the one near the back." They had decided that the biodome should be as far from the main entrance as possible, so these were the first to be inflated. Working quickly, the chief and Rashid had soon attached power cables to the first module, while Georgia checked out the computer controls and moved one of the construction robots.

There was an air of excitement as the chief entered the commands to commence the inflation process. At first, nothing happened. After a few minutes, however, Georgia could see that the module was several feet taller than its neighbor. It continued to expand with no issue and within an hour was fully inflated, standing twenty feet tall with a diameter of thirty feet. It looked like a large marshmallow. There were no windows, but it was not as if there was much of a view at the back of the cave.

Three hours later, the four of them were sitting back in the safety of the MEV for a well-earned break and to renew their air supplies before the afternoon shift. It had been a busy morning, and it was a relief for each of them to remove their spacesuits. Despite their best efforts, dust had crept into the suits and rubbed at their joints. Georgia's elbows were starting to throb. As she talked to Jim, she noticed the captain was looking in her direction.

"Is everything alright, sir?"

"I've been watching you in action today, Pyke. You look more physically able than several days ago, and your whole attitude has changed. I'm not surprised you're questioning the good doctor's diagnosis. If I were you, I'd be doing the same. It's astounding."

"Thank you for noticing, captain."

"I'd like a few moments with you. To have a talk about a few things. Chief, are you okay if we give you a head start in the next module? I won't keep Georgia for long." It wasn't really a question, so Chief Grant nodded and headed back to the airlock, closing the hatch behind him.

Winter sat back in his chair, trying to make himself comfortable. Georgia looked at him suspiciously.

"It's been a while since I've had a good chat with you Georgia. Probably too long, bearing in mind your condition. But I have been closely monitoring your progress. And I have to say it's really impressed me how you've got your head down to support the mission. I didn't expect you to crumble, but I would have stepped in, if I thought you were struggling with the situation."

"You were right to have faith in me, sir. And I am grateful. I want to do as much as I can for the team in the time I have left. Keeping busy and solving problems is all I know, and all I really have left. So, I was relieved when you didn't take that away from me."

"I had grand plans for you, as you know. Even though you didn't intend to stay on Mars permanently, I was hoping you'd change your mind. You're a natural and fearless leader. And an ideal replacement for me one day. I don't know what we will do without you."

Georgia was taken aback. "I know you've always shown faith in me and supported me more than anyone ever has done. But I could never fill your shoes, sir. And I'm sure the general would have a say in the matter of the next person to command Alpha Base."

Winter shrugged. "I'd had several conversations with Control about you. They saw potential in you from an early stage of the mission training. I don't believe they would have blocked your stepping up as leader. Not that it matters now, but I thought you should know. You are highly thought of by more people than you know. And we're all terribly sad."

"I'm not gone yet. You can immortalize me at the right time. Which is when I'm no longer here."

Winter tried unsuccessfully to raise a smile. "I'll do that. But for now, I am pleased to see you back to your old self, at least for a short period. And I promise to speak with you more often. Now I suppose we'd better help the chief before he accuses us of slacking."

Donning their EV suits for the afternoon shift, they climbed into the airlock before exiting back into the cave.

Chapter 28

"You look worried, captain. Is anything wrong?" It was the morning of day five on Mars, and Commander Anders had just arrived at *Endeavour* for his daily meeting with Captain Winter.

Winter wished that he'd learned to control his facial expressions better, but figured it was now too late in his career to do so. "Commander, I've received an update on the asteroid from Ground Control. The effect of Mars' gravity is causing the asteroid to break up and fragment into several large chunks. Most of it will still impact the original crash zone. But that zone has now been expanded and includes Hellas Planitia Any fragments should still impact north of our location but it's too close for comfort. We won't know exactly until several hours before it hits."

"That makes the danger more real," replied Anders, taking a seat. "The good news is that the all habitat modules are inflated and undergoing leak tests. So far it's a positive."

Winter let out a sigh of relief. He knew he had challenged the crew to build the base in an unreasonably short time. "That is superb news, Lars. You've done a very impressive job. Will we have time to move more of the supplies nearer to the base? It will be disastrous if a ship is hit by any asteroid fragments."

"It will be tight, but I'll see what I can do."

"Let me know if we need to divert any resources. Although in reality that will be either myself or Doctor Betts."

"Actually, we're okay resource wise. The issue will be how to keep the rovers operating. We're getting an increasing number of failures that will slow down our ability to move supplies. The chief and Rashid are doing the best they can to swap out the motors. There's no one else that has their expertise." Lars stopped, but Winter could sense that he had something else to say.

"What is it, Lars?"

"It's Georgia. Everyone can see that she is trying very hard to help. But she is struggling. It's not good for her. I'm concerned that she's become a liability. Allowing her to carry on with her tasks is putting some people on edge. They worry whether she's up to carrying out her work and they're concerned for their own welfare."

Winter stiffened. "Who's been talking? No one has come to me."

Anders was flustered at being put on the spot. "It's just general conversation I've overheard. Everyone likes Georgia, you know that. And they feel sorry for her. But the situation is difficult."

"Particularly for Georgia, commander!" Winter could sense his irritation showing and tried to control his tone. "I did give it a lot of consideration, with input from Doctor Betts. After discussing the matter with Georgia, we decided it was best for her physical and mental welfare that she continues. In any event, we need to address the asteroid emergency. Are you questioning my ability to make sound decisions over the safety of my crew?"

"Of course not, captain. I just wonder if, perhaps, you're being more lenient on Georgia than you would be for someone else. With the habitat almost ready to move into, you should reduce her workload."

"Thank you for your advice, commander. I'm planning to let the whole crew rest once we've moved into the base. But for now, everyone pulls together to get the job done. Is that understood?"

"Perfectly, sir." And with that, Lars stood and left the captain's quarters as swiftly as he could.

Winter stayed in his chair to consider his motives, staring at the space where Anders had just been sitting. *Is Anders right? Are my feelings for Georgia clouding my ability to protect her? I thought I was better than that. I will need to speak with Lars later to apologize. I may have been too hard on him, which isn't like me at all.*

Chapter 29

The inspection team of Captain Winter, Commander Anders, Chief Grant, Georgia and Redmayne arrived at what was now Alpha Base shortly after nine am. Their MEV slowed as it reached the entrance to the cave.

Knowing this was there permanent home, Winter took his time to take in all the details. "That is a really impressive entrance. I hadn't truly appreciated how large it was. It should give us plenty of space once completed."

There were nine stacks of pallets lined up neatly either side of the entrance, making almost an avenue. Half a mile to the left, he also spotted the distinct shape of the fusion reactor. A thick black cable ran from the reactor along the ground and into the cave.

Anders spotted where Winter was looking. "As you know, we'll eventually dig a trench for the power cable, but it wasn't a priority in the time we had available. We've not had the reactor running at full capacity as yet either, but the chief assures me it passed all of its commissioning tests with flying colors."

"Indeed it did, commander," replied the chief. "Everything performed just beautifully. We'll end up covering the reactor for protection from the elements. Again, it's not a priority item."

Winter nodded, satisfied with the impressive progress he was seeing so far.

The MEV made its way inside the cave, lighting its way with six halogen headlamps. Straight ahead, Winter could see the main airlock to the command habitat and beyond that, to the right of the tube he could identify the water storage and purifier, as well as the power distribution board.

The autonomous driving system deftly reversed the MEV to the docking port on the airlock, allowing the crew to exit without their spacesuits.

"This is far more practical," admitted Winter as he stepped straight through the airlock into the clean room where spacesuits and equipment would be stored. Through the clean room, the corridor branched off in two directions and Winter hesitated, not sure whether to turn left or right.

"Sorry, sir, let me lead the way," offered Commander Anders. "There will be signage at some point. Left is the command center and right leads through to the common area and beyond that are the personal quarters. We'll see the command center first."

The layout of the base came back to Winter quickly. It was exactly the same as the replica they'd trained in on Earth. The walls of the corridor were a cream color and curved over the top of them. The LED lighting was bright white, but he knew they would change their radiance during the day to help the astronauts adjust between day and night. There was a strange smell that he couldn't quite place. It reminded him of disinfectant. But then, everything had been thoroughly cleansed before being loaded onto the supply ships.

He followed Anders through a door that led into the command center. Once it was fully commissioned, this would be the heart of the base. It was a square room, roughly twenty feet on each side. The various stations were modular and covered three of the walls. On the fourth was a large video screen that would be used for communications. In the middle of the room was a console with a bank of monitors and space for three people to sit. Winter could see that there was still much work to be done. All the monitors were blank and there were spools of yellow, blue and red cable in the far corner. "This doesn't look ready to move into."

"It's not as bad as it looks," said Anders, deflated by the Captain's remark. "There's still some hardware to be brought inside, but Rashid believes he'll have everything working by this time tomorrow. It may not be fully tested, but we should have all environmental systems up and running and comms. The rest we can fix once we're here. In fact, it will be easier, rather than having to travel from the ships."

The chief took a moment to interrupt. "Captain, if you don't mind, I've got some work to perform outside with the power grid. I'd like to get on with that while you carry on with the inspection. You can contact me should you have any questions that the commander cannot answer. I'll take Georgia with me."

"I have no problem with that. I imagine the inspection will take another few hours. Georgia, are you up to this? You've been very quiet so far this morning."

"I'm tired, that's all." Her response was too quick and automatic, but Winter let it pass. "And I've been paying close attention to the commander's guided tour."

"Okay, you two carry on." Winter turned to Redmayne. "Do you have important work as well?"

Redmayne had wanted to stay for the tour, but the captain's abrupt question made it clear he wasn't wanted. "I do need to check the environmental systems outside, the water storage in particular to ensure the purifiers are operating and the stirrers are preventing the water from freezing. Again, you can contact me if the commander cannot answer all your questions."

Once it was the two of them in the command center, Winter sat in what would be his new command chair and looked up at Anders. Taking a deep breath, he said, "Lars, I wanted to find some time to speak with you and apologize for my behavior earlier. It was unwarranted, and you were right. I've had time to reflect on what you said, and I have been giving Georgia favorable treatment."

Anders took the apology graciously. "That's quite okay, captain. I know that it must be a difficult time for you, and you've been under a lot of pressure."

"It's no excuse. You've done a first-rate job to get Alpha Base this far. The whole crew has done a commendable job since we landed.

But I agree that Georgia needs time to take stock. I'm sure she's in denial. I know I would be. But seeing her this morning, listless and with no energy. I can see at first hand that she's struggling to cope. I know she's a fighter but sometimes that's not enough. I should have listened to you, rather than take out my frustration. I will try to do better."

"Thank you, sir. What will you do?"

"I'll have a quiet word with her when we return to *Endeavour*. She won't like it, but she'll have to accept my decision. Now, are you going to show me the rest of the base? I'd like to see where we'll be living for the next two years." Winter stood and shook the commander's hand.

"It would be my pleasure, sir."

Chapter 30

It wasn't going so smoothly outside the habitat. Georgia and Jim had donned their suits and stepped out of the airlock into the darkness of the cave. We should get the lighting sorted as soon as possible, thought Georgia as she stood waiting for her eyes to adjust to the gloom. Although she was holding a flashlight in her gloved hand, there were plenty of cables or boxes to trip over. She watched as Redmayne carefully navigated his way to the water storage facility, part of her expectantly waiting for him to trip. She was disappointed and concentrated on finding her own path.

"We need to determine what's been causing the power spikes we've been noticing," the chief said as he stepped up beside her. I was hoping they'd settle down overnight but they're still causing me worries."

"Any chance it could be the reactor. It's never been properly tested in the field."

"That was my initial thought too. I sent the data to AJ at Ground Control late yesterday and they ran the calculations overnight. She advises that the reactor is functioning normally. There's something else happening here, either with this power grid, the cabling or a connector. We cannot move into the base when there is a risk of power failure. These power spikes prevent us from charging the batteries. I've been over the system with Rashid and we can find nothing obvious. I could do with a fresh pair of eyes, if you have time."

"Always glad to help, especially if it means saving your ass," Georgia said with a smile. "Let's start from scratch and work back to the reactor. Where does the power enter the habitat?"

"Over there," Jim replied, pointing to the far corner of the cave. Georgia looked to where he was pointing and could see three yellow umbilical cables laid on the ground and plugged into a large square junction box on the side of the living quarter habitat. Also visible was the plumbing for the water and waste management systems.

That looks like a good place to start, Georgia thought. She was sure that Jim and Rashid would have done a good job connecting the power cables. It was more likely that a power board was malfunctioning. It was just a matter of finding it. But she had to remain open-minded and not discount any possibility at this stage. Getting the power functioning was too important.

Georgia slowly tiptoed her way toward the junction box, pointing her flashlight to avoid any obstacles in her path. Jim followed, keen to see if Georgia could find the fault that had so far eluded him. With the junction box's front plate removed, Georgia checked that each of the connectors was securely in place. Once satisfied that they were she followed the trail of the power cables as they snaked their way around the rear and side of the cave until they reached the transformer, about halfway to the entrance of the cave. It was about the size of a filing cabinet. On the display panel, all lights were showing green, except for two flickering amber lights that indicated the fluctuating power.

Once Georgia had again tested the connectors were secured in place she asked, "Can we open this up?"

"I wouldn't recommend it. It's sealed to prevent dust and not designed to be opened in the field. We'd have to take it into a clean room to ensure integrity. I've run diagnostics, and it passed with flying colors. You can run them again if that helps."

"I'll have to. You know I trust you, but I have to test everything." She knew that the chief would not take it personally. They were both professional and doing their jobs.

As Georgia started the diagnostic program, Jim received a call from Commander Anders. "Sorry, Georgia," he said. "The commander has a few issues in the science labs that need my attention. I'm sure you can manage without me for thirty minutes."

Georgia watched as he walked back to the main airlock, leaving her to her thoughts as she waited for the diagnostics to complete. She'd worked with Jim for almost three years, since they were both selected for Expedition Two, and she couldn't remember many times when he had been unable to fix a technical problem. So, it was a real shock that he couldn't resolve the power supply issue. I suppose there's a first time for everything, she thought. She had to admit that she enjoyed working with him, even socializing with him as she had over the past few days. Off duty, he was easy to talk to, and he understood her quick sense of humor without being offended. She had to admit she had found it comforting for him to visit her over recent days. She knew he was there because he genuinely cared, rather than because of pity, and that meant so much.

The control screen flashing blue interrupted her thoughts. The diagnostics were complete. Georgia frowned as she looked at the readout. "I don't get," she muttered as she noted that there were no faults with the transformer. She would have bet her daily salary that there was a faulty component inside the large metallic box. Frustrated, she took a deep breath and created a mental map of the electricity grid, starting from the nuclear reactor and ending at the base. If the reactor was causing the power spikes, then it would likely be a permanent issue; they wouldn't be able to get inside the reactor.

So that left the power cables and connectors. Please be one of those, she said to herself, knowing that there were spare replacement parts available. Although she had already tested the connectors in and out of the transformer, there could still be a problem with the connections. Maybe a particle of dust or grit. Georgia disconnected the power cable going into the transformer. It was secured by two thumb sized hexagonal bolts that she quickly undid with the screwdriver in her utility belt. Turning off the transformer and waiting for thirty seconds, she carefully pulled on the power cable, loosening it until it disconnected from the socket. She hoped the emergency batteries in the base could cope for a short period, even if they weren't fully charged.

The connector comprised twenty-four metal pins, each about two inches long and arranged in a pattern that aligned with twenty-four holes in the socket. Georgia shone her flashlight to get a clear look at the connector and the socket but could see no hint of dust. She noticed that two pins were missing from the connector. "Bingo!" she exclaimed, unable to believe her luck. This was likely to be the cause of the fault and would be easily remedied.

After reattaching the connector and turning the transformer back on, Georgia looked around for a speeder to get to the spare parts stored on board *Intrepid* and saw one just at the mouth of the cave. Checking that the speeder had sufficient battery reserve, she headed out toward *Intrepid* which glinted brightly in the midday sun.

Thinking that she would be less than an hour, she chose not to check in with the chief. There was also a part of her that wanted to surprise him with a solution to the power issue. It was a mistake that she was going to live to regret.

***

Redmayne watched silently as Georgia departed on her own and disappeared out of sight. He knew full well that she shouldn't have gone alone but he was not overly concerned for her safety. He had no interest in whatever Georgia may be up to.

If she wanted to kill herself sooner rather than later then that was up to her.

Additionally, he didn't want to be the one to chaperone her around. He had his own priorities and tasks to complete. Being a nursemaid to Captain Winter's pet project was not on his list.

Instead, he continued to test the water supply in the newly constructed tanks. Like the habitat modules, the water tanks had also been inflated and would eventually hold water taken from the Martian subsurface. That was what would make the base self-sustaining for whoever occupied it, and he took that responsibility seriously.

Once the water samples were safely in his pouch, Redmayne quickly made his way back to the airlock. He was eager to test the water to confirm its purity but was even more keen to rejoin Commander Anders to offer his wisdom and encouragement. He was nervous at having left Anders alone with the captain. He still wasn't convinced that the commander had the measure of Winter without his guidance and encouragement.

Chapter 31

Georgia was filled with the familiar sense of euphoria as she sped toward the *Intrepid* on her own. Even though she was cocooned in her spacesuit, the large panoramic visor gave her a taste of forgotten freedom. And this was the first time that she'd been alone in months.

Fifteen minutes later, Georgia pulled up underneath the bulk of *Intrepid* which cast a dark shadow across the Martian surface. Stepping quickly onto the cradle, she pressed the controls to take her up to the cargo hold. As the cradle rose higher, she looked back toward Alpha Base. From where she was, she could just about make out the stacks of white pallets. A thin dark line on the ground revealed the now well-trodden path between the base and *Endeavour*. A plume of dust was being kicked up by one of the rovers. Georgia guessed that it was pulling another load of supplies, with supervision from Joe and Grace. We're already leaving our mark here, she thought.

After reaching the cargo level she keyed in the command sequence and was gratified to see that the cargo doors started to open. She knew the schematics of the ship well. The whole of the internal space was designed for storage, with minimal life support necessary.

Mancuso must have been here already, she thought as she noticed some bare spaces on the floor where pallets should have been. Stepping into the darkness of the hold, Georgia thought she saw some movement out of the corner of her eye. She put it down to shadows as her eyes adjusted to the dim interior.

She could now see racks and racks of equipment, parts and supplies neatly stacked in the eighty feet of usable space above her head. Each item had been carefully selected based on the expected wear and tear of components. In theory, there were enough spares to support Alpha Base for the next ten years in an emergency. However, the food would run out long before then. Even with one less mouth to feed! "Stop being so morbid, Pyke," she scolded herself. "You will fight this."

A mechanical lift ran up the center of *Intrepid*, enabling access to all decks. Unfortunately, it hadn't yet been set up for operations. Georgia was in a hurry and, as the spares she needed were only two decks up, she climbed the access ladder attached to the wall instead. With the only light coming from the open cargo hatch, Georgia switched on her helmet lights before gripping the metal rungs and starting her climb.

By the time she reached the first deck, her arms were burning with fatigue. You're getting soft, Pyke. Get back in the gym, she thought, stepping off the ladder and onto the deck for a break. Shaking her arms to help with circulation, she looked around at the various equipment stocked on this level. It was like an Aladdin's cave and Georgia knew she'd have the opportunity in the future to have a proper inspection with the lights on.

After one minute, she was ready to climb to the next level. As she grasped the rungs, she heard a scraping sound from somewhere above her. It was impossible to sense the exact direction from inside her helmet. She looked up, turning her head to allow the helmet's lights to scan the next level, but could see nothing unusual. It's probably just the ship settling, she thought, waiting for a few seconds and listening for any more movement. However, there was only silence.

By level two, Georgia could hear herself breathing heavily. Relieved that she didn't have to climb any higher, she let go of the ladder and turned around to search for the connectors. She gasped as her light reflected on two large green eyes staring down at her from about ten feet away. The eyes blinked once, and Georgia had a brief moment to see that they belonged to a creature standing on two legs before it quickly retreated behind some pallets. In that brief glimpse, Georgia had time to notice the creature wasn't wearing a pressure suit and appeared to be part organic and part mechanical. Fear prevented her from processing any more information.

Too shocked to scream she turned back to the ladder and clambered down, taking two rungs at a time until she reached the hold, not once looking up to see if she was being followed. Her only thought was to flee as quickly as possible, so she ran to the cradle in a blind panic. It was only six paces across the floor of the hold. However, she caught her foot on the deck plating and before she knew it, she was tumbling through the open cargo hatch. Her gloved hands clawed for anything to grasp and somehow found the cradle's safety rail. She grabbed the rail in one hand but was hanging high above the ground. Swinging her legs wildly she tried to grab the cradle with her other hand but failed, leaving her grip even more precarious.

By now she was panting, causing the inside of her helmet to fog up, the environmental system unable to cope with her rapid breathing. As she tried a second time to get a better grip of the cradle, she chanced a look at the hold but there was no sign of the alien.

She had no time for any sense of relief. Her hand slipped from the rail and she was suddenly falling and staring up at the sky. Despite the low gravity, she hit the ground with enough force to knock the wind out of her. She heard her bones snapping and the intense agony spearing throughout her body overwhelmed her. Through the searing pain she looked up at the towering spaceship and the clear Martian sky, unable to comprehend that she was going to die here, alone. And then she felt nothing as the life slipped from her.

Chapter 32

The captain, commander, and Redmayne had departed the base in the MEV and were on their way back to *Endeavour*. Back outside Alpha Base, it didn't take long for the chief to discover that Georgia was missing. He'd spent almost an hour with Captain Winter and Commander Anders, addressing technical issues on the environmental controls in the crew quarters. There had been a build-up of condensation in several of the quarters, but he was confident that the adjustments he had made would deal with the matter. He now regretted not getting Rashid involved as he could have dealt with it just as quickly, leaving him to the power issues.

Although not surprised to discover she had moved on from the transformer, it annoyed the chief that she had not let him know where she had gone. It was against protocol to be outside on her own. Staring out of the cave entrance thirty yards away, he keyed the comms button on his wrist. "Georgia? Are you at the reactor?" As he paced up and down impatiently waiting for an answer, he noticed the amber lights were still flickering on the transformer. "Come on, Georgia, where are you?"

Still no response. He knew there could be various good reasons Georgia was not replying to his calls. Yet, in her condition, he couldn't help but be anxious for her safety. He flicked his comms to the general channel. "It's Jim at Alpha. Does anyone have eyes on Georgia? She's not responding to my calls."

He still had a faint hope that Georgia had returned to *Endeavour* to rest but Doctor Betts soon dispelled that thought, confirming there was no sign of her on the ship.

Mancuso was next to respond. "Chief, I saw someone on a speeder heading toward the cargo ships a little over fifty minutes ago. They were too far away for me to tell who it was, but it looked like they had come from the base. From the plume of dust, they were kicking up, they were in a hurry."

"Thanks, Joe, that has to be her. Everyone else is accounted for." The chief breathed a sigh of relief. At least he now knew where she had gone. Although why Georgia wasn't replying to his comms requests was a mystery that concerned him. He knew she had been pushing herself lately and had ignored his suggestions to slow down. Maybe she'll pay attention next time, he thought, although he doubted she ever would. He had a more immediate problem, however, when he realized that Georgia must have taken the last speeder.

"Captain, I'll find Georgia. Can someone come by the base and pick me up though? I appear to be stuck here with no means of transport."

***

Winter sat in his chair, brooding. He didn't need the aggravation today. He had just arrived back at *Endeavour* and, although the base inspection had been a success, it had taken longer than planned. All the urgent activities required in order to move in within two days were running through his head. He looked wearily across at Anders who sat silently reading a report on his computer and probably having similar thoughts. "Commander, can you get down to the Comms room? Maybe you'll have more luck using the ship's equipment. You should be able to track Georgia's locater beacon at the very least. I want to know where she is and what she's doing." Anders nodded and headed for the door.

As an afterthought, Winter added, "And if she makes radio contact, tell her to get her ass back here pronto."

Like the chief, Winter was becoming increasingly concerned for Georgia's welfare as the redundancy built into the spacesuits made it very unlikely that a malfunction was preventing her from responding. Which meant that there was another reason she could not communicate.

Anders returned five minutes later, looking confused. "She's not replying and I can't pick up the transponder on her suit. It's as if she's disappeared."

Winter stood to look out of the window at the desolate and unforgiving landscape, fearing the worst. She could be anywhere out there, he thought to himself, hoping the MEV would have more success. It was on its way to collect the chief, with Mancuso and Nicola King already on board. Winter estimated it would reach the supply ships in the next twenty minutes and hoped that would give the search party enough time to find Georgia. Every minute wasted was a matter of life or death. We need to find her. I don't want to lose anyone, least of all Georgia.

There was a sense of guilt at having such thoughts. He shouldn't have any favorites among the crew, yet he regarded her as a surrogate daughter and at the moment he was like an anxious parent, desperately hoping to hear positive news.

What had gone wrong? Was it a physical or a technical failure? It had to be something critical if she wasn't responding, her transponder wasn't working, and she'd not had time to activate her emergency beacon. Despite all of his training, Winter was finding it increasingly difficult to stay rational. He needed answers.

Chapter 33

Georgia blinked. A piercing light was shining directly into her face, hurting her eyes. It took a few seconds for her to recognize that she was breathing and that there was no pain from her shattered legs and arm. Maybe I'm paralyzed she briefly thought to herself. But she could feel her fingers and toes wiggling. Her fingers brushed against strange material. More like rubber than cotton and not a sensation she had noticed previously in the medical bay

She started blinking, trying to get used to the intense light. It was only when she tried to lift her hand in front of her face, she realized she was being held down by restraints. And there was a strange aroma, similar to mouthwash but more metallic.

Fear began to fill her with dread as she surmised that she wasn't on *Endeavour* and her efforts to fight against the restraints proved fruitless. Turning her head away from the light source, her eyes focused on a bank of equipment that she had never seen before—she was in some kind of bubble.

Where the hell am I? And what am I doing here? she thought, trying to remember what had happened. The last thing she could recollect was falling out of the legacy ship. But why? Had her tumors affected her balance and her memory?

"Hello," she called out. "Megan, are you there? Can you come and let me know what's happening?"

But she was met with silence. In fact, it was an eerie silence. She couldn't hear any noises other than the sound of her own breathing.

Georgia gasped as she remembered the alien's face from the *Intrepid*. What was the creature and why was she now here wherever here was? She wanted to cry at the futility of her position and the fear of the unknown. But then she heard a synthesized voice.

"Human. We are not here to harm you," it intoned slowly and deliberately. "Please accept my apologies if we startled you on your ship. You nearly died when you fell but we have... repaired you."

Georgia twisted vigorously around to find the source of the voice but couldn't see anyone or anything. She didn't reply.

"My name is Falmas. I am responsible for this vessel. My associate is Falment. What may we call you?"

Thinking it may be better for her to be co-operative, she replied, "My name is Georgia Pyke. Please tell me what I am doing here and why I am strapped to this..." she searched for a word to describe what she was lying on, but the best she could come up with was, "bed?"

"Again, I apologize for scaring and hurting you. It was not our intention. We saw you and your crew working at your landing site and did not anticipate your presence. A most unforgivable mistake on my part. I brought you to our ship to mend you. Do not be concerned. You will soon be free to return to your own ship."

Whatever creature Falmas was, his melodic voice was very soothing. Georgia still needed answers though. "How long have I been here and what have you done to me?"

"You have been mending for two of your Earth hours. We placed you in our recuperation chamber. It is our first time mending a human. We think we have repaired you properly. You must let us know if you are still in any pain. We will release you now."

The restraints loosened and Georgia could move her limbs. She cautiously flexed and stretched her legs and arms. There was no stiffness and it amazed Georgia that she could not find any sign of the injuries she remembered from falling from *Intrepid*. That's just not possible, she told herself. I should have bruising, broken bones and many internal injuries from that fall. In fact, I should have died! At the very least, my injuries should have taken months to heal and left me in a wheelchair.

At that point she saw her clothes on the floor and realized she was also naked. On an alien ship, in front of aliens who could see her. Feeling vulnerable, she reached down to pick her clothes up and put them back on.

"Thank you for helping me. Can I see you now?"

The wall at the far end of the room resolved itself into a doorway to reveal her hosts surprising Georgia by how humanoid they were, other than being over seven feet tall and their skin being a pale metallic blue color. The two aliens looked almost identical with dark, almost black, unblinking eyes. Short stubby noses and small blue mouths finished the look. They covered the rest of their heads in tight leather helmets. Their limbs, under their uniforms, were long and thin and they were wearing gloves.

Before Georgia could count how many fingers they had, the alien on the right spoke. "Let me introduce ourselves properly to you. We are Sentinels and come from what you would call the Centaur Alpha system. It is our mission to monitor your progress and watch from a distance, as we have done for the past five thousand years. We have recently been directed by the Confederacy to report on Earth now that you are becoming a spacefaring species. The Confederacy is observing several planets similar to yours. Our role is passive, and we are not to interfere with your evolution.

We had not intended for you or any of your crew to discover us. Our observation post sits at the top of the cliff and this ship is cloaked from your equipment and sensors."

Georgia sensed that Falmas was telling the truth. Despite the situation she found herself in, she sensed she was not in any immediate danger. Maybe they had given her a sedative. Even so, their presence was a revelation that she was struggling to get her mind around. "Five thousand years?" she exclaimed. "There is so much history during that period. Surely you have not been here all of that time. There must be others like you."

"You are correct. The Confederacy has sent observation teams at regular intervals over that time. Both Falment and myself have been on duty for eight hundred years. We have seen and recorded many changes across your world."

Georgia was astounded. "How can that be? How old are you?"

"Sentinels are genetically enhanced to endure space travel and long durations. The bodies you see are cybernetic devices that can last many thousands of years. Our heads and brains are the only organic parts, but we don't grow old in the same way that you do."

"That sounds terrible," Georgia uttered before she had time to think. She immediately apologized. "I'm sorry, that was thoughtless of me."

Falmas nodded his head to accept the apology before continuing. "This is normal for our species. The enhancements have made our missions possible. Sentinels derive immense satisfaction from being able to watch and learn as civilizations either flourish or perish."

Falment stepped forward to join the conversation. "Your species' rate of development in the past three hundred years has been phenomenal. There has been intense speculation among our scientists how you have achieved it. They want to know if it is a natural part of your evolution or if there is an outside influence. We tracked your planet's first manned Mars mission attempt. It saddened us it failed but had no part of that failure. As for you, we have been monitoring your ships since you left Earth orbit. We kept a safe distance but understand from your captain's reports to Earth that our ship may have been spotted on several occasions."

"That's right. We thought we had some ghost reflections. Not for one moment did we consider aliens. What will you do with me now that I know about you?"

"That is a minor problem. We are awaiting instruction from the Confederacy. Our actions to repair you have caused some problems.

We will let you know shortly. For the time being you shall remain in this isolation bubble."

And before Georgia could ask any more questions, the Sentinels left the room, and the doorway disappeared, leaving a wall. She sat there, not knowing what to do, but frustrated at being held a prisoner.

Chapter 34

Jim Grant was finding the wait for the MEV to collect him almost unbearable and started walking toward *Endeavour* to meet it. The MEV was visible when it was still two miles out although it appeared to be hardly moving. It was only the huge plume of dust that betrayed that the MEV was barreling across the barren landscape at top speed. By the time it slowed up next to him, the chief was so eager to start the search that he jumped into the airlock without waiting for the MEV to stop completely.

The cabin was grimly silent during the ten-minute trip toward the search area. Instead, the chief, Doctor Betts and Mancuso stared out of the front canopy, eagerly looking for any sign of Georgia or her speeder. There were many speeder tracks from the previous days' activities. Any of them could be Georgia's but it was impossible to discern how recent the tracks were.

Jim slowed the MEV as they arrived at *Challenger*, to allow each of them a better chance of seeing any clues to help them find Georgia. But there was absolutely nothing.

As the MEV reached the first of the supply ships, *Challenger*, Mancuso contacted Captain Winter to inform him they had arrived at the search zone and that there was no immediate sign of Georgia. By now, the chief was struggling to remain calm but knew he and the rest of the team had to focus on finding Georgia alive.

Nicola broke the silence. "Chief, do you know why she would have come out to these ships? What was she working on?"

Jim looked briefly across at her before returning to his search. "I was working with Georgia on resolving some power issues at the base. Commander Anders called me away to assist the captain and by the time I returned she was gone. The power spikes are still occurring, so Georgia didn't fix whatever the issue is."

"She wouldn't have left the job without having found a solution. That's not how she does things. Could she have worked out the problem and required spares or equipment?" Nicola asked.

The chief thought for a few moments, asking himself what Georgia could have wanted from the supply ships. Maybe Nicola was on to something. Whatever it was, it must be related to the power issues. She must have worked out what was causing the problem. His eyes lit up. "That's it! She came here because she found the solution. She just needed some parts."

"Most of the electrical spares are on *Intrepid*," added Mancuso. "If I know where they are then so will Georgia."

The chief couldn't argue with the logic and Mancuso changed course toward *Intrepid* at maximum speed. It's our best lead he told himself, before confirming with Captain Winter that they were heading to a new destination. This has to be it, he kept repeating in his head, almost as a mantra.

Chapter 35

Georgia could not tell how long she had been alone in the room but guessed it must have been at least thirty minutes. In that time, she had checked her arms and legs for any breaks or sprains. There was no pain or bruising at all. It was unbelievable. But not as unbelievable as being rescued by aliens and held a prisoner on their spaceship. She had tried to absorb what the two Sentinels had told her, but it was like being in an incredible dream. She couldn't believe that here, finally, was proof that mankind was not alone. In fact, she thought, they have observed us as we would observe a native Amazonian tribe, or even insects under a microscope.

She thought about the billions of dollars spent on SETI and other searches for extra-terrestrial life, only for intelligent alien life to be right on our doorstep all this time. Georgia laughed at the irony of the situation. *It's a shame this cancer will prevent me from seeing what happens next. Earth will never be the same. I hope this will be a good thing and bring about peace. We're now a very small fish in an enormous pond!*

Georgia continued to pace around the room until the doorway silently appeared and this time only one Sentinel returned. She thought it was Falmas but couldn't be sure until he spoke. "We have our instructions. The Confederacy are displeased with what has occurred and the actions I have taken. We have been instructed to return you in order to minimize any further unintentional contamination of humankind's progress."

"What does that mean for me?" Georgia asked nervously.

"We will return you unharmed to your people. We are not savages."

"I'm sorry, I didn't mean to imply that you were. Aren't you concerned that I will tell my people about you and the Confederacy?"

"We can remove specific sections of your memory. You will have no recollection of what has occurred, and you will return to your ship as if nothing has happened. I can assure you that the process is risk free and painless, so you need not be concerned. Our predecessors have unfortunately had reason occasionally to use the device. We will ensure there is no evidence to show that we have been here. There are established protocols that we will follow."

The news disappointed Georgia. She looked up at him and said, "That's such a waste of an opportunity. There is so much I want to find out about you. Mankind needs to know that they are not alone in the universe. We have asked that question for countless generations. I finally have the answer and you're about to take it away from me. You can teach us so much and help us move forward." She knew she was sounding desperate but continued anyway. "Just look at how you've healed my injuries in hours instead of weeks. I can't begin to imagine what other technology you have. You could help so many people. And you could learn far more from us through direct contact."

Falmas stood, waiting impassively until Georgia took a breath. "We cannot do that. There are rules in place for your own protection. You have to evolve as a species in your own way. Interference by us could lead to unforeseen consequences. You aren't ready for the huge technological leaps we could give you. Humankind must determine its own fate and discover other intelligent life forms in its own time. I understand it is what human parents refer to as *tough love*."

Georgia wasn't prepared to give up too easily. "You would sit and watch humanity destroy itself? Why would you do that?"

As Georgia continued to ask questions, she was aware it was like being back at school, with Falmas acting as the teacher patiently trying to explain a simple concept to the dumbest child in class. It was very disconcerting. "The Confederacy do not see themselves as gods. They do not decide who survives and who doesn't. Over millions of years, they have discovered that less than half of intelligent life develops the technology to discover interplanetary travel. The rest either destroy themselves through war and conflict, or natural disaster. It takes a mature species to understand its place in the universe and truly accept other cultures."

It started to make sense to Georgia. Listening to Falmas and knowing how some of the world's governments would want to exploit the technology gains, she doubted that mankind was ready for the Sentinels or the Confederacy. A Pandora's box would be opened that could never be closed and she could see as much danger as benefit coming from it. For every life saved through medical advances, others would be lost through advanced weaponry.

"Okay, I get it," she said. "The Earth isn't ready for you. But you can wipe my mind and trust that I will say nothing. You have my word on that. Who will believe me with no evidence? Or, if you're still not sure, I can stay with you instead. I've read plenty of alien abduction stories so I know I wouldn't be the first person to disappear."

An odd grunting noise came from Falmas. Georgia wasn't sure if it was laughter or anger, or some other Sentinel emotion. "No Humans have ever been abducted by Sentinels. In addition to research, we are here to prevent any other race from contacting or abducting humans. The stories you have read are false. We do not know why humans lie so much. But you cannot stay with us. It would breach many protocols. And we do not have the food to sustain you."

Georgia shrugged, accepting that she could not change Falmas' mind. She also knew that her friends must be desperately worried about her. "Are you sure I'll still be myself after you wipe my mind? You won't remove everything, will you?"

"We do not believe so. Our records do not show any side effects suffered by the several humans to have experienced it."

Soon, Georgia was laying back down on the platform where she had first awoken. "Before you start, can I thank you for saving me.

You could have left me to die, but you didn't. And now I know that there is other intelligent life in the universe. I will be eternally grateful for the time I have left."

Falmas smiled back before Georgia saw him turn to say something to Falment who was holding a gray device in his hands. She was about to ask what the gadget was for when there was a sudden flash. And then there was nothing.

Chapter 36

The chief was more worried about Georgia than he would have expected, and he wondered about his feelings. He had become closer to her over recent days. But he couldn't be sure if that was due to her being sick and having only weeks to live. He hoped that it wasn't simply pity he had for her. Yet, at the same time, he knew an emotional attachment of any kind would make it very difficult when she died. He had been trying to be there as a friend, as had most of the crew. So why was there a hint of envy whenever he saw her speaking with Mancuso or Redmayne?

His mind wandered back to two days earlier and the exhilaration of racing Georgia across the plain to visit the legacy supply ships. The sense of freedom after having spent so much time in *Endeavour* had been intoxicating but had that elation been because he was with Georgia?

Time to focus on the present, he told himself as *Intrepid* loomed up in front of them with still no sign of her. It would be difficult to spot her if she'd collapsed but if she could grab their attention with a wave, then they might find her. How much oxygen would she have left?

They were only a few hundred feet from *Intrepid* when Mancuso excitedly pointed his finger at one of the landing legs. "Look! There's a speeder. It must be Georgia's."

Jim saw it and then noticed that the cradle was next to the open cargo door. "She must still be up there," he said to the others as he tried to contact Georgia on the radio, once again receiving no reply.

He relayed the news back to *Endeavour*. There was some relief in Winter's voice this time. "At least we now know where she is and why she went there. There's obviously some problem with her radio or her suit. Get up there and bring her home."

As soon as the MEV rolled to a stop, Jim exited the airlock and ran to the access panel to bring down the cradle. "Nicola, you're with me to search the ship. Joe, can you have a look around just in case Georgia is close by."

As they slowly ascended in the cradle, Jim and Nicola had a bird's-eye view of the local scenery, but there was no sign of Georgia. "At least we're narrowing the search zone," said Nicola. "She has to be in here."

Jim's heart was racing in the expectation of discovering Georgia before it was too late. "We need to work fast," he said. "We don't know what state she's in." Neither of them voiced the thought she may already be dead. That was not an option they wanted to contemplate.

On reaching the hold, they made a quick inspection before climbing the ladder to the next level. "She's definitely here. There's her flashlight," Jim pointed to a spot about six feet from the ladder. He picked it up and shone it around the first level before walking around the whole of the area searching for any other clues. "I don't understand why she would have dropped it here though. Let's carry on."

After searching all six levels, there was no further sign of Georgia. Both of them were exhausted and frustrated. It didn't surprise the chief that Nicola was disheartened. He knew exactly how she was feeling right then. "It's a complete mystery. Jim, are you sure we've looked everywhere on the ship? Is there anywhere else we could have missed?"

"Sorry, Nicola, we couldn't have been any more thorough. The only other compartments are in the engineering section directly below the main hold, but I checked the seals on the way in and they've not been broken. With nothing from Joe either we're back to square one again. It's as if Georgia's disappeared into thin air." Unable to hide the disappointment in his voice, he added, "I'll let the captain know."

Chapter 37

Falmas looked down at the human ships from the top of the cliff face. Even from this distance he could see from his optical equipment that three people were searching the ship where Georgia had found him, no doubt looking for their missing colleague.

Beside him, Falment said, "This will not be easy. Timing will be everything if we are to remain unseen. Perhaps we should leave the human here."

"I know that you are not happy with my actions, Falment. But you know that leaving her here to die is not our way. The humans will carry on searching until they find their friend. And then there will need to be an explanation as to how she reached this point on her own. No, she is here because of me and we must do all we can to return her to her crew. I promise to be cautious."

The two of them were sitting in a small silver hover vehicle. It was open to the Martian atmosphere, as the Sentinels' mechanical components meant they didn't require protective suits. Behind them on the floor, Georgia was lying unconscious on the floor in her spacesuit. Falmas knew that their cloaking device would protect them from being seen unless they were too close. The only concern was disturbing the dust, which could send a telltale sign to anyone looking.

"My plan is to leave the human near that ship," he said, pointing to the first ship the humans had passed. "It is within walking distance so her presence there is more explainable than it would be if found here. The three humans will have to pass that way on their return to their own vessel. Maybe they will see her as they travel."

Falmas moved the vehicle over the edge of the cliff and sped down toward their target. Looking to their right, they could see that the humans were climbing back into their vehicle getting ready to head back from their search. Falmas knew the timing would be tighter than he wanted.

He braked at the last minute, hovering just mere feet from the ground. Calmly, he continued to the human vessel and stopped near the base. "This will have to do," he said to Falment before stepping out. They gently lifted Georgia onto the ground and pressed a device to the side of her helmet until she started to stir, before hastily returning to their vehicle. The cloaking device hid all of this activity from any prying eyes.

Falmas moved the vehicle slowly away, careful not to disturb any rocks or dust until he was several hundred yards away then stopped to observe what would happen.

***

Georgia's eyes flickered open and looked up at the pale pink sky, confused. Why was she lying on her back with a supply ship towering over her? Where was she and how did she get here?

Sitting up, she looked round to get her bearings, saw the name of the ship on the nearest landing leg, and was even more confused. She could remember arriving at *Intrepid*, so how did she get to *Challenger*? It made little sense. The tumors must be affecting her brain. She made a mental note to visit Megan as soon as she returned to *Endeavour*. There couldn't be any more similar episodes otherwise the captain would ground permanently.

Once she was standing, she noticed her speeder was missing. "Fuck! How am I going to get back to Alpha?" She tried her radio, but it was silent. Her heads-up display showed she still had more than four hours of air supply. That can't be right, she told herself. The chronometer is telling me I left Alpha Base nearly four hours ago. I shouldn't have more than about sixty minutes of air. My suit must be malfunctioning.

There was no way she could walk back to *Endeavour* before her air supply ran out. Her only plan was to get back to *Intrepid* and hope that her speeder was where she remembered leaving it.

She walked around the base of *Challenger*, lightheaded and nauseous but otherwise okay. To break the silence she talked to herself, something she'd noticed she was doing more often. "Don't panic, Georgia. That's not going to help you. What would you do in the captain's shoes? Surely, he's aware that you're missing and has sent out search parties. It's only a matter of time before they find you."

Intrepid was just over one mile away and Georgia estimated it would take about twenty minutes to walk there at a steady pace. She was feeling more positive that she'd soon be safely back at *Endeavour*, ready to face whatever Captain Winter had in store for her. Her mood improved further when she spotted the MEV driving in her direction. "There we go, Pyke. What did I tell you?"

Georgia ran toward the oncoming vehicle, waving her arms hoping they would spot her. Any doubt that she'd be seen disappeared as she saw the MEV change course to drive in her direction. As she stood waiting for the MEV to pick her up, it was a massive relief to know that she was safe.

The relief changed to surprise when the chief jumped out of the MEV and ran to her. Before she knew it, he was lifting her up and giving her a hug. She could see he was excitedly saying something to her but couldn't hear what it was. She tapped the side of her helmet and shook her head to let him know her comms was not working. He must have seen because he released his grip and indicated for her to follow him.

Once they were both in the airlock and able to remove their helmets, she asked him, "What was that about? Anyone would think you cared."

"Georgia, you've been missing for several hours. We've all been worried sick about you. Especially with your illness. I thought I'd lost you. And I'm not ready for that yet." She was amazed, not only by his words but also by the fact he had tears in his eyes.

Reaching out to take his hand, she said, "I'm going nowhere, Jim. Not yet anyway. I don't know what happened and I guess I'm going to need Doctor Betts to help me figure it out. I don't even know why I was at *Challenger* after I went to *Intrepid* for a replacement connector. But thank you for caring. It means the world to me."

"You can have that conversation with Megan when we get back to *Endeavour*. But please listen to her this time. And Captain Winter wants a word."

Georgia groaned at the prospect.

Chapter 38

Captain Winter was pacing up and down in his cabin on *Endeavour*. He'd spent the past twenty minutes pondering what to say to Georgia and still couldn't decide how to deal with her. His sense of relief was tinged with irritation that she had disobeyed his direct orders and put herself at risk.

Georgia broke the ice. "Before you say anything, captain, I take full responsibility for my actions. I know that I was reckless, but I've learned my lesson. There are no excuses for what I did. I'm sorry for the problems I have caused and for diverting the efforts of the crew."

Winter sat back in his chair while Georgia spoke, absently fiddling with a pen. He knew her well enough to know that she was being sincere. There was no doubt in his mind that the experience would have shocked her. He spoke, gently. "Georgia, I cannot imagine how you're dealing with your condition. Or what is going through your head these days? A terminal illness is something no one wants to face. I can only admire how you've coped, millions of miles from home and loved ones. I've allowed you some leeway because I respect you and because I value your expertise.

"The rules I put in place are to keep you and the crew safe, without further jeopardizing this mission. Ground Control wanted me to stand you down from further active duty and I fought long and hard to support you. But reckless actions like this put me in a difficult position."

"Yes, I understand, sir. You know I am grateful for your support. And I am sorry for the scare I've given everyone, including myself."

"I don't want to take you off duty and waste a valuable resource. I need you. But you have to look after yourself, especially when outside."

"Let me continue working, captain. I gswear that I won't breach your orders again and leave the ship without an escort. I've learned

159

that my symptoms make me dangerous to myself and others. But I can still contribute."

Winter sighed at her tragic situation. He knew the right thing to do was take her off duty. "Okay, I'm giving you one last chance but don't let me down. I won't be able to protect you again. No more going rogue, whatever the reason. Now get yourself checked over by Doctor Betts, listen to what she tells you and take a break for the rest of the day. Dismissed."

**

Georgia hurried down the corridor to see Doctor Betts. "No lectures please, Megan. I've just come from the captain."

"What did you expect? I can't believe you've been so foolish. Now tell me what happened to you. Were there any warning signs?"

"No, none. That's what scares me. I remember going to *Intrepid* to collect a replacement power connector. I thought I could get there and back without being missed as Jim was busy helping the captain inside Alpha Base. It shouldn't have taken more than an hour. The power supply needed fixing so we can move in. The next thing I remember is finding myself on the ground at *Challenger*, just before you found me."

"Have you had any dizziness or signs of fatigue?"

"No worse than since we last spoke. I was feeling nauseous, but that's not been unusual lately."

Megan frowned as she considered the possible causes. "It may be pressure on your brain from a tumor. You need to remind yourself that you're not a well person. You have to take care of yourself. Let me run some tests to make sure you've not caused yourself any further injuries."

Georgia couldn't argue and sat down. "Apart from my headache, I'm okay. All things considered. In fact, I'm actually hungry for the first time in days. Surely that's a good sign."

"Yes, it is, but I'm still going to run some quick tests on you!"

The tests took ten minutes and, other than mild dehydration, Megan couldn't detect any other problems. She prescribed an energy drink, plenty of fluids and some rest.

"Thank you, Megan. You're a good friend. I assure you, this has been a wake-up call and I promise I'll listen to you from now on."

Megan raised an eyebrow. "I've heard that before! And yet, here we are again. You are, without doubt, my worst patient."

Georgia knew it was impossible to defend her own actions. She had been stupid, and she had to change her attitude. "I know that you're right. But trust me, I'm a changed woman."

***

That evening, Georgia sat with the rest of the *Endeavour* crew in the galley and devoured a full meal before eating a second ration pack. She'd had a restful sleep after seeing Doctor Betts and was feeling better for it. Her headache had not returned either. She briefly considered mentioning it to Megan but kept it to herself for the time being.

As she was eating her second meal, Jim came to sit with her. He nodded at her bowl of food and said, "You've got your appetite back, I see. That's a good sign."

"This is the first proper meal I've eaten in days. It's better than soup. I wanted to speak to you. To thank you for finding me."

The chief looked sheepish. "About my reaction when we found you. I was worried about you. We all were. I thought we wouldn't find you in time."

"But you did, and everything is fine. I was more taken aback by your sudden show emotion of emotion. It's a new side to you."

She could see that her comment made the chief shuffle uncomfortably in his seat and wondered if he now regretted his actions. "Actually, it surprised me too. You're right that I usually contain my emotions. Maybe I need to open up more."

"You're not doing a bad job now, Jim," she encouraged, putting her hand on his forearm.

This was new territory for the chief, so he quickly changed the subject. "I imagine Captain Winter gave you a hard time."

Georgia laughed as she put her fork in her now empty bowl. "So that's what you want to know. Did I get grief for being a complete pain in the ass? The answer is yes. Are you happy now?"

Jim held his arms up in defeat. "You can't blame me."

"That damned asteroid has saved me this time. The captain needs all hands to get the base up and running in time. After that, I won't be needed as much and my usefulness will be over." Georgia wasn't sure how true that statement was. It was the first time she'd given it any thought.

Jim shook his head. "I don't want to hear you talk like that. You just need to pace yourself. But you do look well now. Maybe I should see the doctor and ask her for the tonic she gave you."

"Thank you, Jim. I like that you care." Georgia meant it. It reassured her knowing that she would have good friends around her over the coming months. Jim had somehow become very special to her, and she was starting to see him in a new light. "And I like having you around to speak to."

Before they could continue their conversation, Megan walked across to their table and sat down without being invited. "Sorry to break up the party, but can I have a few minutes with my patient?"

Jim blushed and made his excuses.

Megan noticed Georgia looking longingly after him and smiled. "So, what's going on with you and the handsome chief engineer?" she asked mischievously.

This time it was Georgia's turn to blush a bright pink. "Nothing," she mumbled. "We were just talking. He is very easy to speak with. And easy on the eye, I guess."

Megan laughed. "Okay, I won't push you. I actually wanted to know if there's been any more dizziness or discomfort."

"I'm feeling great. Whatever you gave me has worked wonders."

"Are you sure? I know that you're a bad patient and a good liar."

Georgia feigned hurt. "How can you say that? Seriously, I've learned my lesson. And I promise you I am one hundred percent."

"That's great to hear. Remember, it's only been a few hours since your fainting spell. I don't have to remind you that you'll have good and bad days. That just how it's going to be."

"Thanks, Megan. My intention is to make the most of the good times. I don't know how many I have left. But who does?"

Chapter 39

Georgia excitedly went to visit Megan the next morning. "Other than muscles aching I'm ready for another day out on the surface. This couldn't have come at a better time with the move later today."

"That's fantastic." Megan didn't sound totally convinced. "Remember what I told you about not getting carried away, though. This is only a temporary improvement."

"Are you sure, Meg? I honestly haven't been this good in a very long time. Maybe your tests were wrong. Or not calibrated for Mars."

"You saw the results, Georgia. There's no mistake. And no coming back from it. I'm sorry, but you have to face it."

Georgia wasn't ready to have her bubble burst just yet. "But I want a future here on Mars. We're so close to establishing the first permanent colony on another planet and I want to be part of it. And I think Jim has feelings for me. What am I going to do?"

Megan was surprised. "I know you've been working closely with the chief over the last few days. I didn't realize it was anything more than a professional respect for each other. Perhaps you're confusing his sympathy for something else. I can easily see how that could happen."

"That's what I thought, too. But lately he's given me compliments and been very supportive. He was very concerned when I had my episode yesterday. And it's not out of pity. Jim's not like that."

"I don't know what to say. Other than be careful because you're both going to get hurt."

"Maybe this is a perfect relationship for a girl who doesn't do commitment. Or karma? The universe is telling me I should have learned to love a long time ago. Before it was too late. It must have a twisted sense of humor."

She was about to continue when Winter entered the cabin. He nodded and smiled at them. "Ah, ladies. I hope I've not interrupted anything. I've been looking for both of you. Georgia, I wanted to know how you're holding up. You've put in some hard work the past couple of days to get us back on track. And Doctor Betts, I wanted your professional input into Georgia's condition."

"I was just telling Megan that I feel fantastic. I'm convinced I'm on the mend, but she won't have any of it."

Captain Winter looked as doubtful as Doctor Betts who said, "I've spoken to Georgia and explained that some days will be better than others. But there's no remission or long-term cure. She may experience this sense of improvement for a few more days or even a week, but it can only be temporary. It's likely to be caused by heightened adrenaline because of the work and the move into the base."

Winter turned his attention to Georgia. "Are you okay to help with programming the rovers to deliver supplies to Alpha Base today? I'll put you on light duties, but your skills will be invaluable. Doc, I'm assuming you still think she's fit to work."

With Georgia appearing to be in good spirits, Doctor Betts didn't have a valid reason to prevent her from helping.

Georgia smiled and also nodded enthusiastically. "Yes, I'll be back down there as soon as I've changed my clothes. I'm eager to move into the base with the others. Above all else, I can't wait to get my first shower in months."

"That's what I wanted to hear. Head down to Commander Anders and the chief. They're expecting you."

Georgia didn't need any further encouragement and left before the doctor could raise any objections. Megan looked at Captain Winter and said, "I hope you know what you're doing, Liam."

"So do I," he replied.

Chapter 40

Captain Winter was filled with an immense sense of satisfaction as he looked at the crew gathered around the galley, eating breakfast together for the first time. There was an air of excitement among them as they shared stories and experiences. This was, after all their first morning in the base. At that moment in time, they could be anywhere. Work colleagues in a canteen relaxing over a meal before the start of a workday. There were no windows to betray the fact they were deep inside a cave on a planet other than Earth. The normality made it almost surreal.

The first night had reminded him of spending time at summer camp as a child. The experience of camaraderie in a new and exciting environment. As a crew they had worked hard and accomplished far more than he ever expected in the time they'd been given to build the base.

Despite fatigue, Winter knew that many had found it hard to sleep in their new surroundings. He had heard people talking and moving around for some time after he returned to his own cabin but knew it wouldn't take the crew long to settle into a new routine. He was eagerly expecting what they could achieve over the rest of their mission. Winter poured a steaming hot coffee into his personal mug with the face of William Shatner, given to him by Kristen as a joke one week before launch. Being able to use it gave him a sense of connection to her.

He saw Commander Anders sitting at one of the tables, having a conversation with Redmayne. They paused as they saw him walking toward them. "Don't stop on my behalf," Winter said cheerily, while noticing that Redmayne looked annoyed at his interruption.

"Good morning, sir," replied Anders. "I hope you slept well in your new quarters. The base is far better than the mock-ups we saw in Houston. And far more luxurious than my quarters on *Eden*."

Winter had to agree. "Absolutely the best living conditions I've experienced in my time in space. A huge advancement."

"Have you received any updates on the asteroid's track? Tom is keen to set up some experiments."

"Yes, captain," said Redmayne. "This is a unique opportunity for us. Asteroids burn up in Earth's atmosphere. I have a chance to observe what happens in a much thinner atmosphere. Obviously, there will be an impact, but I can also record what happens in the time before it crashes. It won't take long to set up once you give me the approval."

"Relax, Tom. I understand you're eager to further our knowledge for mankind's benefit, but I'm waiting for Ground Control to provide their daily update. It wouldn't surprise me if the asteroid has started to break up and I don't want any of the crew to take unnecessary risks by leaving the cave."

It wasn't the answer Redmayne wanted. "I think that's short-sighted. We may never get this chance again."

Winter was angered by Redmayne's directness. He was not used to being spoken to like that and had to tell himself that Redmayne was a civilian scientist. He'd probably never had to follow orders.

"Mr Redmayne, may I remind you I am in charge here. You may not like all my decisions, but you will have to respect them. I am responsible for everyone's safety, including your own. You will wait until we understand the risk. Is that clear?"

Redmayne paused for a moment, glowering at the captain. "Yes, sir, perfectly." And with that, he stood and quickly left the room.

Winter clenched his fists tightly as the anger rose inside him. "Did you have any issues with Redmayne during your voyage here, Lars?"

"Not really. Although to be honest he kept himself to his quarters most of the flight. He may be overly arrogant at times, but he is highly regarded in his field."

"Can you look out for him? I'm not convinced he took my orders to heart."

"I will, but I'm sure he'll behave. He knows this is a long mission."

"Thank you, Lars." Winter's watch suddenly beeped, indicating he had a message waiting for him. "This will be the latest mission update I've been waiting for. I'll take it in the command room." He stood, picked up his coffee mug and said, "You can join me, commander."

***

Captain Winter keyed in his ID password and the large video screen on the far wall flickered on. "Good to see that everything is working, commander," he said, glancing at Lars. "We'll carry out a full shakedown of the systems over the next few days."

The two of them sat in their command chairs as the captain said, "Computer, play latest message for Captain Winter."

The image of General Stockton resolved itself on the screen, looking directly at the camera. Winter thought he looked even more stern than normal, if that could be possible. It didn't bode well. "Good morning, captain," he began. "I trust you and the crew had an uneventful first night in Alpha Base. I look forward to receiving your update shortly."

The general looked down at some information on his desk before continuing. "As we expected, the asteroid started to splinter about eight hours ago as it began to encounter the Martian gravity field. Our long-range telescopes have detected three rocks, about one hundred and fifty feet across, have broken away from the main body. We forecast two of those to crash into Hellas Planitia at shortly after fifteen hundred hours, your time. I am told that we cannot accurately plot their trajectory, but there is a seventy percent chance that they will crash within seventy miles of your position. We can't be more precise than that, as we do not fully understand the composition of the asteroid. Needless to say, it is far too close for comfort and Expedition Two is to remain in the safety of the base from at least two hours before the asteroid's arrival."

Winter paused the message and glanced at Commander Anders, who was looking as concerned as he felt. "That's an understatement. We've only been here just over a week and we're already being bombarded!"

"It's as if the planet doesn't want us here. We should be safe here though. The lava tube is structurally sound."

Winter had seen the survey reports and knew that to be true. But he had other issues. "I'm more concerned for anything not in the cave. Rocks and debris thrown up from the impact could damage or destroy any of the ships and supplies. Can you work with the chief, Mancuso and anyone else you need for retrieval missions this morning? All urgent supplies need to be brought to the base." As Anders left the control room, Winter added as an afterthought, "Tell Redmayne he can set up his experiments. He'll get a front-row seat for the impact by the sound of it."

Alone in the command room, Winter watched the rest of the message as the general continued his update. "As I mentioned yesterday, the Russians and Chinese have no plans to land until the dust has settled, quite literally, from the asteroid impact. That has not prevented them from going to the United Nations to argue that it is too dangerous for you to be on the planet. They say we are unnecessarily putting your lives at risk. That is ridiculous, but that's not stopped a significant amount of public opinion agreeing with them. The President has made a statement to assure the public that you are safe inside Alpha Base and that we have taken all available precautions. It is imperative therefore that you keep the crew safe.

"There's a lot of tension building and I can't see it going away. We've seen the Chinese Navy increase their presence in the South China Sea and Western Pacific. The Russians have also been moving their military strategically." The general forced a grim smile as he added, "You're probably in the best place at the moment, at least until the Russians and Chinese land on Mars. I've not witnessed this type of aggressive sabre rattling for a long time. Stockton out."

"Oh great!" said Winter to himself. He could see some difficult times ahead with the Russians and Chinese. He wasn't surprised as this had been building for a while. But he had enough on his hands without being a politician. He would have to delegate more of his duties to Anders.

Chapter 41

Seven hours later, the whole crew gathered in the command room, watching the monitor in silence, as the asteroid rapidly approached. The video camera located near *Endeavour* was pointed at the region of the sky expected to see the rocks arrive from space. Everyone in the room was eagerly expecting a spectacular display, and they were not disappointed.

Georgia stood next to Jim. Like everyone in the room, her stomach was knotted in anticipation. There was now absolutely nothing they could do but wait to see what happened. Her expectation was that the mass and velocity of the asteroid would cause tremors. She nervously flicked her attention from the screen to the countdown clock and back again. Unconsciously she leaned several inches closer to the screen, as if that would give her a clearer image.

Emily was the first to spot something. "Top right," she said, pointing excitedly. "There are several pieces streaking through the atmosphere." Georgia looked where Emily was pointing and could just make out the main asteroid moving at high speed, glowing brightly as it encountered the atmosphere. It was soon clear that it was heading a long way north of their position. But there were several other fragments that were flying parallel to it that were heading closer to them, including one that looked as if it would fly directly overhead.

"That one looks far too close for comfort," said Joe Mancuso.

Captain Winter looked over at Redmayne, who was trying to interpret the data coming through on his terminal. "Tom, can you give me any news on the anticipated crash sites?"

Redmayne kept his eyes focused on the information in front of him as he coolly responded. "I'm verifying the trajectories at the moment, captain. At looks as if most of the fragments will land well away from here. The main asteroid will crash over eighteen hundred miles away, so we do not need to worry about that." He stopped to read through more numbers, his brow furrowed as he rechecked the calculations in his head. "That one to the left is likely to crash into the cliff face above us, if we're unlucky, but it may miss the crater entirely. It's too difficult to be sure. And there's one other large fragment that will impact about twenty-five miles short of the ships. I would say that is the one likely to cause some damage. Impact is less than forty-five seconds, so we don't have long to wait."

Redmayne's assessment was unnerving. Although survivable, the asteroid strike was likely to affect the mission for days to come.

The camera followed the fragment that crashed into the floor of the crater. A huge plume of dust and rocks was kicked tens of thousands of feet into the air. The other fragment flew out of sight of the camera, but several seconds later the crew heard a loud rumble and the base shook violently.

Georgia had experienced earthquakes before when she was in Los Angeles and this was no different. The shaking lasted for nearly one minute as the crew gasped and hung on to tables and chairs. She could hear falling rocks rebounding off the top of the base and the joint seals as the structure flexed to deal with the tremors. Georgia held on tightly to Jim's hand. She was waiting for an air seal to fracture and for them all to be asphyxiated.

The shaking stopped as quickly as it began. Jim squeezed her hand to acknowledge that everything was okay and she let go, slightly embarrassed.

"That was more violent than I expected. Looks like we got away with it though," Jim said, trying to break the tension.

The view screen showed a wall of dust that was growing larger and darker by the second. When Winter switched the view to the camera at the entrance to the lava tube, there was no image at all. Georgia ran to the nearest window for a clear view of the entrance and was immediately dismayed at what she saw. "It's pitch black out there," she called to the crew. "The asteroid has blocked the entrance. We're trapped!"

Chapter 42

Other than the communications link to Earth being severed, there was no obvious damage to the base. However, the captain determined it unsafe to exit Alpha Base until they were sure there would be no more tremors.

It wasn't until the following morning before Captain Winter stepped out of the airlock to inspect the damage, along with the chief, Mancuso and Rashid.

The beams of light from their flashlights shone through the thin cloud of dust that filled and drifted around the cave. Captain Winter whistled as he saw the mound of rocks and boulders that was now blocking the entrance to about waist height. Beyond that was a thick wall of dust. "What do you make of this, Jim?"

The chief pointed his flashlight at the roof of the cave. "The lava tube looks secure with no cracks or damage. The rock fall happened outside. Maybe a landslide or debris from the asteroid impact."

Winter agreed, but the news made him anxious. "If the asteroid caused this much debris, then it doesn't bode well for the state of our ships. How long do you need to create a path out?"

The chief gave the matter some thought as he looked at the pile of rocks. "Several hours at least, depending on whether any of the rovers are serviceable and the volume of rocks we discover outside the cave. The good news is that the power cables don't appear to be damaged."

"Okay, get on to it. I'd like to get to *Endeavour* to make sure it's still standing. Then we can worry about the other ships. Let me know when you're ready."

Winter turned and strolled back to the base deep in thought. If the asteroid had destroyed any of the ships, it could critically affect their ability to complete the mission. If the chief couldn't restore communications, he wouldn't even be able to send out a request to be rescued. What would Ground Control's reaction be?

Usually an optimistic man, he was having doubts about whether the mission would be a success. So many things were going against them. But, as captain, he had to keep those thoughts to himself.

***

Winter was sitting at his desk dictating a report which he hoped he'd be able to transmit to Earth at some point. Pausing to gather his thoughts, he looked fondly at the photo of Kristen and Maisie next to his computer monitor. It had been taken on their last vacation, just over eighteen months ago, in Yellowstone Park. It was their favorite destination and had seemed an appropriate place to visit for a final holiday before his mission.

He desperately missed both of them. It was no understatement to say that Kristen was his best friend. She was always there to listen to his problems and celebrate his triumphs. When he'd been stationed on the moon for the one month of training, he'd still spoken with her every day. He couldn't even do that now as the distance between them meant one-way messages and waiting hours for a reply.

With all the troubles escalating back on Earth, he should be there looking after his family. The tensions between the East and the West had turned serious in a very short time. It concerned him he was so far away from those he loved, and he prayed that the world would see sense before his grandchild was born.

Although the mission would always come first, and Kristen was fully supportive of his leading the expedition it didn't prevent him from sometimes wishing he was back on his ranch.

Before Winter could complete his report, Georgia knocked on his door. "Have you got five minutes, sir?" she asked as she poked her head around the doorframe.

"Yes. Come in. What can I do for you?"

Winter noticed that Georgia looked fidgety as she sat down opposite him. He was curious to find out what favor she was about to ask and found her discomfort amusing.

"Captain," it was clear Georgia was trying hard to phrase her question correctly. "You've known me for a long time, and I think you trust my judgement."

Winter nodded but said nothing.

"Doctor Betts has ordered that I take several days' break as she believes the past week has put me under excessive pressure. She says that I need time to recover my strength if I want to fight this cancer. I disagree with that assessment and wish to continue on active service."

"So, you believe you know more than our esteemed flight surgeon, who has over twenty years' experience and more medical qualifications than anyone on this planet?"

Georgia sat forward. "Sir, I know how my body is adapting."

"Are you really okay, Georgia? Honestly? Remember, it's me you're talking to."

"Honestly? I've not felt this good since leaving Earth. Over the past few days I've had more energy, no more headaches and I'm eating regular meals again. I'm no different to any other member of the crew."

"Except for your tumors."

Georgia's face darkened. "Yes."

"What are the doctor's thoughts on your recovery?"

"She can't explain it, which is why she wants me to take some rest. She said it could be a build-up of adrenaline from the recent excitement and is concerned I'll come crashing down."

"I have to agree with her."

"But, sir. We're on Mars. There is no reference source for Megan to base her diagnosis on. There may be other more beneficial causes that we're not aware of."

"You don't know that. We may be on a different planet but you're still human. You're grasping at straws. I don't blame you. I know you want to carry on your duties as a part of the crew, and I admire that. But sometimes you need to pay attention to your colleagues who only have your welfare at heart."

"So, you agree with Megan?"

"I'm taking her advice seriously. As you should. If she says have some rest, then do it. It looks like we'll all be on light duties for the next few days until the dust clears. Enjoy some downtime. You've earned it so don't view it as a punishment."

"Is that your final word on the matter?"

"Yes, I'm afraid it is, Georgia. I can't tell you how happy I am that you're improving but I want you to look after yourself as much as you can. I'll have you working hard again in several days, don't worry about that."

Winter smiled, hoping to break the tension. But Georgia was having none of it. She stood and left the room without saying another word.

Even though the decision had been difficult, Winter knew he'd made the right one for Georgia's sake. After pondering over it for a few more seconds he remembered what he had been doing and flicked on his computer to complete his report.

***

Georgia stormed into her quarters, slamming the door closed behind her. She'd expected more support from the captain. Megan was only doing her job as a doctor, so it was understandable that she wanted to care for her patient.

She was confident that her performance over the past few days merited continued involvement in base activities and there was no need for the captain to keep her cocooned in cotton wool. She knew better than anyone how she was feeling.

It was as if she was being punished for something she hadn't done and so unfair. Georgia vowed to convince Captain Winter to give her another chance once she'd calmed down.

Chapter 43

By early afternoon, the chief had made good his promise to clear the rock fall sufficiently for the MEV to exit the cave, although there was still plenty of work to remove all the rocks. Fortunately, the rockfall had damaged none of the construction robots, and Jim was grateful that he'd had the foresight to park them inside the cave before the asteroid strike.

Captain Winter gathered Commander Anders, Mancuso and the chief to accompany him for the trip. He had contemplated taking Georgia along to check the computer systems but, following their earlier conversation, decided that it would be best to leave her alone. This was, after all, only an initial inspection visit to assess any damage.

As the MEV drove slowly out of the mouth of the cave, Winter spotted Rashid and Harry King continuing to clear the rocks and damaged equipment. Looking out across the plain, he saw that the dust cloud was starting to dissipate quickly. While there was still a thick orange haze in the air, preventing him from seeing all the way to *Endeavour*, visibility was now almost half a mile.

Once they had travelled a short distance, he turned the MEV around to look back toward the cave. There was a large pile of rocks either side of the cave entrance which had crushed several pallets. He didn't know what had been in those pallets and hoped it was nothing vitally important. The rockslide had continued along the base of the cliff wall for almost a mile and the base had been lucky to catch only the end of it. Winter peered up through the clear canopy, trying to see where the rockslide had begun, but a blanket of dust hid the cliff face.

"It looks like we escaped the brunt of the damage, Lars," he said, turning the MEV back toward *Endeavour*.

"We must be due some good fortune," Anders replied grimly. "Let's hope it continues with *Endeavour* and the other ships."

They continued in silence, observing the ground for any obvious evidence of the asteroid. Other than a number of medium-sized boulders that must have been flung from the cliff and which the MEV had to navigate to avoid, there was very little sign of any obvious change. As they moved further from the base, visibility improved and the number of new boulders reduced.

It wasn't long before the towering bulk of *Endeavour* came into view, the sun's rays glinting from some windows running down its port side. From this distance there were no obvious signs of damage and Winter's optimism began to return.

As the MEV pulled up beneath *Endeavour*, they could see the spacecraft was covered by a fine layer of dust, but otherwise seemed intact. Winter and the crew suited up and left the MEV.

"Jim and Joe. Can you carry out a visual inspection of the exterior? Check there are no hull breaches. Commander, you're with me," Winter said as he climbed into the cradle.

As they ascended, Anders pointed at the top of the cliff face that was now visible above the dust cloud. On the edge of the rim, they could see an ugly dark groove cut into the rock. It looked as if something had taken a huge bite out of it.

"That must be where the fragment crashed," Anders said. "It clipped the top of the cliff and carried on along the plateau above where the real damage will be. We were very fortunate. The rockfall would have been far worse if the fragment had struck any lower. We would probably have been permanently trapped."

"Agreed. Perhaps you're right about our luck changing."

Once inside *Endeavour*, it didn't take long for Winter to determine that all systems were fully functional. As expected, he had received numerous messages from Earth, desperately trying to find out if Expedition Two had survived the asteroid. He replied with a summary report of the damage and clarified that everyone had survived. He knew it would ease the fears of everyone at Ground Control and, more importantly, the fears of Kristen and all other family and friends of the crew.

We dodged another bullet, Winter thought to himself. It would have been ironic if we had been trapped in the base when it was supposed to keep us safe.

With the inspection complete, he rode the cradle back down with Anders and climbed back inside the MEV to inspect first *Eden* and then each of the supply ships.

Eden had not been so lucky. Debris had pierced its delicate fuselage, rupturing a fuel tank and destroying two of the main engines. It didn't need the chief for Winter to know that *Eden* would never fly again.

Excalibur had received more extensive damage. A six-foot-wide rock had punctured the ship just below the hold, the hole and jagged metal visible from a distance. As the MEV drew closer, Winter could see that the rock had gone straight through *Excalibur* before ploughing into the solar farm, leaving a black ugly scar across the field of solar panels.

Winter decided that, overall, the damage was a setback rather than a disaster. *Excalibur* was not scheduled to fly again anyway, and the solar farm could be reconfigured, albeit with a reduced power output. It wasn't as bad as he'd feared it could be when he'd woken up that morning.

As the sun began to set, and the MEV made its way back toward Alpha Base, exhaustion began to overwhelm Winter as he finally started to relax. It had been a stressful time for the whole of Expedition Two. Perhaps the mission proper could now begin. He certainly hoped that was the case.

Chapter 44

"You've got your way again, Georgia. The captain has ordered that I conduct another medical on you. Somehow you've managed to persuade him that you know more about medicine than I do."

Georgia had just sat down in the galley for her evening meal and looked up at Megan who appeared to be irritated. It had been a week since the change in her health and there was now no end to her energy. She had quietly been making suggestions to the captain that another medical was necessary to confirm that she was fit enough to return to duty. It had taken several days of persistence to convince him, although Winter had not let her know he would speak with the doctor.

Georgia hovered her fork above her plate and looked directly at Megan. Despite being good friends, there were times when work got in the way of that friendship. "If that's what he thinks is best. When do you want to see me?"

"Give it an hour to let me set up my equipment. Then come down to the medical facility. Are you sure you want to do this?"

"Yes, Megan, I'm certain. It's the only way I can prove to everyone, including myself, that I'm not being irrational or delusional."

"Okay, in that case I'll see you in an hour." Megan turned and left abruptly.

Jim, who was sitting next to Georgia, turned to her. "You know how to keep your friends close. What was that about?"

Georgia devoured her last forkful of lasagna, before speaking. "The discomfort from the tumors has eased off. I don't know how but there's been no pain for days. Megan insists that there is no cure for the cancer I've been diagnosed with. She says I'm fooling myself."

"You can understand why she's saying that. She has the knowledge of expert oncologists and years of research to fall back on."

"I know my own body, Jim. I'm convinced that I'm recovering from whatever I had. I just know it. You've seen me over the past few days. It's not just a new frame of mind. I am genuinely healthy."

"There's no doubt that you're back to your old self again. And that has been great to see. But specialists confirmed your prognosis was terminal. There's nothing I want more than for you to be right about this, but I don't want you to raise your hopes. You need to be realistic."

"I am being realistic, Jim. I don't expect you to understand, just to believe me. I can't explain it, but Megan is wrong. The specialists are wrong."

"And if they're not. Then what?"

Georgia had not considered that option. She was certain she was right. "If I'm wrong, then I'll fight it for as long as I'm able to. You know that I've never been someone who quits. But I would appreciate your support."

"You know that you have it, and always will." Without thinking, Jim reached out and put his hand over the top of hers. No longer surprised by his spontaneous displays of affection, Georgia looked down at their hands touching and smiled.

Looking back at the worried expression on his face, she said reassuringly, "It's going to be fine."

Jim left his hand where it was, and she was pleased that he did. His touch, although surprising, felt good, and she was in no hurry for the moment to end.

"Thanks for caring about me, Jim. It means a great deal to have you on my side, whatever happens. And I want you to know that I'll be there for you too if you ever need me."

The chief smiled. "I never doubted it for a moment. But you should know I'm not the best at getting close to people or sharing my emotions. Telling you I care is a huge step."

Georgia laughed out loud. "Yes, I have noticed that nearly all the men on this expedition are the macho, quiet types. Next you'll be telling me it's easier that way."

"I don't know if it's easier. It's something I've done since I can remember and it's just a habit. I was very awkward with girls when I was much younger. Maybe I never learned to be any different."

"So what's changed?" Georgia realized she never usually cared what other people thought. Why was she so interested in Jim's feelings?

"It's not pity if that's what you think."

Georgia shook her head. "No, that never crossed my mind."

Jim shrugged, trying hard to find the right words. "I've worked with you a long time now and see how you operate. In the early days, I admired your tenacity. You took no shit from anyone around you. During training, you threw yourself into everything. If the instructors wanted a volunteer, you were the first to stick their hand up. You were always the star. And if it sounds like I was a bit in awe of you, that's because I probably was."

Georgia was lost for words. She'd kept her head down throughout training, focused on making it on to the expedition short list. She'd known she was being observed and tested by the instructors. Not for one second had she been aware she was gaining attention from her colleagues.

"I don't know what to say," she spluttered. "I always like to give one hundred percent in everything I do."

"You've given that commitment to everyone on this expedition, and you may have paid for it with your life. But I know that's who you are, and you don't know any other way. You're amazing. Being on this mission with you is very special, and not just because we're creating history for mankind. I'm so happy you're not ready to give up, because I'm not ready to continue without you."

Tears began to well up in Georgia's eyes. She wasn't prepared for this depth of emotion from Jim. They had clicked very early on after meeting but so far it had been nothing more than a platonic work relationship. She quickly wiped her eyes, not wanting to appear weak. "Thanks, Jim. That means so much to me. We should continue this conversation after I've proven to Megan that I'm right. But I can tell you I think you're special too."

She didn't really want to leave at that moment. But the medical confirmation was her priority. And, anyway, neither of them was going very far in the near future. She moved her hand and stood up to leave. Putting her hand gently on his shoulder, she said, "I'll let you know the results either way. But have faith."

"Good luck, Georgia," he called out softly as she left the galley and strode confidently toward the medical center for the tests that would ultimately define what future she had left.

Chapter 45

Megan was calibrating an expensive looking scanner as Georgia entered the base's new medical center. The room was more than double the space of *Endeavour*'s medical facility, with the ability to expand into an additional module as Alpha grew over subsequent missions. A variety of unopened pallets and boxes, together with spaces in a number of racks on the near wall were clear evidence that she still had some unpacking to finish. Most of the equipment had been taken directly from *Endeavour* but there were plenty of additional medical stores on one of the supply ships.

Megan's expression showed it still irritated her at having to perform the medical. "Apologies for the mess," she said in a monotone voice, indicating the boxes. "I wasn't expecting visitors so soon. Rashid was scheduled to help me, but Anders diverted him to help the Kings."

"I see you're pissed at me, Megan. I'm not questioning your medical ability, but I really need to know what's happening to me. I don't want it to affect our friendship."

"Georgia, it's fine. These tests are a waste of time, that's all. I've had other patients who have been in denial of their diagnoses and imagined that they've somehow miraculously cured themselves. None of them have."

"Maybe I'll be the exception that proves the rule," Georgia responded, trying to sound hopeful.

"Maybe," responded Megan, with no conviction. "Hop onto the bed and let's get started."

Doctor Betts spent the next ninety minutes conducting a rigorous examination together with a comprehensive suite of tests. It was clear to Georgia that she was determined there would be no room for doubt in anyone's mind. The doctor quizzed Georgia in depth, searching for any clues on why she considered she had recovered.

Georgia answered each of the questions as honestly and completely as she could. Had she changed her daily routine in the past week, eaten anything that tasted strange or acted differently?

"Other than that we're on Mars, have worked desperately hard to set up Camp Alpha before the asteroid struck and worked through countless minor issues," Georgia responded, ironically, "no, nothing unusual has occurred. Only that fainting experience four days ago. But you checked me out. Has that got anything to do with my current state?"

"I'm not making any wild guesses. Let's just see what the results show."

Finally, all the tests were complete, and Georgia heaved a sigh of relief. "Can you tell me anything now? Any initial findings?"

Megan was looking at a few readings on her computer screen. Absently she replied, "Not yet, Georgia. I'll be sending the information through to Ground Control. I'm only a flight surgeon, not a specialist oncologist. You'll have to wait until morning but I'm sure we'll hear first thing."

"Let me know as soon as you get the results. And thanks again for doing this."

"Remember. Whatever the results, I am always here for you."

Georgia nodded. "Yes, I know."

Chapter 46

Despite being physically exhausted, Georgia lay on her bunk, unable to sleep. There was far too much going through her mind following the medical examination. She knew it had been foolish to have expected Megan to provide the results on the spot. There were blood tests, scans and what had seemed like a million other tests to review forensically before giving the ultimate diagnosis. But the not knowing was eating away at her.

Although confident that she was right, even if it was irrational, there were still nagging doubts that she couldn't quite shake. Alone in her room, in the darkness, listening to the gentle hum of the environmental systems, those doubts began to fester and multiply.

After taking two sleeping tablets prescribed by Megan, Georgia eventually drifted into a fitful sleep, filled with vivid dreams. She found herself back on one of the supply ships. It was pitch black, and she was running away from something. A moment later she was falling and reaching out for something to grab on to, but her hand grasped only thin air. She continued to fall for an eternity, twisting and turning in the air as she fell. Suddenly there was a bright light, and she was lying down in a strange room. It reminded her of a science fiction movie, but she couldn't remember the name. Out of the corner of her eye she could see her left leg was at an unnatural angle with several inches of her shin bone protruding through the broken skin. She screamed, but no sound came out.

Georgia woke suddenly, sweating. Briefly disoriented, she looked around until she remembered where she was. Glancing at the clock on her computer, it surprised her that she'd been in bed for less than three hours. The dream had been so real. She blamed the medication and lay back down. Cuddling her pillow for comfort it wasn't long before she was asleep once more.

The dream was there, waiting for her. She was still in the bright strange room but this time she wasn't alone. Two tall alien looking creatures were leaning over her. They were looking at some type of machine and talking to each other, but she could not tell what they were saying. Her body was being gently lifted before being lowered into a tank of clear viscous fluid. She was completely submerged except for her face. She could sense a tingling sensation across her skin. It wasn't unpleasant but Georgia could not compare it to anything else she'd experienced.

In her dream, she was trying hard to communicate with the alien creatures, but they were paying her no attention. She was becoming frustrated at being ignored. She wanted answers. Why was no one listening to her? In her frustration, she focused on the aliens' characteristics. There was something odd about them. Georgia couldn't decide if they were machine or organic but knew there was nothing to fear from them.

One alien noticed that she was looking at them. He leaned toward her, stretching out one of his long arms. Finally, I'm going to find out what's going on, she thought. The creature opened its mouth to speak...

Georgia was sitting up in her bed again, back in her own quarters. Reaching out for the water bottle she always kept nearby, she took several large gulps and calmed herself down. Even though she knew it was only a dream, there was no way she could go back to sleep again. The clock confirmed it was nearly five o'clock anyway, and she had set her alarm for five thirty. She took two deep breaths and sat with her back resting on the wall trying to remember the details from her dream. It had been so real with colors, sounds and smells as if she was actually inside an alien spacecraft. How could she have imagined something so vivid? Where had aliens originated in her mind?

Georgia idly rubbed her shin where the bone had been broken in her dream and was shocked to find a raised line of skin. She didn't remember ever having an operation on her leg! She hastily turned the light on next to her bed for a better look. With a mixture of fear and disbelief, she could see a six-inch-long scar halfway down her shin. She rubbed it again, the contours feeling strange under her fingers. How was it possible to not remember ever having that scar? And why was it exactly where she had dreamed it would be?

Something was wrong, and this time she was truly afraid.

Trying to keep her panic under control, Georgia climbed out of bed and wandered down the corridor toward Megan's quarters. The corridor was bathed in a soft green light from LEDs in the ceiling, just bright enough to guide people at night. At this early time there was no one else around.

Georgia tapped gently on Megan's door, but there was no sound of movement inside.

"Megan," she whispered loudly. "I need you to check my records. I've found something"

"Now?" came the tired reply from someone who was still half asleep. That was enough of an invitation for Georgia to open Megan's door and turn the light on. "Yes, I have a scar on my shin but I'm sure I've had no surgery. I had just dreamed about it. How can that be?"

Megan sat up in her bed, flinching and put her arm across her eyes to shield them from the sudden light. "Calm down, Georgia. You're not making sense. I'll check for you but let me wake up properly first. Come and see me in thirty minutes. And bring a coffee with you. You know how I like it."

Georgia reluctantly left and sat alone in the galley, going over the dream several times but finding no answers to the questions bouncing around her head. After twenty minutes, she filed a large mug with coffee, added two sugars and walked down to the medical center. She thought she could hear someone in the showers but there was still no movement from the rest of the crew.

Megan was still in her sleep suit with her hair unkempt and looking at Georgia's medical records as she took the coffee offered to her. "There's nothing here to suggest you've ever injured either leg. I can see a distal radius fracture, or broken wrist to you, when you were nineteen but that's all. Perhaps it happened when you were a child. Let me look."

"I broke my wrist when I fell from my horse. It was my fault that time, but I've generally been lucky with injuries," Georgia said as she rolled up her right trouser leg. Pointing, she added, "At the front, halfway down."

Megan leaned over to examine Georgia's leg. "Yes, it definitely looks like you've broken your shin bone at some time, and it's pierced your skin. It would have been a massive trauma, so I'm surprised you don't remember. Especially as this wouldn't have happened when you were a child. It's also odd that nothing has been picked up in your medical records. You are full of surprises at the moment."

Georgia told Megan about the strange content of her dreams. Megan was at a loss to explain the link between the scar and Georgia's visions. "You've been under a lot of stress lately. What with worry about the tumors and getting the base ready. Perhaps you've been suppressing the memory of the broken leg and it's suddenly come into your consciousness. The brain works in mysterious ways."

"But the dreams were so real. I could swear I was actually in an alien ship. And the scar isn't a dream. It's real and physical."

"Let me take a quick scan and forward it to Ground Control to compare against your medical records on Earth. I may not have your complete history on file. It won't take them long to let me know."

"Thanks again, Megan. I know I'm being a pain in the ass at the moment."

Megan chuckled. "Yes, you are. But it's not like you. Give me fifteen minutes to get dressed and sort this hair out and I'll join you for breakfast in the galley."

***

As the pair of them finished their breakfasts, Megan received notification that she had an important message waiting for her on her computer in the medical facility. "That will be your results. I requested that Ground Control make your examination results their top priority. I believe Captain Winter also followed up with his own demand for urgency."

Georgia had a sinking feeling in the pit of her stomach. Their conversation over breakfast had been light, with Megan successfully taking her thoughts away from the impending results. Georgia had also hoped that she would bump into Jim this morning. She was disappointed that, so far, he had not made an appearance. He probably has some early checks to complete for the captain, she told herself. Now, with the results waiting for her in the medical center, she wanted him with her.

Megan downed the rest of her coffee and stood up. "Ready when you are," she said, noticing that her friend had suddenly gone quiet.

"Yes, let's get this done once and for all." Georgia was unable to hide the uncertainty in her voice. She slowly stood and followed Megan back to the medical facility, gray and somber as if she was a convict about to receive a life sentence.

It surprised Georgia to see Captain Winter sitting in the medical facility. He stood as they entered. "I heard your results are back from Earth and thought you may want some support."

"Thank you, sir," was all that Georgia could stammer.

Megan opened up her computer screen to see there were two messages for her. "What do you want to hear first? Tumors or scar?"

Georgia didn't have to think about that one. "Tumors!" This was the big life or death issue. The scar was just a minor mystery in comparison. She watched Megan open and read the response from Ground Control. Her heart sank as she saw Megan stare wide eyed at her screen and put her hand to her mouth in shock before bursting into tears.

Captain Winter must have seen it too because Georgia was aware of his reassuring arm around her.

"How bad is it, Megan? I need to know," she said.

Megan took a few seconds to compose herself before she could speak. Each second was like an eternity to Georgia but to the astonishment of both Georgia and the captain, Megan started laughing through her tears. "It's good. The tumors have gone. You were right. You're clear of cancer!" Megan came around from behind her desk and the three of them hugged and sobbed for joy, their tears flowing uncontrollably.

Eventually they pulled apart and Megan continued. "The oncologists do not understand how this has happened. Your cure is an absolute miracle. Which means you must undergo more tests here and when you return to Earth. The bottom line is, though, the tumors have entirely disappeared. There're no shadows on your scans or abnormalities in your blood. If I didn't know better, I'd doubt you ever had any glioblastoma tumors."

"Surely the specialists have some idea," said Captain Winter. "I'm not an expert but I know that cancer doesn't simply disappear with no treatment."

"You're absolutely right. The oncologists have said little in their response. I'm sure they'll be scratching their heads over this one. There will be plenty of research to find the answer."

"So, I'm cured. I'm not going to die on this planet." Georgia was still trying to absorb the news. Her instincts had been right. She didn't care how it had happened. Now it was time to celebrate life again. "Does that mean I'm back on duty?" she asked, looking at Captain Winter with a huge grin on her face.

Winter looked at Megan, waiting for a nod of approval. "I guess so. I can't think of a good reason to wrap you up any longer. I trust you won't become unbearably smug about being proved right.

"I can't promise anything at this moment," laughed Georgia, almost giddy.

Meanwhile, Megan was reading the second message from Earth. "This isn't possible either," she said, shaking her head in disbelief yet again. "There's nothing in your medical records regarding your leg. More bizarrely still, the scar tissue is fresh. No more than seven to ten days old, apparently. And I can see from the X-ray that your bone is still healing too. Which means you broke your leg since we arrived on Mars. What the hell is going on with you?"

Georgia and the captain were equally dumbfounded. The issue seemed insignificant after discovering her cancer had gone but Georgia's instinct was telling her the two matters were linked. They had to be.

Georgia repeated her dreams to the captain and explained the scar on her leg. "I've been having the dreams for about three nights. Each time it's the same dream but with more clarity. It looks like I'm on one of the supply ships. It ends with me in a strange room with alien creatures. Every time, it's the same two aliens in there with me. I don't believe they're native Martians, but I can't tell you why."

The captain looked astounded. Georgia re-writing the rule book at the moment and he couldn't ignore anything she said. "In this dream, you believe that the aliens healed your leg. You're sure you've not broken your leg before?"

"I'm not imagining this. It feels more like a memory than a dream." Georgia was finding it difficult to explain. She had not given the dreams much thought. Her cancer had taken over her life in recent days and her head was still spinning with the news of her instant recovery. She paused for a moment, to run through the details of her dreams and see if she could remember any more details. "It may sound farfetched but what if I didn't faint when I went to *Challenger*? And my dreams really happened. What if the aliens exist and they healed my broken leg when I went missing?"

Megan shook her head. "If your dream is real, you would have fallen nearly eighty feet to the ground and broken more than just your leg. I'd have expected multiple contusions and internal trauma. You wouldn't have survived."

"Yes, I know that." Georgia's mind was spinning as she tried to fit the pieces of the puzzle together. "Maybe the aliens fixed more than just my leg. They could have performed some type of total body scan and repaired all my other injuries as well."

"And removed your tumors? Are we considering this as likely? That Martians or aliens exist and are watching us? It's more than just a little farfetched. Why did they choose you? Why don't you remember what happened?"

"Agreed, captain. I can't answer any of those questions. But do you have a better alternative?" Georgia looked to Megan for any kind of support, but she was not ready to give any kind of opinion.

The captain also looked as if he was totally out of his depth." I don't have an answer. I won't discount anything. But intelligent and advanced alien life is a huge leap of imagination. If they really exist, then I don't know if I'm thrilled or scared witless. Doctor, you've been quiet for a while. What are your thoughts?"

"Honestly, sir? It's possible Georgia may be on to something. I can't explain the tumors or her broken leg that has been miraculously cured. Her recovery is so implausible that alien intervention is almost the most rational answer. I'm not saying that is the only explanation. But I don't have a better one."

The captain stood silently for several moments, assessing his available options. Finally, he had to admit that he needed more facts.

"There's enough evidence to give some credence to that theory. If it's true, then that opens up a whole new set of problems. I need to get guidance from Ground Control on what we do next. How do I inform the crew without causing panic? If aliens exist, are they Martians or from somewhere else entirely? I, for one, am already worried that we are being monitored by an advanced alien species. For the time being, we keep this quiet."

Georgia sat there stunned. The existence of aliens would explain a great deal about her new lease of life. The past few days had been a rollercoaster of emotion and she was overwhelmed by the experience.

Captain Winter clapped her on the shoulder. "Georgia, I understand that your cancer recovery is momentous, and I am sure you want to share it with the whole crew. Can you wait until I have spoken with Ground Control? We'll need to create a plausible explanation for your cure."

Chapter 47

It took Ground Control over eight hours to reply to Captain Winter's report on the possible existence of aliens and their involvement in the cure of Georgia's cancer. The response, classified TOP SECRET, came in a video and forty-five pages of detailed instruction on what information they could share and with whom.

General Stockton's video summed up the thoughts from Earth. The general looked somber as he sat upright with his arms resting on the desk in front of him. He was flanked on either side by Mission Director James Ford and Chief Medical Officer Deborah Grainger.

Winter had gathered Commander Anders, Doctor Betts, the chief, Professor Redmayne and Georgia in the control room to watch the message, although he had not shared the reasons why. The six of them sat expectantly in front of the monitor.

"Captain Winter," began the general. "Thank you for your report this morning. As you expected, it garnered a great deal of interest here and at the White House. There had been much conjecture from Doctor Grainger's team around Pyke's miraculous medical recovery. Her test results sent through yesterday astounded the whole team and were double-checked to ensure there had been no mistakes." The general paused and looked across to Doctor Grainger who continued.

"Captain, none of my specialists has been able to offer any explanation for the sudden and complete remission of Pyke's multiple glioblastoma tumors. We compared her previous results when the tumors were clearly present. There is no way that she should ever have recovered, let alone so quickly. Then, as if one puzzle was not sufficient, Doctor Betts sent through a second with the request to examine Pyke's medical history for a fractured tibia, together with a scan of what appears to be a very recent injury."

In the Alpha command room, Georgia could sense Jim and Redmayne glance at her as they tried to absorb the news about her health. She ignored the attention and focused hard on the screen.

The general coughed to interrupt. "It's fair to say that Doctor Grainger and her team are embarrassed at their failure to provide any reasonable answers or explanations on Pyke's latest condition. We worked overnight and consulted the most eminent global experts, all to no avail. It was determined that we have to carry out a detailed research program to understand if there is a local cause and if there is any associated danger to the crew."

The mission director carried on. "No one considered the possibility of alien intervention. Not until we received your latest report. Pyke's account of her dreams, linked to her recovery, makes a compelling story to explain what may have happened to her. While we are not conceding that intelligent extra-terrestrial life exists, it is considered a highly possible scenario at the moment. It fills in a lot of gaps. But it also leads to several concerns and questions.

We've spent several hours briefing the president and the United Nations in a session behind closed doors. They are extremely worried about what impact the news will have on the public. There was unanimous agreement that there would be panic and global instability. With no hard evidence it would be reckless at this stage to mention the possibility of alien life on Mars."

The general interrupted yet again. "We have drafted an emergency protocol that comes into effect immediately. It expressly forbids anyone associated with the mission from publicly sharing any news on Pyke's health, her dreams, or any speculation about an alien presence. I'm sorry but that means we will monitor all your personal transmissions to loved ones on Earth. For the time being at least. A copy of protocol has been sent to you to share and implement with the whole of Expedition Two. There are no exceptions. I will release a more detailed version over the next few days.

"Should intelligent alien life exist and be observing you, we have no idea what their intentions are. If Pyke is correct and they are nearby it would appear that they want to keep themselves hidden. The last thing we want to do is antagonize an advanced civilization. Which means you are not to actively seek out the aliens in an attempt to confirm their existence. We cannot know what the reaction might be. At the moment, they are taking a passive role and we should keep it that way. If Pyke did encounter them, it was likely an accident. Even if they are responsible for her recovery you should proceed with extreme caution. Too much is at stake."

Mission Director Ford nodded. "We designed these protocols for your protection, as well as the safety of Earth. We need to prepare properly for first contact, if that's around the corner. I know we're asking a lot of you and your crew to continue as if nothing has changed but I'm sure you understand. Good luck."

The image on the screen froze as the message ended.

Captain Winter leaned back in his chair, unsurprised by the orders. There was a stunned silence from his senior crew. "Any questions?" he asked.

There were plenty, particularly from Anders and Redmayne who both wanted to know about Georgia's health and why there was so much talk about aliens.

Georgia patiently recounted her experiences over the past few days to a disbelieving audience. She noted that Jim was the only one that congratulated her on her recovery. He looked genuinely pleased for her and she felt a pang of guilt that she'd been unable to share her good fortune sooner.

Anders and Redmayne were angry that the captain had kept them out of the loop. Redmayne, in particular, was adamant he should have been told. "Captain, if Georgia had an encounter with intelligent life, it affects all of us. As chief scientist on this mission, it falls on me to study any alien life, from bacteria upwards. This could be a momentous discovery for humankind and you're hiding behind bureaucrats millions of miles away on Earth."

"There are processes that we all have to follow. Even you," replied Winter, who was becoming increasingly agitated by Redmayne's arrogance. "You heard that the United Nations is concerned about the public reaction. Don't you agree that this information needs to be controlled? Especially when we have no hard evidence. There could easily be an entirely different reason for Georgia's recovery. Why needlessly stir up public paranoia?"

"I don't care about sharing the information with the public. But you should trust your crew. It's obvious to me that the only rational explanation is alien interference. How much more proof do you need? We're wasting time here when we could be working out what the aliens want and how we can contact them. I don't need to be afraid. If they saved Georgia's life, then they are obviously benign."

"We don't know that for sure." Winter was finding it harder to control his frustration.

"Tom's right," added Commander Anders. "You should have shared this sooner. We could have started this debate this morning and been ready for that message."

"And do what?" asked Georgia. "We know nothing about the aliens or where they may be hiding. They could have an underground complex or their own craft. They may be long gone or even a figment of my imagination."

Jim sprang up from his chair excitedly. "Georgia, remember on day six, we were on speeders returning from the supply ships. You thought you spotted something metallic glinting from the rim of the crater. Maybe that was them. What do you think?"

Georgia had forgotten about that moment. "I don't know," she pondered. "It was the briefest glimpse and could have been anything reflecting in the sun."

Winter had had enough by now. "We can spend all day debating who should have been told and when. It makes no difference now. The facts are, we have a mystery around Georgia's recovery that we won't solve by sitting here. Aliens may be the answer, but no one knows for sure. The guys in charge on Earth, our superiors, have put in place some procedures to avoid public panic based purely on conjecture. And they have ordered us to not piss off any aliens that are here. I don't have a problem with that. And neither should any of you. So, Redmayne, wind your neck in and get back what you're supposed to be doing. I will share the information with the rest of the crew, but we proceed as normal. Does anyone have any issues with that?"

Everyone else in the room sat in stunned silence. They'd never seen Captain Winter so riled. But they could not argue with his concise rationale.

***

Redmayne stormed out of the command room, marching his way to his science lab. "The entire world is controlled by idiots," he muttered to himself. He slammed the door and locked it before pacing up and down. He'd not been this fired up for a very long time. Why wasn't it obvious to everyone that mankind was on the verge of a momentous event? They would miss out on a unique and epic opportunity. Landing humans on Mars was insignificant compared to establishing contact with an intelligent species from another planet. It was a subject that had been debated by the best scientists and theologians for hundreds of years. And finally, when the answer was within touching distance, the world's leaders were found wanting, unable to hold their nerve and be brave enough to take the next step.

He banged his fist on the wall in frustration, denting the thin aluminum structure. He didn't enjoy being prevented from what he knew was the right thing to do. At least the Russians had more of an imagination. He was confident they would take a different view if they were in charge of the mission.

He needed to contact the *Andropov* to get clear instructions on how they wanted to handle the matter, which meant going to *Eden* and using his personal communicator. It was too late in the day to make that journey, so he'd have to wait until the morning.

His anger softened when he noticed that his computer screen was flashing to show a message waiting. It was from the mysterious Alex and requested that Tom use all haste to locate the aliens. Once found, Tom was to transmit the co-ordinates and await further instructions.

These orders, while Tom wasn't sure how he would complete them, justified his decision to align his work with the Russians. He may not agree with their ideologies but they, along with the Chinese, had the imagination and bravery to make the hard choices when needed. The Russian and Chinese leaders weren't soft like those in the West, and that would be decisive for the future of Earth. They wouldn't have allowed the multiple errors and corruption that led to Expedition One failing, thereby killing his beloved Laura, the pilot on that ill-fated mission.

What he had in common with the Russians was that he also knew how to be patient before exacting his revenge. For six years, the anger and resentment had been building, and he was now closer than ever to completing what he'd set out to do. Snatching the aliens away from the Americans would be the icing on the cake.

And the Russians knew how to reward citizens for their loyalty.

His calmness restored, he set to work, researching any possible clues from Georgia's report and medical tests. He hoped there would be something that he could discover that no one else would. That would make all the difference he needed.

Chapter 48

At the end of an emotionally draining day, Georgia lay in her bed, staring at the ceiling. As with Tom Redmayne, she was frustrated at the orders to not search for the aliens. She wanted closure and certainty to allow her to move on. She needed to know if she had actually encountered aliens. Instead, there remained a big question mark over what had happened to her and she was nowhere near close to finding an answer.

She was convinced that, as her dreams had been so intense, they had to be genuine memories. Yet there were still enough gaps and inconsistencies to cause confusion over what was real and what was in her imagination.

Georgia considered what her father would have thought about her current situation. She could still remember the Bible classes he had taken her and Jackson to from an early age. Her father had been a devout Christian and could recite whole passages from the Bible. As a young girl, Georgia couldn't understand why he took the word of the Bible so literally. To her, the events described were just stories. She didn't consider them to be true. He had tried so hard to convince her that the scriptures explained God's will and that religion was an essential part of making the world a better place. Her simple questions often made him angry, but he never gave up on preaching to her.

She wished he was still alive to see what she had achieved. She missed the arguments they'd had and believed he had enjoyed the verbal sparring but had never accepted her opinions. Would he believe in the existence of aliens? She was sure he wouldn't have.

As she thought fondly of her childhood, Georgia managed to drift off to sleep.

In the middle of the night, her dreams returned yet again.

***

Captain Winter called a team meeting after breakfast. There had been no more overnight updates from Ground Control on how to handle the situation on Mars although he was sure that there was an ongoing debate as to what was the best course of action. That was fine with him. It meant he could focus on the day in hand.

He was pleased to see a room full of eager and energetic faces as he entered the common room again.

"I hope you are well rested. I know that the news yesterday was a lot to take in for many of you. Heck, I'm not sure if I've fully got my head around it all. Does anyone have any further questions that I can answer or address with Ground Control?"

"Yes, I do," said Joe Mancuso from the back of the room. "I've looked at the protocols issued yesterday. They're very restrictive on what we can say and transmit back to Earth to friends and on public channels. And there are clear orders to not actively seek any possible alien life. I didn't see any guidance on what we should do in the event that the aliens, if they exist, make contact with one of us. Do we run away or act friendly?"

Winter noticed a few nods of agreement around the room. Mancuso wasn't the only one to give the matter some thought.

"A great question, Joe. I don't think the rule makers back on Earth thought that far ahead. I read the protocols too last night and you're right; it's a list of controls on what not to say and do. They've been written to prevent widespread panic back home. I doubt anyone on Earth believes aliens exist. I'm far more open-minded and if Georgia believes that she had an alien encounter, I take that very seriously.

As to your question, if there are aliens and they make contact, I'm not sure we should ignore them. Where can we run to? My preference would be to befriend them. What does everyone else think? I'm open to any other options."

Georgia was the first to speak. "I agree with you, sir. Their intentions are peaceful. And if their technology is more advanced than ours, then they could have killed us long before now if they'd wanted to."

Redmayne had a different view. "Everyone here is talking as if aliens exist and we'll bump into them walking round the next corner. But there's no evidence other than Georgia's recurring dreams and a wild guess that her cancer was cured by alien intervention. Now, I'm the first to hope that aliens really are on this planet but the odds of that being the case are infinitesimally small. So, a debate on what you should do when you meet one is a waste of time."

Commander Anders agreed with Redmayne. "We have more pressing priorities establishing the base and setting up the propellant depot. I don't believe that aliens are here watching what we do. We just need to focus and carry on with establishing this base. It's our primary mission still, as far as I know."

They were the only dissenters among the crew. Winter had the impression that everyone else in the room had a certain level of anxiety on the subject. He wanted to retain calm in the room. "We honestly don't know what we're dealing with. There's no point second guessing ourselves and worrying about something that may not exist. However, until we know for sure, I suggest that everyone here use their discretion. In the unlikely event of alien contact do not show them any hostility. Ask yourself, 'What would that fine Captain Winter do?' And the answer is to be respectful and welcome them with open arms." His disarming comment broke the tension and raised a laugh in the room as he'd intended.

They spent the remainder of the meeting assigning tasks for the day. While Winter thought the commander's view on the aliens was extreme and unnecessary, he did agree that they should establish a normal base routine to complete the long list of urgent open items that had been overtaken by the intervention of the asteroid. As it was his idea, it was impossible for the commander to dodge responsibility for implementing the routine when the captain craftily passed it to him.

***

Georgia was assigned with Jim to collect the power couplers and relays for the Sabatier Reactor which were stored on *Challenger*. Getting the reactor working and creating methane for the rocket propellant was now one of the priority tasks to show that the ships could refuel and return to Earth.

Within thirty minutes of Captain Winter's meeting finishing, the pair of them were in the MEV, driving out of the base toward the distant supply ships.

The chief took it upon himself to break the silence. "I didn't have time to congratulate you properly on your amazing news yesterday. You're full of surprises but I cannot tell you how thrilled I am that you're totally cured."

"That's okay," she replied. "I know you were busy. And the day went in a mad blur. I can't take it all in still. Thanks again for your support, and our conversation the other night."

"I don't know what came over me. I wasn't sure if I'd overstepped the mark and I didn't want you to be awkward around me."

Georgia giggled. "Don't be silly. What you said was sweet. It was wonderful to see a different, softer side to you. Knowing how you feel will make the rest of my mission far more enjoyable. Especially now that I'll be hanging around for a long time."

Jim blushed for the second time that week. "I hope we can have many more of these moments together."

He looked down at the control screen to confirm their route. Georgia could sense he had something else to say.

"Yes, what is it?" she asked.

"I wanted to ask about the alien encounter you've been having dreams about. Do you think they're real memories or are they dreams caused by the medication you were on?"

"I can't be one hundred percent. The dreams are as real as a memory with all the senses that go with it. But they stop at a certain point and I can't get past it. It's to do with the aliens. I can see and hear them, but I can't interact with them. The harder I try, the quicker I wake up. My gut feeling is that the dreams are actual memories. I hope I can prove it. Both to myself and everyone else." Georgia went silent again, contemplating everything she had been through as they completed the trip to *Challenger*.

She was grateful that the chief gave her the space she needed to process everything that was happening to her.

                                        ***

Once inside *Challenger*, Jim turned on the lights and told Georgia that all the parts they needed were on the third level. With the power on, they were both able to take the central elevator to the correct level and find the bins they needed.

As Georgia was dragging a pallet containing the relays to the lift, the lights suddenly cut out, and they were in complete darkness. Jim switched on his helmet lights and said, "I hope that's just a fuse. I'll look in the engineering section and have this fixed in no time. Are you okay with loading the other pallets on to the lift?"

Georgia gave no reply.

Jim swung his head round so he could see where Georgia was standing. It looked as if she was frozen to the spot. "Georgia? Are you okay?"

His words broke the trance that she was in. She turned to face him and whispered, "This is how it happened. I encountered the alien in the dark, on *Intrepid*. It's all coming back to me. I was there in the darkness, and the huge alien came out of the shadows. Oh my God! I can remember everything."

Georgia started trembling and Jim rushed over to her, putting an arm round her and drawing her into him as much as the cumbersome spacesuits would allow. His eyes darted around in the blackness, but he couldn't make out anyone or anything that shouldn't be there.

"It's okay now." He tried to sound reassuring. "There's nothing here now and I'm with you. You're not alone."

Georgia straightened, quickly gathering her composure. "I know, Jim. I have memories suddenly rushing back into my head. It's like I have broken a dam. I now know what really happened to me. I need to tell the captain."

Chapter 49

Everyone had reconvened in the common room to hear Georgia share her update. There had already been whisperings of what had happened to her, but they all stood in eager silence, waiting to hear the truth.

"As you know, there's been plenty of debate about whether my dreams were real. At first, I thought they were just dreams. But there was an inexplicable overlap with what was happening to me, such as a scar on my leg exactly where I had dreamed I broke it. Then, when I was back on *Challenger* this morning with Jim, it suddenly all fell into place." Georgia paused, glancing around to see that her audience was rapt. She took a deep breath and continued.

"When I went missing last week, it was because I did encounter an alien creature exploring the cargo hold." The room was in utter silence as she grabbed their complete attention. "I was there to find parts to fix the power issues being experienced at the base and was searching for the parts I needed. When I saw the alien, I panicked and ran to escape but somehow, in that panic, I tripped and fell out of the hold. I remember hitting the ground hard and being in unbearable pain. My suit was compromised, and I knew I was about to die. I must have passed out, either from the pain or through lack of oxygen. The next thing I remember is being on the alien vessel and they were carrying out some procedures on me that healed all of my injuries."

"Did you see what they looked like? What did they do to you?" Redmayne was clearly a convert and keen to get as much information as possible, although his questions echoed the thoughts of nearly everyone else in the room.

"They didn't insert probes or carry out any other unsavory tests if that is what you're referring to." There was a ripple of nervous laughter around the room.

Georgia smiled and recounted the conversations she'd had with Falmas. Everyone looked at her with eyes wide. The story was so unbelievable yet, they knew it must be true. The Sentinels weren't Martians at all, but from another planet in a distant part of the galaxy.

Georgia continued. "They've been observing us since we left Earth. Their role is to watch over mankind's development and evolution while remaining unseen, with no interference. They told me their species has done so for five thousand years. Falmas, the leader I think, did not expect to run into me on *Intrepid*. He said he had an obligation to fix my injuries as he believed it was his fault, although they could have easily just left me there and no one would have been the wiser as to what had happened. However, they were too good at healing me, possibly through lack of knowledge of our physiology, because they not only fixed my injuries, but they also removed all the cancerous cells from my body. Their technology is far superior to anything we could even dream of."

Commander Anders asked, "You say that you were on the Sentinel's craft. Are you able to remember where it was or how many other creatures were on board?"

Georgia shook her head. "Sorry, commander. I was unconscious when I was taken to their craft and when they returned me. It has to be close by though if they're watching over us but far enough away that we can't see it. There was no sensation of movement or weightlessness, so my best guess is that they're on the surface somewhere. Probably looking down at us from the rim. As for crew, there's just the two of them. Apparently, Sentinels travel in pairs and there's a special bond or link between them."

"That's useful to know if Earth allows us to go searching for the Sentinels. Ground Control may take a different view with this latest information," said Captain Winter. "'What more can you tell us about your experience on their vessel? Either about the Sentinels or their technology."

"There is so much to remember. I was too much in shock at the time to take it all in or to ask the right questions. I wasn't prepared for the encounter."

"You're now the resident alien expert," joked Winter. "I'll be ordering you to write a handbook."

"I'm not sure we'll get another chance. Bear in mind the Sentinels have been watching humans for thousands of years and what happened to me was pure chance. It makes you think about documented records of aliens throughout history. But I don't believe the Sentinels want further direct contact. They see it as contaminating our evolution."

"Yet they rescued you and then returned you to us. What did they expect?"

"They tried to wipe my mind so I wouldn't remember. I'm sure they didn't anticipate that my subconscious brain would recall some events. And my experience on *Challenger* today really kick-started my memory. I doubt Falmas would be impressed that I remember so much about them."

Redmayne spoke up again. "Maybe I was wrong yesterday. There is now enough evidence for me to believe in the existence of aliens. Thanks to you, Georgia, we finally know that we are not alone. Which is all the more reason we should go out and discover where they are, make contact, and convince them to share their technology. Imagine what a difference they could make in our society. Medical advances for a start, with you as a shining example. But also, what about the eradication of hunger? No more famine or suffering."

Georgia suspected Redmayne was trying to push his own agenda. Despite his objections earlier, he had been giving the matter a lot of thought. "Their culture doesn't view it in the same way. Maybe they don't see us as an advanced civilization. Helping us would be cheating our natural path. Falmas compared it to the tough love you might give your child. We have to learn to overcome the challenges that are affecting humans on Earth. Demonstrate that we have the capability and resolve to deal with those problems before taking the next step as a society. If we were given all that technology on a plate, with all our problems solved overnight, what would we have learned?"

Captain Winter agreed with Georgia. "You're right. Although it may seem inhuman for the Sentinels to allow people to die and struggle, those issues are of our own making. And we should be the ones to work it out. What we should take away is that there is a future in space for us if we can survive as a species. It's an ambitious goal that we should strive for."

"That's all well and good, captain," sneered Redmayne. "Tell that to the people who are needlessly suffering when there's the possibility of dealing with it overnight."

"You don't know that for sure. What other consequences may there be? How do you know for sure that the aliens' intentions are completely benign? History has shown on many occasions that the best of intentions does not always work out well for the weaker party. It will be for the politicians back home to decide what may be best for us all. You should bear that in mind."

"So, you won't be making any recommendations in your report?"

"Not that it's really your business, but I'll be stating the facts as Georgia has shared them with us. And I will be sharing some thoughts of the crew. It's important for Ground Control to understand the motivation and stress that we're going through. While I respect your opinion, it doesn't mean that I or anyone else has to accept it."

Georgia spent the next hour detailing the rest of her experiences on board the alien vessel and answering a multitude of questions from the crew, most of which she couldn't answer. There was a mixture of astonishment and fear at what they had all heard. As the session wrapped up, Winter looked around the room to assess how the crew was handling this latest development. The looks of astonishment didn't fill him with confidence. He knew he, along with Doctor Betts, would have his work cut out to ensure there was no unnecessary panic.

Chapter 50

Redmayne excitedly returned to his quarters and opened up his computer tablet. He knew that the latest confirmation that aliens existed and were on Mars would be eagerly received in orbit and back on Earth. The Russians had been seeking the last part of the puzzle, and here it was. He would now have to step up his research to discover where the alien craft was. At least he now knew what he was looking for. And Georgia's theory on the probable location made sense. If he was observing a culture and didn't want to be seen, then where better than from high on top of the cliff.

His mind filled with possibilities. When he'd applied for the mission, he had just wanted to share all the expedition's secrets with the Russians, allowing them to seize an advantage and foothold. The last thing he had expected was to discover the existence of alien life. He still couldn't quite accept the fact that they were here on Mars, watching him and the rest of Expedition Two. Or, as they had told Georgia, that they had been watching for thousands of years on Earth. But that was a clue. To have been observing humans for such a long time, the Sentinels must have some kind of stealth technology that shielded them from being observed. It may not have mattered for most of Earth's history but with the invention of telescopes, radar and the widespread use of cameras then it was reasonable to expect that the Sentinels would have been spotted in the past one hundred years.

Which meant that it wouldn't be a straightforward task to locate their craft now. If he was correct, then it wouldn't be visible to the naked eye or from standard optics. Otherwise, it would be visible from satellite imagery. Redmayne set his mind to working on possible solutions, although he couldn't ignore the fact that the Sentinels' technology was far superior to anything on Earth. It wouldn't be easy to bypass whatever they were using.

As he considered the problem, he also thought back to Georgia's revelations. He'd had so many more questions but had not wanted to arouse too much suspicion. He was confident that he could figure out some answers on his own and didn't want to give Georgia more credit than was necessary.

There was a huge part of him that was envious that Georgia had been the lucky one to be in the right place. In fact, the more he thought about it the more pissed off he became. It should have been him that made first contact. He was confident he'd have managed the situation better. He would have gotten more information out of Falmas about their technology, culture and ship. Instead, it had been Georgia. Someone with no imagination who was incapable of understanding the bigger picture. She may be an expert with computers and robotics, but that really was the extent of her skills. It was a sad waste for mankind that she had been so lucky to have the encounter.

When he was a young child growing up in Johannesburg, he'd often looked up at the stars and wondered if life existed on other worlds. To his childlike logic, it had made sense that among the millions and millions of planets in the universe there had to be other intelligent life. It would be a lonely universe otherwise. But with the Earth just a single planet on the edge of a vast galaxy he had grown up doubting he would ever have a satisfactory answer to his question.

Now the opportunity to establish contact with an alien race was within his grasp. He could feel it. And to be one of the first people to make contact was hugely important for him. No more playing second fiddle to any other scientists. He would be instantly famous, his face known around the world. The history books would forever include his name as a scientific legend, alongside the likes of Galileo, Sir Isaac Newton and Leonardo da Vinci. Mankind would forever learn about how he changed the course of human history.

Calming himself down, he composed a message to Alex updating the information on the Sentinels, detailing what Georgia had just told him and confirming he was working on discovering the Sentinels' craft. He didn't expect an immediate response as it would be the middle of the night in Moscow when the message would be received. But he knew the message would garner the highest attention.

Chapter 51

Redmayne left Alpha Base unnoticed early the next morning while the others were having breakfast. He was not a regular in the common room at mealtimes and so his absence wasn't seen as unusual. Carrying a small spare air supply and two cameras, he took one of the speeders from its charging mount and headed out in the direction of *Endeavour*.

The sun had only recently risen above the far rim of the crater. A few fine wisps of cloud at high altitude managed to soften the effects of the rays. Much like the rest of the crew, he had become accustomed to the sun appearing far smaller than it did on Earth. Long shadows played in front of him and a fine layer of mist coated the surface that created an eerie quality as he sped out onto the plain but would clear as the sun heated the ground.

Half a mile short of *Endeavour*, Redmayne swiftly changed direction and headed toward *Eden*. He was confident that no one would be watching him. During his time in Moscow, he had been trained to hide his tracks. He could never be too careful. His excursion was filed as scientific research in case anyone questioned where he was.

Redmayne was keen to test his theory on how the Sentinels avoided detection with a dampening field. Working late into the night, he had calculated how to oscillate the amplitude of light that could be detected by a series of sensors. It would be a simple matter of attaching the modified sensors to one of the science drones stored on *Eden* and flying it above the rim of the crater. If Georgia was correct, the Sentinels' craft couldn't be too far from the edge and within three miles from the point exactly above Alpha Base.

The sensors hadn't been built with his plan in mind, and the modifications took much longer than expected. It was shortly after lunch when, sitting in his lab aboard *Eden*, he was finally happy that he had securely attached the sensors to the drone and would work as he wanted. Checking the time, he estimated there was still sufficient daylight that day if he hurried to launch the drone.

He went to his old science lab on the ship to retrieve a controller. Five minutes later, the drone flew out of the hold door and sped rapidly toward the sheer cliff face, gaining altitude as fast as it could. Through his VR headset, Redmayne had a perfect view from the drone's twin cameras. He slowed its assent as it approached the rim and carefully rose several feet, turning the drone slowly left and then right for any sign of the alien ship.

With the plateau looking as barren as Hellas plain, offering no clues to the location of the Sentinels, he tried his luck and headed west, checking all the time for any trace of the ship.

His gamble soon paid off and several minutes later he spotted the telltale shimmer of the dampening field and, within it, the unmistakable lines of an alien craft standing out against the rugged Martian landscape.

This is too easy, he thought smugly. He lowered the drone to within ten feet of the ground and hovered in the same spot, looking for any sign of action or response to his presence. After one minute, there was no change, so he edged the drone forward very slowly, making sure that he was recording everything he could see. When the drone was within fifty feet of the alien craft, static interference started making the image blur and freeze. He immediately decided he was too close and backed the drone away until the image improved. Satisfied the drone was back at a safe distance, he carefully circled the craft. It appeared to be a smooth, metallic wedge about two hundred feet long, with several bulges randomly placed alongside the side. There were also some strange markings that he didn't recognize. Probably their language, he determined. Most surprising for Tom was that he couldn't see any windows, doors or obvious means of propulsion.

This is incredible, he thought. If we can access this craft and replicate its technology, the future for humanity will be changed. The Americans are crazy to give this up so easily. The Russians will know what to do with this technology and will most likely rule the world with it. Perhaps they will give me all the credit and make me a hero. I'll be able to call more of the shots with Alex from now on.

As there had been no response to the drone's presence, he raised its altitude to get a better view of the ship from above. From this perspective, it intrigued him to see that the alien craft looked like a gigantic droplet laid on its side. It was like some sort of optical illusion and his mind couldn't understand how the design could do that.

Redmayne was now impatient to see inside the craft, but he still had not found the entrance. That would have to wait for another day, and he knew he had taken too many chances already. It was time for the drone to return. He had to get back to the base before darkness fell.

He waited ten minutes for the drone to return, recovered the detectors and, satisfied with his day's work, sped back to the base just as the sun sank behind the crater rim for another day. That was cutting it finer than he'd planned but he was able to park the speeder, access through the airlock and return to his lab without bumping into anyone.

Chapter 52

Captain Winter called Commander Anders to his room for their daily briefing session. Winter was surprised that Anders was several minutes late. He was normally so punctual.

"Is anything wrong, Lars? You look on edge today."

"Yes, I'm good thanks, sir. I just didn't sleep well. It's a bit discomforting knowing that we're being secretly observed by an advanced civilization. I know how a lab rat feels now. What's the update from Earth?"

Winter knew there was more to Anders' mood than met the eye, but he let it pass. He was sure Anders would speak with him when he was ready. "No change as regards our Sentinel neighbors. General Stockton has acknowledged that aliens probably do exist, but the only advice is to proceed with caution, whatever that means in practice. The protocols remain in place while the United Nations decides how to inform the public without causing a mass panic."

"Surely this news can't stay private for long. It's bound to leak sooner rather than later."

"Agreed. But I imagine the politicians cannot decide among themselves what to do. They're probably trying to work out how they can benefit from this discovery. Most nations will want to be the first to start a relationship with an alien race. Or, at the very least, prevent any other country from being first. I can't begin to conceive the advantage a single country would have."

"There's enough tension already. I can see one side forcing the issue to gain that advantage."

Winter nodded. "We may be in the best place for the time being," he said ruefully. "I don't want to be in the middle of any conflicts. Just as long as they launch the next supply ships. Hopefully, it will get sorted out peacefully, but I don't hold out much hope at the moment. How's the crew holding up, by the way? You spend a lot of time with them. Are they concerned?"

"They're doing well as far as I can tell. Handling the news professionally and getting on with their tasks. The crew needs some time to adjust to the base, and some stability for a while. I'm willing to take on more responsibility to ensure the crew is adequately supported."

"Thanks, Lars. For the time being, however, I want you focused on rectifying the snag list on the base. Use Rashid and Grace. Maybe include Emily. No doubt her injury is driving her mad. There must be something useful she can do inside that will keep her busy."

"But you know that I can do so much more than that. I can't understand why you're holding me back."

The sudden outburst shocked Winter. "Commander, I have no doubts about your ability. For now, though, I've given you orders which are determined by the necessities of the base. I expect them to be carried out. I hope I'm making myself clear."

"Very, captain." Commander Anders stiffly saluted and left the room, staring straight ahead.

That wasn't like Anders at all, Winter thought. He's not been himself lately but that may be simply down to stress. Winter made a mental note to speak with Doctor Betts on the subject. Maybe she could have a talk with Lars and discover if anything was wrong.

***

At that same time, Redmayne had his own concerns to address. The response from Alex was not one he had expected. Someone in the Russian camp either had a warped sense of humor or they were seriously overestimating his skills. Although he had the utmost confidence in his own abilities, this was going to be the ultimate challenge for him. The location of the Sentinel craft was no longer enough. The Russians wanted to know they would have access to the craft when they landed.

Tom was disappointed that he had not anticipated this request. Once the Russians committed to a landing on the plateau so close to Alpha Base, there would be an international outcry. Time would be of the essence to control the situation, which meant there would be no time to waste attempting to contact the Sentinels and gain access. There was also the probability that the Sentinels could relocate their craft. Finding them again would be like looking for a needle in a haystack with the Russian lander forced to return to the *Andropov*.

He sat at his science station, absently tapping a pen on the corner of the desk, working out in his mind how he could regain control of the situation. He was not sure what options he had. He doubted the Russians would expose him if he refused to help or failed in his attempt unless they decided he was no longer a valuable asset. His strong position was now looking more tenuous.

Reaching the plateau, five miles straight up, was the easy part. A two-person jetcopter was stowed on *Aquarius* for surveying the terrain outside the crater. He was sure that it hadn't yet been unloaded though and knew he would require the help of someone else as the jetcopter was large and unwieldy.

The only person likely to assist him was probably Commander Anders, but it was a dangerous game he was playing. Taking the jetcopter was a one-way ticket; he'd never be able to offer an adequate explanation to Captain Winter. That stakes were that high. He would have to succeed and join the Russians or fail and be confined to quarters for the rest of the mission. He knew which option he preferred.

The tough part was figuring out how to convince the Sentinels to welcome him aboard. That required further thought and careful planning. But the rewards for success would be immense. He was convincing himself that such rewards far exceeded the risk of failure.

Redmayne discovered Commander Anders in the common room, reading some reports on his tablet device while eating a protein bar. "Lars, have you got a few minutes?" he asked.

Anders put down the tablet on the table in front of him. "Yes, Tom. If it's urgent"

"It is. I've been giving a lot of thought to the aliens. I'm really concerned about the safety of all of us. Don't you think it's reckless of the captain to not carry out some level of reconnaissance so we know where we can go. It's as if we're walking around in blindfolds when we could bump into an alien at any moment. We still don't know for sure if they're hostile or friendly."

Anders nodded in agreement with Redmayne's sentiment. "I spoke with the captain about this earlier. Neither he nor General Stockton are overly concerned and aren't willing to do anything. To me, they simply don't have a plan and instead are happy to stick their heads in the sand. By the time they do decide, it will be too late."

Pleased that the commander didn't agree with the passive approach being taken by the captain, Redmayne saw there was an opportunity to manipulate those misgivings. "You saw how the captain rejected my suggestions out of hand last night. There was no need for the stance he took."

"Yes, I noticed. I tried to support you, but Captain Winter was having none of it. And now he's side-lined me, giving me the snag list to resolve instead of more important tasks. He could have given this job to the chief or even Rashid."

Redmayne nodded, knowingly. He looked around the room furtively to make sure no one was in earshot before saying in a low voice, "I don't know about you, Lars, but I've seen how the captain speaks to you and the jobs you're assigned. You're clearly not the favorite."

"I'm sure that's not true. Everyone on this expedition has an equal say." The commander didn't sound convinced, so Redmayne twisted the knife.

"Is that what you really believe? Captain Winter keeps Georgia close, along with the chief and the doctor. They were the people who knew about Georgia's dreams and suspicions before you were told. Even Joe Mancuso gets the plum jobs. You saw in the meeting that they spoke with one voice. Winter didn't listen to either of us. You're supposed to be second in command and I'm chief scientist. He should give us both more respect than he does."

"Tom, I can see you're frustrated. We have to trust that the captain is doing the right thing. He won't let anyone come to harm."

"Your loyalty is admirable. How can you know for sure we're safe? Georgia has nearly died twice, and we were all at risk because of the asteroid strike. It was only thanks to you that this base was operational in time to save us. I'm not sure if the captain is up for the task. He's counting down the days to his retirement."

The commander looked frantically around to ensure no one was listening to their conversation, before whispering, "I hope you're not suggesting mutiny. This is the twenty-first century, not the eighteenth. You can't take over the ship and leave the captain marooned on a passing moon."

"That isn't what I'm saying," replied Redmayne. "But I am convinced you would be a stronger leader than Winter. You're younger and have more ambition, I'm sure. I trust you far more."

"You'll find out if you can wait for the next crew rotation."

"Yes, but that may be too late for us! I simply believe we need a different approach with the Sentinels. It wouldn't hurt to find out a little more about them. Who knows when our next opportunity will be to encounter aliens? Perhaps not during our lifetime. Maybe you could go down as the person brave enough to make contact. Georgia doesn't count as her encounter was accidental."

Anders thought about it for a moment. Redmayne could tell he'd struck a chord and that the commander had a secret desire to see his name be immortalized. "What would you say if I told you I have discovered the location of the Sentinels' ship?"

Anders' mouth flopped open. "I would say that's impossible. How could you possibly do that? We thought they camouflaged it to avoid detection."

"I am chief scientist for a reason, Lars," Redmayne replied smugly. It is hidden by a form of cloaking technology. But I sent out a drone yesterday with some modified sensors. And I found it!"

"You did what?" Anders was incredulous. "That was incredibly stupid. And against explicit orders."

"Nothing's happened so far, so I got away with it."

Anders' shock quickly turned to suspicion. "Why are you telling me this now? You could have kept the information to yourself. Or shared it directly with the captain and let him decide what to do."

Maybe he wasn't as gullible as Redmayne thought, but without skipping a beat he replied, "Because I need you for the next step. And I'd like you to help me make contact with the Sentinels. Their craft is up on the ridge and the only way to get to it is with the jetcopter. I was hoping you'd help set it up with me and then we can go for a test flight."

"I'm not so sure about that. It's a big step and it would leave us exposed if the Sentinels spot us. Let me give it some thought."

"Thanks, Lars. That's all I could ask for. The last thing I want is for you to do something you're uncomfortable with. Although I'm sure it will be viewed well on your record if you establish more details about the aliens or save crew members." Redmayne decided to stop there. Pleased with himself, he left Anders to his thoughts. He'd planted enough seeds, but he couldn't push Anders any further.

***

Georgia had been running on the treadmill for about fifteen minutes when Jim walked in ready to start his own workout. She removed her headphones and smiled at him, as he dropped his towel on the weight bench and started his warm-up exercises. "Are you following me?" she asked.

"Would it be a bad thing if I was?" he replied with a wink. "It's far more fun exercising with a friend."

"Ah, is that what I am now? A friend. What was I before?"

Jim flinched. She was always too quick for him. "You were a colleague. Now I've promoted you. You should be honored. I don't have many true friends."

"I do feel honored to be in such an exclusive club. Now stop stretching and get running with me. Friend."

They spent the next thirty minutes continuing their friendly banter as they ran together. They were so absorbed in each other they hadn't noticed how much time had passed until Georgia's timer rang out. By now, her body was flushed, and she wasn't sure if it was from the exercise or Jim's close proximity. Either way, she knew that she was enjoying his company and didn't want it to end.

She stepped from the treadmill and tried her luck. "I'm in need a shower after that run. Care to join me?"

Jim was clearly surprised by Georgia's sudden request but quickly recovered his composure and stopped his machine. Giving her a big smile, he said, "Why not? I can always run again tomorrow." He collected his towel and followed Georgia to the shower room.

Chapter 53

Redmayne was awake early again. He still didn't know whether his plan would succeed, but he had to start as soon as possible. He was sure he'd said enough to convince Commander Anders. But Anders was a weak man and, therefore, not entirely reliable.

The significant issue of accessing the Sentinel craft also still needed to be addressed. He had hoped for some divine intervention to help guide him to an answer but, as yet, he was sadly disappointed. He climbed out of bed and crept down the corridor for a quick shower, hoping it might invigorate him for the day ahead.

Once showered and dressed, he made his way to the control room where, as expected, Anders was checking on the latest instructions received from Ground Control overnight. The commander looked up from his computer screen and gave Tom a suspicious look as he entered the room.

"Good morning, Lars," said Redmayne in his most friendly tone. "I trust you slept well. Have you given any more thought to our conversation yesterday?"

Anders frowned. "I knew it wouldn't take you long to chase me for an answer. Yes, I've had some time to consider your suggestion and, weighing it up against the interests of the crew, you have my approval and my assistance."

"Thank you. That means a lot to me. I know you won't regret it."

"I hope that I won't. This could go badly for both of us if we're not careful."

"So, you'll help me offload the jetcopter this morning."

"I've been checking the daily tasks and I've nothing that can't wait or be delegated. The same for you. The question in my mind is what you intend to do once you reach the ridge line?"

Tom hesitated before responding, not sure how Anders would react to his next suggestion. "That's a really good question. I want to try to make contact with the Sentinels. They don't appear to be aggressive so I'm hopeful that any risk is very small."

"Wow, I didn't expect that so soon. Although I guess I should have expected that, coming from you. You've never been backward at coming forward."

"What did you think? If I just wanted to monitor them, I could have used the drone to place sensor equipment! No, this is a moment for bold leadership. Are you up for that challenge, commander?"

Secretly, Anders wasn't sure that he was. But the lure of making history was very attractive. And the risk was worthwhile. If successful, how could he be court-martialed for failing to follow orders. He'd be a public hero, celebrated by billions. "Okay, let's do it. Do you expect the Sentinels to respond? They may just ignore our requests for contact. Have you given that any thought?"

"Very perceptive. That's what I've always admired about you, Lars. You can always detect the key issues before anyone else." Tom was fairly sure he wasn't going over the top with his praise. "I have given it some thought, but still don't have an answer. To be honest, I don't really know what to expect. But we should give it a try."

Anders was flattered that Redmayne could see his qualities. "It would be best if we have some kind of plan ahead of the game. Other than knowing the location of their craft, we'll be traveling blind. Have you considered speaking with Georgia? As the only person who's spoken with the Sentinels and been inside their ship, maybe she'll have an insight."

"I don't want to get too many people involved and raise suspicions. Georgia wouldn't help us, anyway."

"You're probably right. It's a shame because she is the only real link we have to the Sentinels. If only there was a way to convince her to help."

That gave Tom the seeds of an idea. Anders was right. Georgia was their best and only hope of contacting the Sentinels. They would hopefully recognize her from their previous encounter and allow her access. The issue was how to get Georgia in the right place at the right time. It would not be easy and would involve making her do something against her will, but desperate times called for desperate measures.

"Leave that with me, Lars. I'll meet you at *Aquarius* at eleven o'clock."

Chapter 54

At the daily team briefing in the common room, Winter completed his update to the crew and requested that Commander Anders assign the task list for the day. Once all tasks had been allocated, Winter finished the meeting by asking if anyone had any questions.

Doctor Betts was the first one to raise her hand. "Sir, don't you find it strange that we've still had no further guidance on what to do with the Sentinels?"

"Good question, Megan. Normally, I would agree with you, but the major powers have more significant problems to deal with close to home. As I understand it, tensions have flared in the South China Sea with the Chinese and American navies facing off. Unsurprisingly, the Russians are supporting China and accusing President Foley of warmongering. Added to that, there have been food riots across parts of southern Europe and an increased number of power outages across Africa, Japan and India. So, while the issue may be close to our hearts, I'm afraid it's way down the list of priorities on Earth."

Megan nodded. "That makes sense globally. I expected more of a response from General Stockton. Discovering new intelligent life is a potential game changer for everyone."

"Exactly. But as far as Ground Control is concerned, they have the situation contained from the public and can choose when to provide further guidance."

"It sounds as if it's the wrong time to go public. It's already a potential powder keg back home!" added Mancuso. "Imagine throwing aliens into the mix."

"I can't see there being an all-out war," replied Winter. "But there's plenty of instability at the moment. The Chinese have been threatening to show they're a power to be reckoned with for some time. They may have Russian support, but I don't know how keen the Russians would be to get dragged into a war between East and West."

Anders shook his head. "They wouldn't get a choice if all hell kicked off. They'd have to back the Chinese."

"Okay, guys," interrupted Winter. "We could debate this all day. Are there any more questions before we get on with our duties?"

Harry King stood up and asked. "Captain? Talking of the Russians and Chinese, do we know what's happening with the *Andropov*? It's been in orbit for a week now. Do we know what they're doing or when and where they'll be landing?"

"Ground Control are in the dark. The only news coming out of Moscow and Beijing is that they're carrying out in-orbit tests and reconnaissance. There was the delay for the asteroid which made sense at the time although to be honest I'm surprised that they've not landed already. But as always, they're keeping their cards close to their chest. I doubt we'll know their plans until they've landed."

Georgia added, "Don't you find it strange to come all this way and then wait for days on end? They already have a landing site with their own cargo ships and equipment in place. Are they waiting for something else to happen?"

Redmayne, keen to change the subject, asked, "Like what, Georgia? There's no delivery service out here." His attempt at humor fell flat, but he continued anyway. "They may have some kind of technical issues with their landers and don't want to risk any of the crew. I sincerely doubt they would publicize the fact that they have any malfunctions."

Captain Winter stepped in. "Okay, that's enough for now. There's plenty to do. Commander, do you have all the assistance you need today?"

Anders cast a quick look at Redmayne before replying, "I could do with borrowing Georgia this morning. I'm heading out to *Aquarius* to check on the construction robots we'll be using on the facade. I know that's a few weeks away, but I want to get ahead with ensuring the robots are fully functional. We may even be able to get them working on a few other tasks."

His request surprised Georgia. This was the first that she'd heard of the construction robots being needed so soon. They were her babies though, so it made sense for the commander to require her help. It might also give her the opportunity to get to know him better. She'd not spent much time with him, and he often acted awkwardly around the female members of the crew. Several hours with him would give her a chance to understand him better, and maybe to share some of her ideas with him.

"Jim, is that alright?" she checked. "You don't need me today?"

"You don't need my permission," he laughed. "I'm sure I'll survive just fine without you."

Chapter 55

Redmayne watched the MEV drive away from the base with Anders and Georgia on board. He felt a knot in his stomach as he accepted that there would soon be no going back from his course of action. Despite his concerns about whether Anders would pull through, he'd had no other choice but to rely on the commander.

His mind was still working on a plan to contact the Sentinels. The more he thought about the problem, the more convinced he became that Georgia was the key to making it happen.

Redmayne had already determined that for his devious plot to work he needed to create a distraction that would delay the crew. This would allow Anders the time to unload and start assembling the jetcopter with the unwitting help of Georgia and allow time to reach *Aquarius* undetected. This was an aspect he had thought through in detail overnight and had then required some work in his lab to manufacture what he needed.

The biodome was attached to the base at the rear of the cave, and therefore furthest away from the external airlock. It would be the perfect spot to trap as many people as possible, ensuring no one would see him departing. He allowed himself a moment of satisfaction at being so resourceful. Rising to the challenge imposed by Alex was proving to be fun.

Making his way swiftly through the base, Redmayne was soon through the connecting tunnel to the biodome. The lighting here was harsh, and it took several moments for his eyes to adjust. The moisture in the air was clammy compared to the air-conditioned environment of the base. It reminded him of a forest after a heavy rain shower and he had a sudden urge to be back on Earth.

Putting that thought quickly to one side, he found Harry and Nicola King tending to the plants in the aquaponics bays. "Good morning, Harry," he said cheerfully. "How are the seedlings coming on? You have an amazing setup here."

Harry looked up, surprised. "Tom? You've not been in here before. We're making steady progress. The majority of the plants have traveled well and coped with transplanting from *Eden*. It won't be too long before we have a small crop and can start eating fresh vegetables rather than the processed mush we've had to endure."

"That's fantastic news." Redmayne feigned enthusiasm, while his eyes darted around scanning the area. "I'll let the two of you get back to work. I just came down to check on your amazing work."

"Thanks. We're really proud of what we're achieving here. I'm sure we can make the base become sustainable." It was clear that Harry wanted to start a conversation, but Redmayne was in a hurry and had seen what he needed.

There was a small gray fuse box just inside the biodome. He must have walked straight past it as his eyes adjusted to the glare. With the multiple lights, heaters and aquaponic equipment, the biodome will be drawing a lot of power, he thought.

Making sure that he wasn't being watched by the Kings, he walked across to the fuse box before pulling a small device, about the size of a matchbox, from his pocket. He deftly opened the fuse box, slipped in the device, and wedged it between two cables. Satisfied the device was securely in place, he sealed the fuse box before closing the door. Then, satisfied he made his way swiftly back to the science lab.

Redmayne had set a timer on the device. He now had ten minutes to gather all that he needed and make his way to the main airlock. He had calculated that would give him more than sufficient time before all hell broke loose.

However, he hadn't factored in Grace who was in the lab, looking at a research paper on the computer screen. This was all that he needed. He looked at his own computer and was relieved to see that there were no messages waiting for him. "What can I do for you?" he snapped.

Startled, her head jerked up to look at him. "I was just checking on the specifications for the Sabatier Reactor for Rashid. He says he can improve the efficiency," she replied nervously. "Perhaps you can help?"

"Not now, Grace. I've got far more important things to work on. Can't this wait?" Redmayne looked at his watch, anxious to get away.

"The captain was happy for me to do the research. Maybe I can help you instead, if you like."

That was the last thing he wanted. "No, it's okay. Carry on, but touch nothing of mine. I have some expensive equipment here." Before Grace could reply, he picked up the few items he needed and headed to his quarters for the communicator.

Frustrated that he had wasted too much time, he hurried from his quarters without a second glance knowing he wouldn't be returning.

Redmayne avoided anyone else in the corridor and reached the airlock just as the device in the biodome activated.

The device he had left contained two volatile chemicals that had been kept in separate vials. At that moment, the vials snapped, combining the chemicals causing an instant thermal, chemical reaction. The heat was so intense that the device exploded, ripping through some cabling in the fuse box. Although the explosion was small and contained, its effects were dramatic.

Power was immediately cut to the biodome. The lights went out and all the equipment stopped, leaving the Kings in an ominous pitch-black silence.

"What's happened?" said Nicola, a trace of panic in her voice.

"Some sort of power failure," replied Harry, sounding calm. "Just stay where you are. The emergency supply should kick in almost immediately."

Harry wasn't to know that the emergency supply had also been damaged by the explosion. Acrid smoke was now pouring from the fuse box, setting off an alarm and causing the fire seal to close off the biodome from the rest of the base.

Captain Winter was in the control room when the alarms sounded, informing him that there was an emergency in the facility. The computer schematic in front of him showed that the issue was in the biodome, but he was unable to raise the Kings.

Over the internal Comms system, he ordered, "Emergency in the biodome. All hands meet me there."

This was exactly the outcome Redmayne wanted. He slipped into his spacesuit at the airlock and exited the base. Within a minute he was on a speeder making his way toward *Aquarius* and thrilled that his plan was working out so well.

Chapter 56

It wasn't working out so well for the Kings. To Harry's surprise and dismay, they were still in darkness over a minute after the power had failed. He knew that something was seriously wrong.

Nicola had been silent, waiting for the lights to come back on but was freaking out. "I can smell smoke!" she suddenly screamed out.

Harry could smell it too and he fought hard to control the panic that was rising inside him. A fire would be catastrophic and potentially life-threatening. "Nikki, talk to me. I'll come to you and follow the sound of your voice. You need to stay calm. I'm sure Captain Winter is on his way with help."

"Harry, I'm scared. I don't want to die. We could suffocate in here if there's a fire. Where are you?"

Harry touched her arm, making her jump. "I'm right next to you. We're not going to die. There are enough emergency procedures in place to keep us safe."

The sounds of the door being opened suddenly broke the silence before Captain Winter's voice rang out. "Harry? Nicola? Are you in here?"

"Yes, captain. We're at the rear of the biodome but we can't see anything. There's smoke, so there may be a fire."

"Okay, stay there. We'll come and get you." Two beams of light shone across the room, eerily silhouetting the plants and equipment. The captain and Doctor Betts hurried through the biodome, flashlights in hand. "It looks like there was a short circuit in your fuse box," Captain Winter said. "It must have taken out the backup as well. That's where the smoke is coming from but there's no risk of fire. I'm sure the chief will soon have it fixed."

"Thanks, sir. We were worried there for a few minutes. It's no fun being trapped in complete darkness. I hope we can get power on quickly for the sake of the plants."

"I suggest you take a break until then. Megan, would you care to take them for a drink in the galley?"

"Just what the doctor ordered," she replied.

***

Winter escorted Megan and the Kings out of the biodome, stopping next to the charred fuse box. The chief had the door open and was examining the insides. "There's extensive damage. Much of the cabling and trunking has been destroyed. We'll need a replacement box as well as to swap out some of the power cables."

"That's no small job. How long is it likely to take?"

"The rest of the day. But there's something else. There are clear signs of a chemical reaction and fragments that don't belong in that box. It looks as if it is deliberate."

Winter stood up and took in a deep breath. "It was sabotage? I can't believe anyone would do that. Or why!"

"I can't answer that. I'll send Rashid for the replacement parts while I carry out a few more tests to confirm my suspicions."

"Get it done. I have to report this immediately. Ground Control need to know."

Chapter 57

Georgia's time with Commander Anders in the MEV was not helping her change her perception of him. If anything, it was confirming her view that there was something strange about the man. As soon as she had entered the cabin to set off from the base, he had been nervous and fidgety.

She had spent much of the past few months with Captain Winter and Jim. Both of them were strong, resolute men. Capable leaders and charismatic. Anders was almost entirely the opposite. To be fair, he was an excellent organizer and had ensured Alpha Base was built early. But he hadn't convinced her that he was a leader. He tried too hard to be liked and, for her, that was a fundamental flaw. However, she knew she was stuck with him for the foreseeable future on Mars.

As the MEV sped from the cave into sunlight, she started a conversation, hoping that he may open up to her. "Commander, how are you settling into life on Mars? Is it what you expected?"

Anders continued to look out of the front canopy at the landscape as he spoke. "It's exactly as I imagined. Barren and inhospitable. But I was prepared for every eventuality. I think it's important to be able to quickly adapt to your surroundings."

Georgia was intrigued by his statement. "In training, they always taught us to be ready for the unexpected. But then, no one had ever landed on Mars. The only information was what the various landers provided. We've done very well since we arrived."

"I wasn't referring just to the environment, Georgia. We also have to adapt to the circumstances and even the people around us. I thought you would know that, especially after what you've endured in recent days. You're a perfect example of someone able to adapt and survive."

His comment stung Georgia. It was personal and unexpected. "So, according to your logic, everyone needs to adapt or die? Do you begrudge the fact that I survived cancer?"

"Of course not. I simply believe some people find it difficult to deal with whatever is thrown at them. That doesn't mean they're less capable than you or I. But it may make it harder for them and affect others around them."

It was clear to Georgia that Anders had someone in mind, but he wasn't going to name that person. She was sure he was talking about the captain though. She had seen how Anders had butted heads with him several times in team meetings. Especially lately. She changed the subject as the MEV continued to speed across the Martian surface.

"You said that you wanted to evaluate my construction robots. What tasks did you have in mind for them? I can program them to do many tasks, although they're designed mainly to build the main structure at the entrance to the base. I wasn't aware of any other urgent activities for them."

There was a long pause and Georgia was thinking he had not heard her. He wasn't the easiest person to have a conversation with. She was about to repeat her question when he finally replied. "I want to advance the construction. But before I make the recommendation, I thought it would be a useful exercise to unpack and inspect them. Because we'll have to unpack the jetcopter to access your robots, it may be worth assembling that at the same time."

That prospect raised Georgia's suspicions. What was Anders really up to? She wasn't aware of any valid reason to use the jetcopter now. There was enough work to establish the base before venturing further afield. The drones were sufficient to cover a large area around the base should the scientists wish to carry out any research. The only reason to use the jetcopter was to fly up over the edge of the crater.

And, as far as she knew, there were no intentions to do that within the next three months.

Unless you wanted to go Sentinel spotting. Anders wasn't the type to make such a radical decision on his own though. Or to go against the orders sent from Earth. Something else was going on here that she was unaware of.

She decided to not push the matter for the time being and instead let it play out. She was sure she would discover the truth soon enough. The rest of the journey to *Aquarius* continued in silence with neither of them wanting to do or say anything that may arouse the other's suspicions.

Chapter 58

As they ascended the side of *Aquarius* in the cradle, Georgia stared into the distance back toward the base. It appeared so far away from here, with several of the ships acting almost as markers between her and what was now home. She was still trying to work out what Anders was really up to and why he had brought her with him. The whole situation was making her uncomfortable.

In the distance she noticed a small plume of dust rising above the landscape. She recognized it as the distinctive sign of someone driving a speeder quickly across the landscape. Whoever was riding the speeder was heading in their direction and she estimated would arrive within the next ten to fifteen minutes.

"Are you expecting anyone else to assist us?" she asked, pointing at the dust cloud.

Anders was evasive. "No one in particular. But they may be after urgent parts on one of the other cargo ships."

His answer didn't convince Georgia. She could tell that Anders was lying, and she knew she had to get back to Alpha Base. But how?

Once inside the cargo hold, she waited for her opportunity. All she needed was to distract Anders and she could make her way back to the MEV and find out what the hell was really going on. Once the lights were switched on, she could see how full they had packed *Aquarius*. She had not been inside this ship since it had been sealed on Earth and had forgotten how much equipment had been loaded.

Her three construction robots, together with various building attachments and spare parts were located on the first level. They were humanoid, standing six feet tall, although their legs and arms could extend for greater reach They resulted from many years of research into robotics. For the construction phase of the mission, where much of the work would be performed on the Martian surface, the robots were a safer option than the crew. There was the constant danger of damage to spacesuits from sharp building materials and tools that could quickly kill an astronaut or render them unconscious. Robots were sturdier with replaceable components. They could also operate at night when it was too cold for the astronauts.

Georgia had been closely involved with their development for five years. One of her main roles on the mission was to maintain the robots, ensuring they completed their primary tasks. They would then be re-purposed to perform other potentially hazardous jobs.

Because the robots were connected to the ship's power supply for the journey to Mars, Georgia was confident they would be fully charged and ready to go at her command.

However, Anders wasn't immediately interested in testing out the robots. His eyes were firmly focused on the jetcopter. Because of its size, it was on the main level of the hold but, contrary to what Anders had said, was not causing an obstruction.

"I'd like to get the jetcopter out now," he said. "It will be easier to test on the ground. Georgia, can you give me a hand with the winch mechanism?"

"I thought we were here for the construction robots. I'd like to take a look at them and make sure they survived the landing. That is what we're here for after all."

"Of course it is. But the jetcopter is going to take longer to of-fload. I want it done first." Anders' tone suddenly changed as he exerted his authority.

He didn't faze Georgia. "You know, I've been thinking about the urgency to unpack the jetcopter. The captain has never mentioned using it since we landed. I know its main purpose is to allow us to travel up to the plateau. And there's something else bothering me."

"Pyke, we don't have time for this. Just follow my orders."

"Not once have you asked me any questions about the Sentinels or my time with them. I know you want to, but you've avoided the subject. Why is that?"

"I don't know what you're talking about."

"You don't want the construction robots at all. You plan to seek the Sentinels and you need me to help you. I'm not prepared to do that." Georgia defiantly made her way back to the cradle, intent on heading back to the MEV.

Anders quickly stepped in front of her, grabbing her arm tightly. He was six inches taller than her and used his bulk to prevent her from moving forward. "Wait! You don't know what you're talking about."

Georgia looked him squarely in the eyes. "Let go of me now, commander. I'm going back to Alpha to talk about this with Captain Winter. Your behavior is out of order. Let me through."

Reflexively, Anders released his grip. "Okay, just hear me out. You're right. The plan is to take the jetcopter up over the ridge. Tom wants to contact the Sentinels. To ensure that it is safe for us here but also to take our first steps in communicating with an advanced alien species. He's the one on his way here now."

"Are you mad? The captain would never sanction this. And the Sentinels don't want to make contact. They made it clear that their role is purely as passive observers. They'll avoid any interaction with us."

"That's your opinion. We could miss out on an amazing opportunity for mankind. The captain is playing it safe, listening to politicians who have no idea what it is like out here. You can be part of the brave new world, Georgia. You're young and intelligent. Surely you can see how cooperation would help Earth and solve many of the problems that people are facing. Even save lives."

"I don't know what Tom has been saying to you. But you're making a huge number of assumptions. Do you really believe the public is ready for this news? And are you prepared to force the Sentinels to do something that is against their beliefs? How would that make us look in front of the many other alien civilizations out there in the universe? How do you know that all of them are friendly? You need to consider your actions carefully. It can't just be your decision or Tom's."

"I have thought about this a lot, Georgia. More than you know. I trust Tom to not screw this up. We'll be cautious. And if the Sentinels aren't prepared to talk with us, then we'll leave it. I'm trying to keep the crew safe. I want to show how it should be done."

"I'm not sure this is the right way. Let's go back to Alpha and talk this through sensibly."

"The time for talking is over. If we don't do this now, then someone else will. Why do you think the Russians or Chinese haven't landed yet? I'm sure they're making their own plans to make contact. Do you want either of those nations to have direct access to alien tech? Can you imagine what they'll do with it?"

They hadn't noticed that Redmayne had made his way up in the cradle. He was now silhouetted against the door of the hold, with the tall brown cliff behind him.

"Georgia, I see that you don't agree with our plan," he said in a mocking tone.

She turned angrily to face him. "This sounds like your doing. The commander doesn't have the balls do this on his own."

"You're wrong. Lars has very progressive views on this subject. He wants to benefit mankind as much as I do. I'm surprised you're not more supportive."

"I agree with the concept. What I object to is the reckless way it's being implemented by the pair of you. You know that you'll both be court-martialed for this. The captain won't accept insubordination."

"We'll see," said Redmayne. "But we're wasting time. Commander we need to get the jetcopter set up while we still have time."

Georgia didn't like where this was going. "Can I go now? I won't help you."

"Oh, but you will. You're the key that will give us access to the Sentinels. You'll be coming with us." Redmayne pulled a six-inch knife from the bag he was holding, its metal blade glinting in the beam from one of the overhead lights. "Somewhat primitive but it could puncture your suit if you don't co-operate."

Anders wasn't prepared for this latest development. "What are you doing, Tom? You don't have my permission to commit any violence. We're doing this to save lives, not threaten the crew. Put the knife away."

"It's okay, Lars. No one will get hurt. I know what I'm doing. Georgia, I am truly disappointed that you don't share the same opinion as I do. Afterwards, you'll see that I am right."

Georgia took a pace toward Redmayne. "I doubt that very much. And I really don't like being threatened."

"I thought it was the only way to grab your attention. Now, I really am sorry, but we are going to have to detain you. It's in your best interests to prevent you from doing something you'll regret."

Redmayne bent down and pulled on the access panel at his feet. The small door in the floor swung open, revealing a series of steps that led down to the engineering section of the ship. There was little space down there, but it provided access to the rocket engines in case of any problems.

"If you don't mind. I'd prefer it if I knew where you were for the time being," he said, waving his knife to indicate he wanted her to take the steps down to the space below.

Bewildered, she looked around at Anders for some support. She was sure this wasn't what he wanted.

"I'm sorry, Georgia," he said resignedly. "You should do as Tom says. I promise you won't be harmed but we need time to prepare the jetcopter."

Outnumbered and with little option, Georgia reluctantly stepped through the access door and down into the engineering section. As Redmayne closed the hatch behind her, she switched her helmet light on and found somewhere to sit to contemplate her fate.

Chapter 59

Back inside Alpha Base, the chief entered the control room in search of Captain Winter. Mancuso was laid on the floor under a desk, running cables while Emily, still on crutches, stood over him holding the cabling layout. She turned and asked, "How bad is it down there, Jim?"

"Not as bad as it first looked. The soot and melted plastic were quite dramatic, but it's a simple job of swapping out the box. Rashid will get it done in the next few hours."

Mancuso stopped what he was doing and sat up. "I feared the worst when I heard the alarms going off. Thank goodness no one was hurt."

The chief agreed. "You can thank the designers for implementing many safety measures. Have you seen the captain?"

"He's in his quarters."

Jim headed down the corridor and knocked on Winter's door.

"Good timing, Jim. Come in and take a seat."

"Thank you. I can confirm that the fire was caused deliberately. Someone planted a small chemical device on a timer. The chemicals were highly combustible when mixed. There's no way this was an accident."

The chief noted that the captain didn't appear shocked by the news. "That confirms the report I've just received from General Stockton in response to this matter. Ground Control picked up some encrypted transmissions between this base and the *Andropov*. Not through our own communications equipment. Someone here has their own device to communicate directly with the Russians or Chinese."

"We have a traitor?"

"Apparently so. But we don't know the identity or their intent."

"The fire was never designed to cause extensive damage other than disrupting power to the biodome. Whoever planted it knew what they were doing and that we would be able to repair the damage."

"They must also know that we'd realize it was sabotage. They're therefore willing to accept discovery. It only requires a process of elimination among the twelve of us."

"Which means they must have a plan of escape. But where? And why reveal their hand now?"

"I was giving it my attention just before you entered. I doubt the person responsible is still on the base. The fire was a distraction to allow them to get away and carry out whatever their real plan is. It's the only reason that makes sense."

"Commander Anders and Georgia are at *Aquarius*. Could it be one of them?"

"I can't see Georgia or Anders behind this. They're not spy material. I would bet my career on it."

"Is anyone else missing?"

Captain Winter coldly replied. "Tom Redmayne."

Chapter 60

Redmayne was becoming increasingly frustrated at the time it was taking to set the jetcopter up for flight and was struggling to control the anger rising inside him.

He looked at his watch for maybe the twentieth time. He had no idea how effective his pyrotechnic display had been back at the base. What he could be sure of was that the captain was aware not only that there had been deliberate sabotage on the biodome but also that he was the most likely culprit. It was unlikely that Winter had established a motive, but it wouldn't be long before the captain sent out a search party to apprehend and return him to Alpha Base.

He was pleased that he'd had the foresight to plant a radio jammer near *Challenger* which was preventing communications between the base and *Aquarius*. The last thing he needed right now was for Anders to discover what he'd done.

Pausing briefly, he raised a hand to shield his eyes from the sun, which had reached the highest point in the sky. Peering into the distance he could see a cloud of dust, confirming his suspicions. "Lars, we need to hurry up. We're going to have company soon. If we can't take off in the next ten minutes, we may never get the opportunity again. And you'll find yourself confined to quarters for the rest of the mission."

Anders was feeling dispirited. The situation had escalated badly as soon as Redmayne had arrived at *Aquarius*. The realization was dawning on him that Redmayne had manipulated him, and it shocked him that he could have been so stupid. Locking Georgia away had not been part of his intentions. He'd been naive to think she would agree to their plan.

His career was now hanging by a thin thread. The only way to redeem it now was to follow through, achieve contact with the Sentinels and be seen as a hero. That appeared more unlikely as the minutes ticked away.

Unloading the jetcopter and lowering it to the ground had been the easy part, especially with two of them to move the machine into place. But they lacked the technical knowledge of either the chief or Rashid to make sure all the equipment was properly connected and flight worthy. Like Redmayne, Anders had read the manual during training on Earth, but had not expected having to assemble the jetcopter.

H stood back to take stock. The jetcopter looked complete. Its jet-black structure comprised a small oval platform that could carry two astronauts standing up. A pair of tall thin jets on either side used compressed nitrogen to power the machine into the sky. An avionics system that kept the vehicle vertical and even allowed for it to be piloted remotely, if necessary, enhanced fundamental controls.

Anders looked at the machine doubtfully, still attempting to guess what Redmayne's plans were. If there was only room for two, what would happen to Georgia? There was no way that he would let the jetcopter take off without him. He wasn't going to be left behind to face the music with the captain. As commander, he was second in command and should give Redmayne instruction. He knew he had to re-assert his authority and take control of the situation, although the oncoming dust clouds were worrying him. Too late, he knew he should have thought this through properly.

Grudgingly accepting his fate, he said, "Tom, all the struts are locked in place and the jets are fully primed. It will be airborne in less than five minutes. What are we doing with Georgia?"

"She's coming with us. It may be a tight squeeze, but the jetcopter has enough power to carry three people. Or you can stay here if you'd prefer. I'm going to get her now and persuade her to do the right thing. Just make sure you're ready to go."

Anders didn't appreciate being given orders. Especially by an arrogant civilian scientist. If this plan was successful, he would make sure he would never have to follow orders again. He stared at the cradle as it carried Redmayne back to collect Georgia, wishing he could turn the clock back twenty-four hours.

***

Georgia was using her time in captivity wisely. After she'd recovered from the initial shock of her situation, it didn't take her long to come up with a plan of escape. Although she had never been in this part of the ship before, she remembered the schematics, or at least the main parts. She was sure that there were some narrow access tubes behind one of the consoles in the engineering section.

The design of the supply ships meant that the huge fuel tanks took up all the available space to allow for the maximum amount of fuel to be loaded for take-off. There were, however, two tunnels that could be crawled through to inspect the fuel tanks for cracks and to swap out sensors. She was positive that one of the tunnels ran the full length of the ship down to the rocket motors and that there was an access panel at the base of the ship. She wished Jim was there because he would know for sure. If she was right, when she reached the bottom, she would need to jump twelve feet down to the ground, but that wouldn't be a problem in the reduced gravity.

Georgia quickly began to reach around the console until she found what she was looking for, a small pressure door. Wedging her feet against the upright, she found enough leverage to move the console far enough to wriggle her body around and through the door. Peering past the door, she saw a vertical shaft with a series of rungs in the wall opposite. Looking down, all she could see was darkness. But she knew the bottom was no more than about sixty feet below. It was a better option than waiting for Redmayne to return and take her with him to meet the Sentinels.

***

So it was that when Redmayne opened the access panel in the hold, he vented his anger in an almighty scream as he found she had disappeared. He rushed down the steps to see if she was hiding in a corner, before spotting how she had escaped. "Damn you, Pyke. You didn't need to make it hard for yourself."

Still in a rage, he headed back to the cradle, pausing briefly to set another one of his little traps. After all, he had no intention of ever returning.

***

Several times on the climb down, Georgia thought she would become trapped. The shaft was incredibly narrow and was never designed for someone in a cumbersome spacesuit. The protective insulation covering the air supply on her back kept snagging on the joints where the sections of the spaceship had been welded together. This was a part that the public never saw and so the attention to detail wasn't the same as the external skin of the ship, where the joints were seamlessly welded.

She cursed yet again as she struggled to free herself before continuing the slow climb down. As she neared the bottom, she would stop every couple of rungs and extend a leg, reaching out for the floor. Because the shaft was so tight Georgia had found it impossible to tilt her helmet forward. She was reliant entirely on touch. But it couldn't be much further to go.

Eventually, her outstretched boot touched something solid and she knew she'd gone as far as she could. Fortunately, the shaft opened out and she was able to kneel down and find the escape hatch which was secured in place by two sturdy levers.

Georgia gripped one of the levers and pulled with all the strength she had. The lever didn't budge and after a minute of exertion, Georgia was panting hard. She stopped and sat back to take a break, realizing she needed to try a different approach.

Wedging herself against the wall of the shaft, she found she could push the lever with the sole of her boot, allowing her to put all of her weight behind her effort to loosen the lever. After plenty of grunting and exertion by Georgia, the lever slowly started moving. After pausing again to get her breath back, she gave one final effort, and the lever shifted to the 'open' position. Georgia repeated the exercise on the second lever and the door of the hatch finally swung open on its hinges.

Looking down, Georgia could see the ground below between three huge rocket motors. They would hide her until she reached the ground, but then it would be pure luck if they spotted her before safely making it to the MEV. She slid out feet first, lowering herself as far as she could and controlling herself with her arms. When she could slide no further, she counted to three before dropping to the ground, flexing her knees for the landing.

She stayed on her feet but, as she stood upright and turned to see where she was, she came face to face with Anders who was staring directly at her.

"You are very resourceful. I'll give you that," he said. "You could have waited and taken the cradle with Tom."

With Redmayne not there, Georgia thought she may have a chance. "Lars, you don't need to do this. Don't let Tom ruin your career or get you killed. This is all about him. He wants the prestige and fame. He doesn't care about you."

Georgia could see hesitation in the commander's eyes, so she continued, walking slowly toward him, but also closer to the MEV. "You saw what he did with me. He was prepared to force me at knifepoint to do what he wants. Is that the person you want to be associated with? He's lost his perspective. Please don't do the same."

Georgia could see that Redmayne was descending in the cradle. She was running out of time to convert Anders. But she knew she was close and finding his weak spot.

"It's too late," replied Anders. "We've come this far now. I may as well see it through. If you come peacefully, I will tell the captain we forced you. You'll be in the clear. I'm prepared to take responsibility for my actions."

Georgia shook her head. "I can't do that. It's not right. You're making a huge mistake." She then spotted two speeders in the distance, still several minutes away. At least rescue was on its way. "Look, the captain will be here soon. He's not going to let you fly off. You'll have to come back to the base and face the music. At least stand down voluntarily."

Redmayne stepped forward brandishing his knife in one hand and a length of thin cable in the other. Georgia noticed the wild look in his eyes, and she was genuinely afraid. "Good try, Georgia, but all you've done is piss me off, which wasn't a wise thing to do. I really need you to come with us now and not cause any more trouble. We have destiny waiting for us. So, if you don't mind, I need to tie your hands and then we'll be on our way."

As Redmayne bound her hands in front of her, Georgia could see the determined expression on his face through his visor. He was adamant that nothing would get in his way. It appeared she was out of options.

Chapter 61

Captain Winter and the chief were travelling as fast as their speeders could take them, with Mancuso about fifteen minutes behind. The speeders bounced lightly across the bumpy terrain and Winter held on as tightly as he could, a grim expression across his face as he concentrated on not falling off. This was his first experience on a speeder, and he wished he'd had more time to practice. He knew that Jim was keeping pace with him to one side, but he kept his eyes focused directly ahead at *Aquarius*.

He had no idea what he was about to face when he arrived. While there was little doubt in his mind that Redmayne was the traitor, he was confused about Anders' involvement. Could they be working together? Whatever the answer, they had been very thorough so far, including jamming communications. He was going in blind and was sure that their approach would have been seen by Redmayne. He was not in a position of strength, but there was little alternative if he wanted to save Georgia.

As if reading his thoughts, the chief said, "We should be here in the next five minutes if we can keep this speed up. What's the plan when we get there?"

"Be cautious and take it one step at a time. Redmayne is cornered, which makes him unpredictable. As for Anders, I don't know what he's playing at. I have a bad feeling about why they've selected *Aquarius* and taken Georgia."

"The jetcopter? You think they're making their way to the Sentinel craft?"

"That's the only conclusion that makes any sense of the attack on the biodome. It was merely a distraction to give them a head start. Setting up the jetcopter will take some time. I just hope we're not too late to stop them. If they take off, then it's game over. And Georgia could be lost to us."

As they drew closer to *Aquarius*, Winter could see the MEV and the jetcopter. Two people were on the ground and a third was in the cradle, coming down from the hold. If the jetcopter was ready to fly, then he was cutting this very fine.

He tried communicating with Redmayne again but received no reply.

His only hope was for Anders to have second thoughts once he spotted him and the chief. For sure, the speeders were kicking up enough dust and pebbles to be seen from a good distance. Their presence would either deter Redmayne from further action or cause him to press ahead with his escape. Most likely, it would be the latter.

"Chief, stay at top speed until the last possible moment. I want you to disable the jetcopter while I deal with Redmayne and Anders. Hopefully, I can talk them out of doing something really stupid."

"And after that?"

"I don't know. But the focus is on stopping that jetcopter and saving Georgia."

Chapter 62

Anders' resolve was rapidly deserting him. Out of the corner of his eye he could see the two speeders steaming in at top speed. It was now or never. But Tom's knife made him nervous. He didn't want anyone to get hurt.

"Georgia, please get on the platform. If you do as Tom says, then there's no need for anyone to get hurt."

Redmayne waved the knife closer to her suit. Just one nick and it wouldn't take more than a few seconds to depressurize. He was looking like a desperate man. She was no longer sure what he was capable of and didn't want to find out. If only she could delay him long enough for the captain to arrive.

She walked slowly toward the jetcopter, following Anders but with Redmayne behind her, pushing her forward roughly. Anders climbed on to the jetcopter's small platform and started strapping himself into the safety harness.

Georgia protested. "There's only enough room for two. Leave me behind. I can talk with the captain. Explain why you're doing this."

Redmayne gave her another poke in the back to encourage her forward. "It will be a tight squeeze. You can stand between the two of us. But hold on tight because there's no harness for you."

Georgia stepped up on to the platform, immediately leaning forward and barging into Anders, causing him to lose his balance and fall off the other side. She tried to jump over him, but Redmayne quickly reached out and grabbed her ankle, causing her to fall to the floor hard. Instinctively, she kicked out with her left foot but failed to connect with Redmayne.

"That's enough," he shouted. "Try that again and I'll tear your suit open. Now stand up, slowly."

Georgia stood as Anders got to his feet next to her looking shaken, his suit covered in fine brown dust. He silently checked his own suit for any damage but there was nothing obvious. He climbed back on the jetcopter, cautiously avoiding contact with Georgia.

As she stood in the middle of the jetcopter, Georgia hoped she had done enough to allow the captain to reach her in time.

***

Winter was dismayed to see the brief skirmish on the jetcopter but was equally pleased that Georgia was still alive. The distraction she had caused would give him and the chief enough time to reach the jetcopter before it escaped. He pulled up several yards away, stopping as Redmayne waved the knife in his direction.

"That's close enough, captain. You don't want anything to happen to Georgia."

Winter knew he had to take control of the situation quickly. He looked across at Commander Anders for any sign of assistance, but he seemed to be supporting Redmayne. He hadn't expected that from his number two.

"Tom, I don't know what you're doing, but it won't work. Let Georgia go and return to the base. We can sort this out there with no one getting hurt."

"You know I can't do that. You'll lock me up."

Winter knew there was no point calling Redmayne's bluff. He was desperate and appeared set on completing his mission. But maybe there was still hope for Anders. How much did he actually know? He endeavored to find out. "I know you're working with the Russians, Tom. What deal do you have with them? Will they take care of Georgia and Lars? I assume the Russians are coming to collect you."

Anders reacted, turning to face Tom. "You didn't tell me about the Russians! You convinced me this was for the safety of the expedition."

"It is for the expedition. Don't listen to the captain. He's lying and will try anything to save his precious Georgia Pyke," Tom sneered. "I don't know what he's talking about."

"Commander," continued Winter. "Ground Control have intercepted several transmissions between the *Andropov* and someone on the base. If it's not you, then it has to be Tom. He's a spy and has been working with the Russians all along. Everything he's told you is a lie. He intends to lead the Russians to the Sentinels."

As Winter was speaking, the chief slowly dismounted from his speeder and started walking sideways, behind the MEV. Tom spotted what he was doing. "That's far enough, chief. Just stay there where I can see you."

Winter turned to glance at the chief and said, "do as he says, Jim."

The chief stopped and glared at Redmayne. "You'll have me to answer to if you hurt Georgia," he said, unable to hide the raging anger in his voice.

Chapter 63

Georgia was feeling extremely vulnerable, wedged between Anders and Redmayne, with the latter waving his knife in an increasingly erratic way. She was powerless to do anything but trusted the captain to resolve the situation, especially with Redmayne outnumbered. The only thing she could do was stay calm and wait for a chance to escape.

She could sense that Anders was doubting his involvement as Redmayne's true plans were laid bare by the captain. She could see what Captain Winter was doing and was sure that Anders was an unwitting victim of Redmayne's deceit. Maybe there was still a chance that Anders would help her.

***

Winter pressed forward with his tactic of talking directly with Anders. "You can't trust, Tom. He's using you. He's used all of us. Did you know that he set a small bomb off in the biodome this morning? No one was injured but there's plenty of damage. Do you want to be associated with someone so reckless?"

Anders looked stunned by this latest revelation. "Is that true, Tom?"

"Yes!" Tom realized this was no time for pretense. "I needed to allow us time to get the jetcopter ready. You can see that. But I didn't harm anyone. It was just a small device in the fuse box. It was never dangerous. I wasn't going to harm anyone."

Anders couldn't believe what he was hearing, although it was all starting to make sense. Tom was using him, and he would use Georgia. And then, in all likelihood, he would be discarded and left to face the consequences. All to help the Russians complete a power play with the Sentinels. His own ego had blinded him. Was it too late to make amends?

Commander Anders stared across at Redmayne and said, "I can't go through with this. I'm not a spy or a traitor. You should listen to the captain and step down. It's over for me."

Anders unbuckled his harness and started to step from the jet-copter. Georgia saw an opportunity to follow, but Redmayne anticipated her intentions.

"Not so fast," he said, grabbing her arm again. "You're staying with me. I'm not finished yet."

Georgia cried out in pain but was powerless to free herself from his grasp. Anders froze on the edge of the jetcopter's platform, no longer sure what he should do but unable to leave Georgia with Redmayne.

Captain Winter saw the chief use the distraction to move quickly out of sight behind the MEV and spoke again to ensure Redmayne's continued attention. "There's no need to hurt her. You're only making this worse for yourself. Do you really think you can escape on your own?"

Redmayne, still holding tightly onto Georgia's arm, maintained his resolve. "The commander is weak. I always thought he would let me down. Which is why I have a backup plan. In two minutes, the *Aquarius*' main fuel tanks will purge themselves of any remaining fuel. That fuel will combust in the rocket chambers, destroying everything left here on the ground. I suggest you spend that time wisely by running away as far as you can. And leave me alone."

Winter couldn't be sure if Redmayne was telling the truth and was weighing up the risks when the chief sprinted from behind the MEV and jumped on the cradle, pressing the controls to ascend.

"Leave the engines to me," shouted the chief. "Save Georgia."

"Yes, save your beloved Georgia," mocked Redmayne, undeterred by the chief's actions. "Jim won't be able to stop the purge and the engine blast will fry you. Let me go, and she lives. If you try to rescue her, she dies. It's very simple, really."

The position looked hopeless to Winter. He looked up to see that the cradle was already a third of the way to the hold. The chief was cutting it fine to cancel the engine ignition. If he failed, it would be too late to save any of them.

Redmayne was also well aware that the time for talking was over. The jetcopter's engines were now up to pressure and ready to take off. Their power vibrated through the soles of his boots. As he fastened the buckle on his own harness, he said to Anders. "Commander, step down now. If you're not with me, then I don't need you."

Anders' mind was in turmoil. Without thinking about what he was doing, he lifted his foot to step from the platform. But his boot caught in the foot restraint and he lost his balance, tipping backward toward Redmayne and Georgia.

Out of the corner of his eye, Redmayne saw what he thought was Anders attacking him and instinctively raised his hand to protect himself. Before he knew what was happening, his knife slid through Anders' spacesuit. Anders' momentum carried the knife deep into his side and he gasped in agony. In one movement, Redmayne withdrew the knife and pushed the still falling Anders from the platform.

The commander had felt the cold burn of the steel enter his side as he struggled to regain his balance. He was momentarily confused by the strange sensation. When the stabbing pain engulfed his body he gasped in agony, intent only on survival. He tried to move but his legs began to buckle under him. At the same time, air was sucked violently from his lungs and he was unable to take another breath.

Georgia watched in horror as Anders slumped to the ground, unaware he'd been stabbed until she saw the blood spray across the control panel in front of her. The knife had not only delivered a fatal blow; it had caused Anders' suit to decompress rapidly. She knew instinctively as he rolled weakly on the ground that he had seconds to live before he suffocated.

Redmayne stared in disbelief. He told himself it was an accident, but there was no time to consider his action. His careful planning was quickly unraveling, and he had to take off and get to the Sentinel ship. Without another thought, he shoved Georgia back on her knees with one hand. Tucking the knife back in his bag, he quickly wiped the blood from the control panel and started to key in the flight sequence for the jetcopter.

Chapter 64

The chief was watching in impotent anger at the action quickly unfolding below him. The scene had quickly descended into a disaster, and he silently vowed to deal personally with Redmayne when he got his hands on him.

He tore his eyes away to check how far above him the entrance to the hold was. He did not know how much time he had to stop the fuel purge, but it couldn't be more than sixty seconds. This would be tight, but he knew that anything within three hundred feet of the rocket engines would be incinerated.

Ignoring what was happening below him he leaped from the cradle as soon as it reached the hold. He knew the controls he needed were in the engineering section and recognized, as soon as he saw the floor hatch open, that Redmayne hadn't been bluffing. This was real.

He depressed the personal comms channel to warn Captain Winter. "Tom's done it. Get out of there now."

***

Captain Winter knew he was out of options. He'd seen Anders fall and knew immediately from the fountain of blood that there was no hope of saving him. The chief had only just reached the hold and the jetcopter's engines were nearly at full power.

As the jetcopter began to hover a few inches off the ground, he heard Jim's frantic message. "Tom's done it. Get out of there now."

He knew that it was now or never if he was going to rescue Georgia and himself. Spotting that Redmayne was no longer holding the knife he sprang forward, quickly closing the gap to the jetcopter.

As the machine continued to rise slowly, Winter desperately lunged and dived to grab Redmayne. Grunting with the effort, he was able to hook his arm around Redmayne's leg, but found himself hanging precariously from the jetcopter. His weight caused the machine to lurch to the right, dragging his boots across the Martian dirt.

At the controls, Redmayne increased power to the engines to stabilize the jetcopter and send it up into the air. There was a flurry of sparks as the jetcopter collided with *Aquarius*, leaving a deep gouge along the body of the supply ship.

Conscious that the captain was tightening the grip on his leg, Redmayne aimed a kick at Winter's helmet with his free boot, missing by inches as he fought to find his balance.

The jetcopter was now more than thirty feet in the air and struggling to level out. Winter, his legs swinging dangerously close to the plumes from the engines, shifted his weight and grabbed hold of a railing with his other hand.

Georgia, still stunned by what had just happened to Anders, was fighting to keep her balance as the jetcopter continued to sway erratically. But seeing what the captain was trying to do lifted her hopes. Looking into his eyes, she could see his fierce determination to save her.

***

Bending his knees to cushion the landing, the chief jumped down to the engineering level under the cargo hold. The control panel was directly in front of him, but the screen was blank. Redmayne had lied to them. A devious diversion to take him out of play. Jim cursed at having been fooled again so easily.

Bitterly, he radioed the captain again. "It's all clear sir. The bastard lied to us."

He spun around and sprang back up the narrow steps to the hold, hoping there was still time for him to stop Redmayne. He stepped back to the open hatch to get a clear view below him. As he saw the jetcopter rising, his mind quickly calculated its trajectory. Maybe there was one final opportunity open to him.

***

The jetcopter violently careened into *Aquarius* again, causing Winter to loosen his grip on Redmayne's leg. Georgia, her hands bound, couldn't keep her balance and rolled to the floor on her side, almost sliding from the platform. It was only the fact that she braced her legs that kept her from falling. She looked back in helpless despair as Redmayne kicked out again at the captain's helmet, this time his boot connecting heavily. A thin crack appeared across Winter's visor, as Redmayne prepared for another blow.

Georgia saw the Winter's visor and screamed, "No, Tom! You're going to kill him."

Redmayne stopped at Georgia's words and looked down into Winter's face.

"Tom, please don't do this," the captain pleaded. "There has to be another way. Just land this thing before anyone else gets hurt."

"Please Tom," urged Georgia. "Whatever you need, I'll do it."

Winter could see the momentary doubt in Redmayne's eyes disappear, only for his dark resolve to return.

"I wish it was that simple, captain. But we both know there's no coming back from what I've already done. If I land now, you'll prevent me from completing my mission. I am truly sorry." And with that, he took another swing at the captain.

Winter moved his head to the side to dodge the kick, but his grip slipped from the railing. His fate was now clear, and he regretted he would never see Kristen and Maisie again, or meet his grandchild.

Knowing that he had failed her he made eye contact with Georgia for the last time. From the haunting look of despair in her face, it was obvious she also knew.

The captain's visor shattered catastrophically as Redmayne's boot lashed out and connected. His helmet exploded as air escaped into the ultra-thin Martian atmosphere, sending shards of plexiglass outward in all directions. Winter's hands went to his face as oxygen was forcibly sucked from his lungs and he slid from the edge of the jetcopter and plummeted to the surface. He had lost consciousness by the time he hit the ground two seconds later.

"Noooooo!" Georgia screamed as she tried to get up from her position. She was in shock at what she had just witnessed. Filled with anguish and hatred she swore that she would kill Redmayne for what he had done and glared up at him with loathing in her eyes.

If Redmayne noticed her look, he ignored it. He was far too busy fighting the controls and gaining altitude. His focus was on getting away as quickly as possible.

***

The chief was balancing on the edge of the cradle as the jetcopter continued to weave and ascend in his direction. As he saw Winter fall, Jim understood that he was the final hope of preventing Redmayne's plan from succeeding.

Without the weight of the captain, the jetcopter rose rapidly toward him. The chief could see Redmayne was intently looking at the controls and must have forgotten that he was there. His brain quickly calculated the right moment to leap from the cradle and take Redmayne by surprise.

At that second, however, the device Redmayne had planted in the hold exploded. Although the same as the device used in the biodome, Redmayne had attached this one to the valve of a pressurized oxygen cylinder. The cylinder erupted in a ball of flame which instantaneously filled the hold and enveloped the chief. While his suit effectively repelled the flames, the shockwave from the explosion catapulted the chief from the cradle and into thin air. He somersaulted helplessly past the jetcopter, watched in disbelief by Georgia and Redmayne.

Before he hit the ground with a sickening crunch, the chief's final words were, "You must stop him, Georgia."

Chapter 65

The chief's voice was cut violently short by the sound of static.

Georgia stared at the edge of the platform in anguish. She knew from her own experience that Jim had no hope of survival from this height. She looked up at Tom, anger flaring in her eyes. "What have you done?" she accused.

Redmayne was visibly shaken. The last sixty seconds had escalated rapidly into something so unexpected. He'd never planned to hurt anyone, let alone kill three people. Yet here he was. A murderer. There was no coming back from that. He'd known all his victims. Been friends with them in his own way. Not for one moment had he thought he'd turn into a killer.

He couldn't look at Georgia. He wasn't sure how he could look at himself in the mirror again. Instead, he focused on controlling the jetcopter as it rose steadily into the air above the plain, heading for the cliff face. "I'm sorry. Believe me, I didn't want any of that. If they'd let me leave, they would still be alive."

From her position on the floor, Georgia could no longer see *Aquarius*. Only wisps of smoke from the explosion. "Don't you dare blame any of them. They were all good men, and you gave them no choice. You caused all this to happen. I will make you pay." She struggled to loosen her ties, hoping to make good her promise. Redmayne flinched instinctively, but she remained securely bound.

They continued to climb in silence. Redmayne had nothing to say and was trying his hardest to forget the final expressions on the faces of the now dead men. He reminded himself to focus on the mission in hand. It was now even more important for him to succeed so that the deaths were not a needless waste. He also desperately needed the Russians to save him and give him sanctuary. He couldn't return to his life in Alpha Base. They would kill him for sure.

The ridgeline drew closer above them as the jetcopter continued to climb ever higher. There was no time to take in the view, even at this altitude. Redmayne was calculating how far away the Sentinel ship was and hoping that it had not moved location since the previous day. That would be disastrous. The Russians would never land just for him.

Once they'd passed over the top of the cliff and were traveling across the plateau, Redmayne plugged the modified sensor into the jetcopter's computer and looked at the screen waiting for the telltale shimmer of the alien ship. He flew in a zigzag pattern thirty feet above the ground to give him the best visibility. After several minutes of searching, Tom was worrying. However, as he passed an ugly brown rock outcrop, the sensors picked up the ship, and he was able to breathe a sigh of relief.

Slowing the jetcopter down, he brought it gently in to land with a bump about fifty yards from the alien craft. He didn't know if the Sentinels could detect him or not but hoped that they would react to make his job easier.

His first task was to contact the *Andropov*. He pulled the communicator from his pouch and synched it with his suit comms. "Redmayne to *Andropov*. Come in, please."

There were a few seconds of delay before a man's voice responded. "This is Alex. I assume you have some information for me."

Redmayne tried not to betray his nerves. "Yes, Alex. I'm at the location of the Sentinel craft now. You should be able to obtain the co-ordinates from this transmitter."

"Is the craft secure?"

"Not yet. But I have the key," he replied, looking down at Georgia for the first time. She was lying on her side but no longer glaring at him.

"Excellent work, my friend. The *Kiev* is ready for undocking on the next orbit. I am told it will be with you in seventy-five minutes. Today will be the day that shakes the world."

"Indeed, it will, comrade. I look forward to celebrating with you." Redmayne knew that the Russians had a supply of vodka on board the *Andropov*. It had been too long since his last proper drink and he needed it after what had just occurred at *Aquarius*.

With the Russians on their way, his next and hardest challenge was to access the Sentinel vessel. "I'm sorry for interrupting your thoughts, Georgia, but now is the time I require your help."

Before she could react, Tom had lifted her to her feet and was pushing her roughly off the jetcopter's platform. With her hands still tied in front of her, it was all that she could do to keep her balance as she stumbled forward.

"Keep walking. I still have my knife."

"You're insane if you believe I will help you and your communist friends. Leave the Sentinels alone."

"That's not an option. You either help me willingly or we do this the hard way." He knew that Georgia would resist so thought a little reminder might help. "You've seen what I'm capable of so don't make this difficult for yourself. Captain Winter made the mistake of underestimating me, and it ended very badly for him." He regretted the threat immediately as the final image of the captain came back to him.

"Threats won't work on me, Redmayne."

Tom had no doubt that Georgia would be tough to crack. She'd proved that too many times and she wouldn't be as easily manipulated as Anders had been. "You've been inside their craft. Just get me access. Show me the way in and I'll release you. You can have the jetcopter and return safely to Alpha. I promise I won't harm you if you help me."

"You're wasting your breath. The Russians will have a wasted trip and probably won't be too impressed when they find out what you've done."

Georgia must have walked through a force field because the Sentinel's ship suddenly appeared less than forty feet in front of her. Automatically she stopped in awe just as Redmayne bumped into the back of her. The craft was metallic with a smooth surface that shone in the sun. Its weird series of curves and edges gave it a unique quality, unlike anything either of them had seen before. There was still no sign that the aliens had detected their presence.

Tom was speechless at what he saw. This close, it was more impressive than he could have possibly ever imagined. The technology inside would keep him occupied for the rest of his life.

It was the motivation he needed to complete what he had to do. "Okay, Georgia, you have one last chance. Get in touch with the Sentinels."

"I'm not going to help you. And you won't make me change my mind. Kill me if you have to but that still won't get you inside."

"I'm ready to bet it will," Redmayne replied smugly. And without another word, he turned off the air supply to her suit.

"What have you done?" she said as the heads-up display in her helmet turned red. She had less than a minute's air in her suit to draw on.

"I said you'd help me. Let's see if your alien friends will let you die when they've already saved you once. For your own sake I really hope I'm right about this."

Georgia tried to stay calm. Panic would only result in using her remaining air quicker. She sat on a boulder and waited, desperately hoping that Tom was wrong. She'd rather die than let the Russians exploit the Sentinels. Or let Tom succeed in his mission. The man was a murderous traitor, after all.

It wasn't long before she was gulping for air, her lungs desperately searching for that last bit of oxygen. But there was none. Her chest heaved but to no avail. Uncontrollably, she fell to the ground, rolling around in the dust. Her erratic movements soon slowed until they stopped completely. She lay there staring at Redmayne's dusty boots, feeling defeated but strangely calm knowing that his plan had failed. She'd already faced death several times since arriving on Mars. This was finally her time. Her vision grew dark. And then there was nothing.

Redmayne ignored what was happening to Georgia. She was just a means to an end now, and he didn't need to see her death throes. Instead, he was intent on spotting any reaction from the alien ship but there was none. Any hopes he had to get on board were fading fast. It looked as if Georgia's would be another senseless death on his conscience.

He kicked the ground in anger and screamed at the Sentinels' craft. "Damn it! Why don't you fucking save her?"

Chapter 66

Georgia opened her eyes, blinking at the bright but somehow familiar lights. She was lying on her back, still in her spacesuit but with the visor removed and her hands untied. She reached up to wipe the tears from her eyes.

Rather than relief, she was filled with utter dismay. Falmas did not understand what he had done or what Tom's plan was. The Sentinels had played right into his hands, because of her. She had to warn them.

Sitting up made her head swim, and she thought she might be sick. The nausea soon passed though, and she was able to stand and look around the room to get her bearings. The muscles in her chest and legs felt as if they'd been squeezed and twisted but she was otherwise okay. Of greater concern as she looked around the empty room was where were Redmayne and the Sentinels. She had no idea how long she had been unconscious or if Redmayne was even aboard, but only she knew what he was planning.

Georgia walked slowly around the edge of the room. The walls were bare and there was no obvious door so instead she looked for a switch or mechanism. Her fingers deftly felt along the wall but frustratingly there was nothing.

"Falmas? Are you there?" she called out. A few seconds later, the wall in front of her dissolved to make a doorway leading into a wide corridor. Standing there were the two Sentinels with Tom standing close behind them. Georgia noticed that Falmas stood stiffly and silently.

Redmayne spoke, his eyes bright with excitement. "Georgia, I've just had a guided tour. This craft is unbelievable. Its engines alone are unimaginable. They warp space, allowing faster than light travel without the relativistic issues that Einstein predicted. It's totally revolutionary. No more chemical rockets." Georgia had never seen Tom so animated. He was a different person again. Someone she no longer recognized.

"Tom, I don't think the Sentinels will just give up their technology. Do you?"

"They will be forced to share what they know. The *Kiev* will be here very soon, and the Russians have very persuasive techniques for finding out what they need to know. Of course, it would be much better for everyone if Falmas simply co-operated. There could be a grand powerful alliance between Russia and the Confederacy. Imagine that? They would be stronger as respectful allies."

Falmas turned to Tom, speaking calmly and confidently. "The Confederacy will not allow that to happen. Is it wise to threaten them?"

"It's not a threat; it's an offer. I am sure that both sides can find areas of mutual benefit. If not, then we'll just have to figure out how everything here operates. However long that takes."

Georgia stepped slowly forward, keeping eye contact with Redmayne. "What's happened to you? You nearly killed me. And for what? To piss off alien races that could eradicate humanity as easily as we wipe out an ant colony?"

"Yes, I'm sorry about what I did to you," Redmayne conceded. "But I was proved right, wasn't I?" He paused as if waiting to be congratulated for his insight. "The Sentinels have compassion. They've invested too much time studying Earth on behalf of the Confederacy. I'm sure that there is something more to the research that they're not telling us. And for that reason, they won't wipe us out."

Georgia could sense that Redmayne was becoming lost in his arrogance, prematurely bathing in the knowledge, fame, and power that he thought was coming his way. Perhaps she could use that against him. But she needed to know how he had overpowered the two Sentinels. They both towered over him yet had not tried to resist him.

"Falmas, why have you let this man take control of your vessel. You outnumber him. Surely you can do something."

"Sentinels are not trained to fight. The Confederacy has other races to do that. We are merely researchers, or historians if you would prefer. There was no contingency to encounter humans directly. Perhaps that was an oversight."

"Yet you saved me again. Why?"

"That was another mistake on my part. I had not expected your colleague here had intentions that were so negative and aggressive. But I could not see you die. It would have been because of us again. I may live to regret that decision."

"Good try, Georgia," sneered Tom. "You see. It will be too easy for me and the Russians to discover all that we need to know. Then we can go out and conquer the universe."

"And what about helping humanity?"

"Not for me to decide. But I'm sure those that want to be helped will be. For a price."

"How very noble," Georgia sneered.

Redmayne smiled back. "Enough of this chat. I have to secure the vessel. You," he said, pointing at Falmas. "As you care so much for Georgia, get in there with her while your crew member here shows me around." Tom roughly pushed Falmas into the room, causing the alien to stumble. "Now seal this door. I want no surprises."

Falment waved an arm, and the door became a solid wall again. Georgia and Falmas were trapped.

Chapter 67

Georgia slumped down in defeat and looked up at Falmas with sorrow in her eyes. "You shouldn't have saved me. You don't know what you've done."

"That is your opinion. I had no choice."

"But now you've lost your ship because of me. And when the Russians get here, they'll strip this vessel apart for all the technology. When they've done that, they'll more than likely experiment on you to extract all the information they can. If you've been studying us for countless millennia, then you know what humans are capable of. We stop at nothing to get an advantage over others. Redmayne has already killed three of my colleagues today."

"I appreciate your concerns. The situation looks grim at the moment. But it will be impossible for anyone else to enter this vessel. Falment will not let that happen."

"But your presence is now known. You'll have humans rolling up outside in a matter of minutes. Surely the Confederacy won't tolerate that. Will they send re-enforcements?"

"If we do not report within ten of your hours, then you are correct. The Confederacy will send a contingent of warriors to rectify the matter."

Georgia wasn't sure she was keen on the approach Falmas proposed. "What exactly does that mean?"

"A search unit will arrive to assess the situation and then take the appropriate steps. In this instance, that action is likely to involve purging the area."

"Again, I don't like the sound of that. It sounds like a clinical operation."

Falmas nodded. "In many ways it is. This vessel will be remotely swept for any sign of organic life or infestation. If any life is detected, other than myself or Falment, the ship will be flooded with gamma particles. This will be lethal to all biological life aboard, including myself. The planet will also be cleansed in the same way to eradicate any signs of our presence."

Georgia was shocked. "So, all human life here will be destroyed. Even those in my base."

"It may be a crude and brutal approach but that is how the Confederacy keeps itself hidden from emerging civilizations. We have conducted the process several times in your Earth history and these were treated as natural disasters."

Georgia put her head in her hands, desperately trying to formulate a plan. "Oh my God. We need to get out of here and stop Redmayne, so that you can prevent that from happening. How can we get out of this room?"

Falmas sat next to Georgia and put an arm around her. "This room isn't a prison. We only gave your colleague the impression that it was. There is more than one door out of here. However, it is small, and designed for the maintenance droids on this ship."

"Now you tell me you also have robots. Okay, so show me how to escape."

Falmas walked over to a wall on her left and pressed what looked like a blank spot in the wall. A small opening, more a hatch than a door, appeared. It was far too small for Falmas and Georgia feared that it would be too tight a squeeze for her too. "You want me to get in there?" she asked in disbelief.

"There is a maze of passageways that allows the droids to access all parts of this vessel. I will give you the directions to my personal charging station." Falmas unscrewed a finger from his left hand and passed it to Georgia, who stared at it in astonishment. "You will need this. It will allow you to open and close doors as you have seen me do."

This was the half-chance that Georgia needed. She still had to overpower Redmayne but hopefully she'd be able to take him by surprise.

"Thanks, Falmas, this makes all the difference."

With Falmas' directions fresh in her mind, Georgia knelt down and slid through the tiny hatch on her stomach.

Chapter 68

Redmayne was in the Sentinels' flight center with Falment. There was an array of consoles and equipment in front of him. He couldn't begin to guess how any of it worked, but he knew he would have fun taking it apart. The only equipment he recognized was a large screen which appeared to show the location of each of the Expedition Two and Legacy ships, Alpha Base and several objects moving in orbit. Presumably, those were the *Andropov* and the *Kiev*, with the latter appearing to be heading in his direction.

Checking his watch, Redmayne calculated he had less than ten minutes before the *Kiev* landed with a shipload of Russians expecting an open door to the Sentinels' craft. It would be embarrassing for him to fail to fulfill his promise.

Falment had been uncooperative so far. Redmayne looked up at the towering Sentinel. "Help me out here. I'm trying to be reasonable. I need you to switch off the cloaking device and open the main hatch. Is that really too much to ask?"

Falment stood impassively still, staring into the distance and acting as if Redmayne wasn't even in the room. Although the Sentinel didn't understand this human's behavior, it was obvious he was dangerous.

"He's not going to help you" a voice called out behind him.

Tom spun sharply around, briefly surprised to see Georgia standing in the doorway to the room. "I should have known you'd escape. You've had luck on your side these last few days. But it won't do you any good this time."

"You're wasting your time, Redmayne. The Sentinels will not give up their craft for you or anyone else. They're sworn to protect it and themselves. You've killed good men for nothing and trapped yourself here."

"I'll work it out for myself," Tom shrugged in response.

"How long will that take? The Confederacy will be sending a sanitation squad long before you learn any of the symbols. We'll all be dead. Try to be smart. You're beaten."

Tom's eyes flashed in anger. "This does not end now," he raged. "Don't try to talk me out of this or trick me. I will succeed because I am better than you and not afraid to do what needs to be done."

He angrily swung his knife into Falment's leg. There was a clang of metal hitting metal and the knife became firmly lodged. Tom attempted to pull it out but could see that it was stuck fast. He glared up at Falment whose only reaction was to look back down at him with a knowing smile on his face.

"No one else needs to die today, Tom. Give it up now," Georgia continued calmly, but keeping a safe distance from Redmayne who in his present rage he was unpredictable and dangerous.

Having lost any semblance of reason, Redmayne let out an angry roar and charged at Georgia with his fists raised. This was what she had been hoping for. She waited until the last minute before stepping to the side and bringing her knee up. Using all the anger and hatred inside of her, her knee connected with his chin with a satisfying snap. Redmayne flew past her and was unconscious before he hit the floor.

Georgia looked down at him lying still on the floor, controlling the impulse to kick and stamp on him. But she was in a hurry.

"Falment, can you release Falmas? We need to get this vessel away before the Russians arrive."

Falment ran to the door and asked, "What will you do with your friend?"

Georgia thought about her options for a moment. "He's no friend of mine and has no place with us at Alpha Base. I'd like him brought to justice for what he's done but there are no laws here. I could kill him but that would make me no better than him. If you don't want him either, then I suggest we just leave him here. The Russians will mete out their own justice."

Falment disappeared around the corner, returning seconds later with Falmas. "Falment has told me your plans, and I am in agreement." He glanced up at the big screen. "We must be fast. The Russian craft will be landing in a couple of minutes."

***

Redmayne slowly came around, still slumped on the floor. He could sense himself being manhandled and was aware that someone was trying to put his gloves on. His chin throbbed with pain and his front teeth were loose.

Opening his eyes, he saw that Georgia and the two Sentinels were standing over him and his helmet was already back on.

"Good to have you back with us," Georgia said coldly. "You'll be pleased to know I won't kill you, even though you deserve it. There's nothing worse than being a traitor and a murderer and I don't honestly know how you can live with yourself." She was content that Redmayne looked confused and scared. That was the least he should be feeling.

Redmayne recovered some composure. "I knew you were a kinder person than me. It's your weakness. What will you do with me? Leave me with these creatures?" He gestured at the Sentinels. He was in no position to argue or struggle at that moment and was genuinely afraid of what the Sentinels may do with him.

"They don't want you either. I can't blame them. But you don't really represent the best in mankind, do you? So instead we will throw you out with the trash."

Redmayne looked even more confused.

Georgia sighed at having to explain herself more clearly. "We will leave you here for your real friends. Maybe they'll take you back to the *Andropov* with them and allow you to explain how you failed them."

Redmayne wasn't sure what the Russians' reaction would be, nor was he keen to find out. He was no longer of any use to them and would be surplus to requirements. There was a very good chance he'd be pushed through an airlock eventually. But it was the best option he had. He slowly stood, defiant to the last. Leaning in close to Georgia's face he said, "We'll meet again. This is not over with."

Georgia stared back coldly into his eyes. "You really don't want to meet me again. I may not be so generous next time. Now get out." Georgia stepped aside to let Redmayne pass and for Falment to escort him off the vessel.

Falmas said, "Now that you know our existence we will return to the Confederacy. We will be assigned a new mission, but I fear we may need to be re-programmed."

"I am sorry to hear that. You have been so kind to me, and I would have liked an opportunity to spend more time to get to know you."

"It is enough for me to know that you are safe. You represent the best in your species, and I know now that I made the right choice to save you. I can make arrangements for another vessel to take you to my home world."

Georgia was taken aback but knew there was only one answer. "Thank you, Falmas, that is a very kind offer. A few days ago, I would have accepted it without hesitation. But I'm needed here with the rest of my crew. We've lost a lot of good people today. The base can't afford to lose any more if it's going to be sustainable. But I will keep your secret safe."

"So be it. We will return you to one of your ships."

"Can you make it *Aquarius*. I have to recover my crewmates."

***

Redmayne found himself laid on his back staring up at the Martian sky. He thought he saw something metallic shimmering briefly above his head, but it quickly vanished. Must have been an optical illusion or reflection on my visor, he thought. He lay there for several more seconds, listening to the whirring sound of his oxygen pump, confused by his surroundings. Sitting up and looking around at the barren rocky landscape he realized that he was very alone. He struggled to remember what had happened to him and suddenly he could see Lars Anders' face, a look of shock and pain across it, and his own knife stuck in Anders' side.

Tom threw up inside his helmet as he remembered the captain and the chief both dying because of him too. Vomit trickled down the inside of his visor, before settling around his neck seal. The smell made him retch again.

The deaths had been necessary. He'd been cornered and forced to react quickly. Now he knew for sure that he had made the wrong choices. He'd never seen himself as a killer. What had he become?

His orders from Alex surfaced in his mind again. He was to secure the Sentinel ship. But there was no sign of it or Georgia. Had he failed? Why couldn't he remember? He was filled with too much remorse and confusion to rationalize his position.

A weaker man would have buckled, but he was a survivor. The situation looked bleak now, but he'd find a way through. He saw the *Kiev* approaching and hoped it was to rescue him because he couldn't return to Alpha Base.

So, he stood straight and tall with a new resolve to deal with whatever the future threw in his direction. There would be other opportunities to deal with the aliens. He was sure of it. They would be back, now that mankind was becoming an interplanetary species. They'd want to watch humans, either through fear or interest. He hoped it would be the latter as it would be a weakness he could exploit.

Chapter 69

Falment joined Falmas and Georgia back in the flight center as the viewscreen showed the Sentinel craft gently rising into the sky. Georgia could not sense the movement or sound and guessed that was down to more alien tech.

The screen showed Redmayne sitting up from where he'd been lying on the ground. "Did you pass the human through the neurolyzer?" Falmas asked.

"Yes, he was unaware of what was happening until it was too late. He appears to have survived the process." For Georgia's benefit, he added, "Your colleague will not remember the past sixty minutes and should have no recollection of anything that occurred on this vessel."

Georgia laughed bitterly at the irony of the situation but could not enjoy the moment because of the grief she was struggling to keep under control. Redmayne had achieved nothing but disruption and murder. She could only hope the neurolyzer would be more effective than it had been on her, although it would be a step toward justice if he had the odd nightmare as she had done.

She noticed the knife still stuck in the side of Falment's leg. "Does that hurt?" she asked, pointing.

Falment looked down to see what she was referring to. He smiled and shook his head. "No, we have no pain receptors. The blade caused some very minor damage, but my systems have automatically bypassed the affected area. I will carry out repairs on our journey home."

"In the same way you repaired me?"

If Falment was surprised that she remembered her previous visit, he didn't show it. "The nanobath is very effective," he said.

"More than you could ever know," she muttered to herself.

The Sentinel ship flew majestically over the ridge, allowing Georgia to appreciate the depth and size of Hellas Planitia. From here it looked like an enormous clay bowl. The base of the crater was so far below them that she couldn't make out many details and the scene reminded her of flying across the Arizona deserts back on Earth.

As the craft swooped down, the tall white supply ships were soon visible. A spider's web of thin dark lines between the rockets and leading back to the cliff showed the regular routes the astronauts had been taking.

The craft landed softly only one hundred yards from *Aquarius* but if anyone was on the ground, they appeared to be unaware of their presence. Falmas and Falment escorted Georgia to the hatch and watched patiently as she climbed back into her spacesuit and tested all the seals.

Falment pointed to the jetcopter he had brought on board. "I thought you may need your machine more than your friend."

"Thanks both of you for all your help. I wish it had been different, and that you didn't have to see the worst of humanity."

"You forget that we have been watching you a long time. We have witnessed far worse behavior, even though we still do not understand it. We will wait here for a short time until we receive confirmation from the Confederacy that we must return. And I also want to ensure your safety."

As Georgia closed her visor she asked, "No neurolyzer this time?"

Falmas smiled appreciatively. "I really don't think that is required." He tapped a panel and the wall immediately became a doorway, with a ramp leading down to the ground about twenty feet below. Without another word, Georgia stepped through the door. Eager now to check on the carnage she had witnessed, she almost ran down the ramp.

There was still no sign of anyone but the MEV and speeders were still parked up. She noticed that the exterior hatch on the MEV was open, so she made her way in that direction.

"Hello, is anyone here?" she checked on her comms. Megan was the first to respond.

"Georgia? We thought you were dead. I'm in the MEV. You need to get here fast."

Georgia was concerned by the urgency in the doctor's voice and sprinted the rest of the way. The MEV airlock took forever to pressurize. As soon it was safe, she opened the internal door to the cabin to what looked like an operating theater. Megan was kneeling over Jim, who was lying on the floor in a pool of blood. It was apparent that she was desperately trying to save his life in the tight confines of the cabin. Mancuso was standing over her, holding a bag of plasma with a tube leading down into Jim's arm.

As Georgia entered the cabin, Mancuso looked across with a solemn expression and slowly shook his head. Tears started forming in Georgia's eyes as she knelt beside Megan and saw Jim's condition.

Without looking round, Megan said, "I'm sorry, Georgia. There's nothing I can do for him other than ease his pain. He's broken his back and received crush injuries to his legs. I don't know how he's still alive."

Georgia put her hands up to her face in horror at what she saw. Jim's legs and arms were placed in unnatural positions. His face, covered in deep scratches, was deathly pale. He was breathing through a tube the doctor must have inserted.

"Is he conscious? Can he hear me?"

"No. He was unconscious when Joe found him."

Mancuso spoke. "I saw him fall from the jetcopter. I was with him within seconds, but he was already in a bad way. The doctor told me to bring him here so that she could stabilize him. I'm sorry I couldn't do any more."

Georgia patted him reassuringly on the leg. "That's okay, Joe. None of us suspected Redmayne was capable of such actions. He had us all fooled. The captain and Anders have already paid for it with their lives."

Megan nudged her. "You need to say your goodbyes."

"I don't know if I can. There's been too much loss in one day. Jim has been so close to me the last few days. I'd hoped we'd have more time together."

"If it's any consolation, I know he was very fond of you and would have wanted more time as well. You changed him."

"It's not right he has to die." Tears were rolling down her cheeks, but she didn't care. Life had become very unfair.

"Fuck!" Mancuso suddenly exclaimed from nowhere. "What is that thing?"

Megan and Georgia looked up and saw Falmas staring down at them through the roof. Georgia plugged in her comms device. "Falmas, what's wrong?"

"We have been monitoring your vehicle and are aware of the injuries to your colleague. I may be able to help."

"Yes, of course. Why didn't I think of that? You healed me."

Falmas shook his head. "These injuries are more severe. His body is totally broken and his limbs crushed. Even our technology cannot repair those injuries."

Georgia's heart immediately sank. "What can you do?"

"I believe we may can save him. However, it will mean replacing his body parts with artificial components."

"He'll become half machine, like you?"

"Yes, precisely. It will require placing him in stasis and taking him back to our world where the procedures will be carried out."

"How do you know it will succeed? Have you done this before?"

"I'm not aware of similar instances but I do know what is involved. In theory, there is no reason why the melding process won't work. It will be physically painful for your friend, but he will retain his memories and sense of self."

"So, he'll still be the same person. Just in a different mechanical shell."

"It is your choice. But you must decide now so we can transfer him to my ship before his brain functions are lost."

Georgia quickly shared the Sentinel's offer with her colleagues. Megan said, "I don't know if I should be horrified or astounded. It's a tough call to make but it's the chief's only chance of survival. Bury him or send him to the stars to be remade."

Georgia looked down at Jim, knowing that he would want the opportunity to live. But was the cost too great? He'd be alone on a planet, light-years away with a new mechanical body. Was that really a life he would want?

"I've made my decision. Falmas, please do what you can for him. He is special to all of us."

"I understand."

***

Georgia escorted Falmas as he carefully carried Jim back to the Sentinel ship. Megan and Joe followed a few paces behind but stayed at the bottom of the ramp, their eyes staring at the backs of Falmas and Georgia.

They carried the chief to the room she had first found herself in and laid on the bed. Holding back tears, she removed his helmet before lifting her visor. Leaning across, her tears started again as she gently kissed his forehead and whispered, "I hope you can forgive me." With one last lingering look, she pulled herself away and left Jim in the company of Falment who looked impatient to begin the procedure.

As she left the craft for the second and final time, Falmas said, "We will take the best care we can. I promise."

Georgia looked down at the doctor and Mancuso as they waited at the bottom of the ramp. The sun was sinking on the horizon, casting long shadows. She sighed. "Will you let me know if you succeed?"

"Probably not. I don't know what my future holds but it will not be in this sector again." Falmas looked resigned to his fate. "I don't regret my actions," he added quickly. "It has been an honor to have an opportunity to speak directly with your species. I have learned more in the past week than I have in the previous five hundred years."

"Perhaps you need to consider your research methods," replied Georgia, slightly bitterly. She had many regrets bouncing around her head at that moment.

Falmas nodded, and she started walking back down the ramp, briefly turning and waving when she reached her friends. Falmas closed the door, and that was the last she saw of him.

Chapter 70

Nobody spoke on the long journey back to Alpha Base. The MEV took the lead with Doctor Betts on board. The bodies of Captain Winter and Commander Anders had been lifted up and placed in the airlock. Joe and Georgia rode speeders on either side, as if in silent tribute to their fallen comrades.

Georgia was lost in thought, with the key incidents of the day replaying over and over in her mind. She had always seen herself as a loner, finding it difficult to forge relationships with people and had accepted that was how she was, not relying on others. However, she was now more isolated than she had ever been. Captain Winter had become her mentor, without her even acknowledging it or thanking him. She could see now how his easy manner had bypassed the natural barriers she put up to protect herself.

She wasn't quite sure how to define what Jim meant to her. He was more than a colleague. She had developed emotional feelings for him. There had been potential for more, and it would have been fun discovering how far that could have gone. Instead, that potential had been cruelly snatched away by that traitorous Redmayne. She wished she had killed him when she'd had the chance.

Had she done the right thing allowing the Sentinels to take Jim. They were his one slim prospect of survival. But would he want a life so far away from any other humans? Was it better than being dead?

***

Doctor Betts had communicated with Alpha Base to explain some of what had happened. It was therefore no surprise that the surviving members of Expedition Two were somberly waiting for them as the MEV docked back at the base. Megan allowed herself a few tears before composing herself, stepping through the airlock and past the bodies to open the hatch to Alpha Base. She was aware of the crew lining the corridor but kept her head low as she walked toward the control room. She couldn't find any words that would reassure anyone.

Georgia and Mancuso entered the base via the secondary airlock and arrived in the control room shortly after Megan. Georgia looked around the room at the remnants of Expedition Two's crew, all staring at her expectantly. Eight of them left from the original twelve.

She spent the next twenty minutes running through what had happened, sharing all the facts she knew. Doctor Betts and Mancuso filled in the details for the time that Georgia had been on the Sentinels' ship. The crew listened in silence, too shocked to speak and mourning their lost colleagues.

Once Georgia had finished, a nervous Rashid tentatively asked, "What happens now?"

It was a simple question, but Georgia didn't have an answer. She looked at Megan for help but was met with a shrug of her shoulders. "We carry on. That's what our friends would want us to do. We all came here on a specific mission to prepare Mars for colonization and we will see it through, despite the adversities we have faced today as well as any new ones that will come our way." She meant the words but wasn't sure in her head how they would actually achieve it. That could wait for another day. The crew had no more questions and accepted the position.

"Doctor, can you come with me to the captain's quarters. We need to advise Ground Control of what's happened and the fatalities. I don't envy whoever has to speak with the families."

Once inside the captain's room, the two women hugged each other and sobbed uncontrollably, slowly rocking from side to side. Now was the time to mourn the losses.

Chapter 71

At exactly midday the following day, the Expedition Two crew assembled to bury their fallen colleagues and to pay their last respects. Two graves had been dug by the construction robots near to the cliff face just under one mile from Alpha Base. Everyone bowed their heads in silent prayer as the two bodies, wrapped in the flags of their native countries, were lowered into their final resting places.

Georgia, newly promoted to command for the rest of the mission, said a few heartfelt words about each of the men. Her epitaph for Captain Winter had come straight from the heart. She had not needed to prepare anything for him. Emily Pope had helped her out with words for Commander Anders as she hardly knew the man.

"Before we leave," she added. "I'd also like to take a moment to remember Chief Jim Grant. He may not be dead, but he is lost to us forever and will be missed as much as the captain and the commander. Jim fought as hard as anyone to establish our camp. I have a lot to thank him for." She paused so she wouldn't start crying again. "The three of them have left big shoes to fill. But I know that each of us is up to the task and I hope that you will support me as much as you did the captain. If I make mistakes, and I will, remember I'm not Captain Winter and am not trying to be. But I will do my best. Thank you."

The crew dispersed and trudged in silence to the MEV, leaving Georgia and Doctor Betts at the graveside.

"I would say congratulations on the command, Georgia, but I know this isn't how you wanted it."

Georgia took a long last look at Captain Winter's grave. A temporary marker with his name had been placed on the ground until they could make a more permanent gravestone. That's enough time for grieving, she told herself. Time to focus on the living again. With that she turned and started walking to her speeder.

"Command was something I never considered. Giving orders and taking care of everyone else's welfare was not part of my mission brief. Apparently General Stockton sees qualities in me that I wasn't aware of."

"I'm sure the captain would be proud of you. He saw you as a surrogate daughter." Doctor Betts stepped on to her speeder, as the last of the crew climbed into the MEV.

"Let's see how I do. I want him to be proud of what we achieve before Expedition Three arrives. There's a lot of work to be done, especially with only eight of us. Only then will I know if I was the right choice." Georgia fired up her speeder and set course for Alpha Base, with Megan keeping pace by her side.

"You're a popular choice with the crew. They've not shown it yet because of the deaths, but they'll be very supportive I'm sure."

"Thank you, Megan. I know you'll be overworked with counseling and your physiology research, but I would appreciate it if you could be my deputy. I value your judgment more than anyone else's here."

"You've got it." Megan gave her friend a beaming smile of encouragement. "We'll get through this together. Did Ground Control confirm if the Russians picked up Redmayne?"

Georgia could barely control her annoyance." Would you believe the Russians are denying all the accusations about their involvement with Redmayne? He wasn't working under their instructions or even in contact with the *Andropov*. They're asking how they could know that Redmayne was up on the plateau rather than here. Apparently, yesterday's flight was a trial run for their lander to shake out some system issues. They touched down briefly but went straight back to the *Andropov*."

"So he's dead."

"Officially he and Jim were killed in the same accident that killed the others. Neither side is willing to go public about the Sentinels.

Personally, I think the bastard made it back to the Russian ship. Part of me wishes I'd killed him when I had the chance. I was tempted for a brief moment."

"You did the right thing, Georgia. I hope the Russians left him to die a slow lingering death as his air supply depleted, but people like that always get a lucky break. He'd better hope he never meets me again though."

"Either of us," Georgia said grimly. She noticed that the MEV had raced ahead of them and was entering the base. There was nothing urgent for her to hurry back for today. Anyway, gliding over the bumps and rocks at high speed wasn't as much fun without Jim.

<<<THE END>>>

GET EXCLUSIVE CONTENT

Building a relationship with my readers is the very best thing about writing. I occasionally send newsletters with details on my current projects, new releases and special offers.

And if you sign up to the mailing list, I'll send you a copy of Deception, my prequel to the Mars Frontier series. You can receive this novella, for free, by signing up at www.paulrixauthor.com[1]

---

1.   http://www.paulrixauthor.com

ABOUT THE AUTHOR

Paul Rix is the author of the Mars Frontier human colonization series. His online home is at www.paulrixauthor.com[2]. You can connect with Paul:

on Twitter at www.twitter.com/PaulRix8[3]

on Facebook at www.facebook.com/paulrixauthor[4]

or email at paul@paulrixauthor.com if the mood takes you.

2.   http://www.paulrixauthor.com

3.   http://www.twitter.com/PaulRix8

4.   http://www.facebook.com/paulrixauthor